Practice
to
Deceive

Also by Janet L. Smith
Published by Fawcett Books

SEA OF TROUBLES

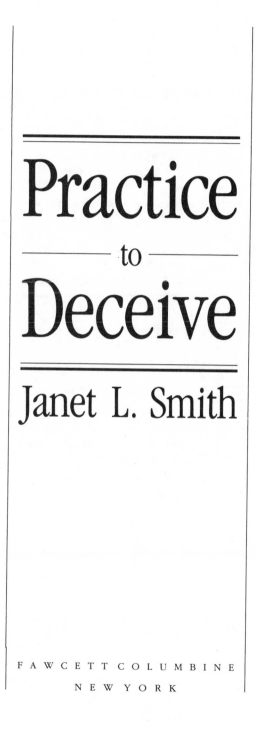

Practice

— to —

Deceive

Janet L. Smith

FAWCETT COLUMBINE

NEW YORK

A Fawcett Columbine Book
Published by Ballantine Books
Copyright © 1992 by Janet L. Smith

Library of Congress Cataloging-in-Publication Data

Smith, Janet L.
Practice to deceive / Janet L. Smith.—1st ed.
    p. cm.
ISBN 0-449-90744-9
I. Title.
PS3569.M537518P73   1992   91-58998
813'.54—dc20   CIP

Manufactured in the United States of America
First Edition: July 1992
10 9 8 7 6 5 4 3 2

To my father,
Clyde Smith, who is
nothing like the fictional fathers
in this book.

Practice
to
Deceive

Chapter 1

Enjoying a rare moment of relaxation, Gordon Barclay swiveled in his chair and watched a loaded freighter make its ponderous way across Puget Sound. For most men turning sixty meant winding down, taking fewer risks, planning for oblivion. To Barclay it seemed as if the ride had just begun.

He heard a light rap on the door—Nancy with his letters to sign. He pivoted so he could watch her from the corner of his eye while pretending to scrutinize a document. Her dress was one he hadn't seen before, a pink flowery sort of thing with a lace collar and made of a silky fabric that swung playfully on her narrow hips. She laid the letters on his desk.

"The Wilson interrogatories went out today, and I called and confirmed the trial date on Mastriani. Word Processing says your brief and jury instructions will be done by five."

"I'd sure be up a creek without you, my dear, wouldn't I?" He took the stack of letters from her and quickly scribbled his signature on each one. He hated proofreading and trusted that her typing was accurate.

"How was lunch at Fuller's?" asked Nancy.

"As usual, the restaurant was sublime, the company ridiculous." Barclay lowered his voice. "I trust you'll never tell Walt Wiley at Trans-Pacific Casualty what I really think of him."

"Your biggest client? I'd never dream of it. Did he wear that awful seersucker suit again?"

"No, today's was worse—blue and white houndstooth made

of some sort of fabric that looked like spun Styrofoam. He ordered homogenized milk with lunch, made them cook his tournedos of beef *well done*, and asked the waiter for more bread four times. Oh, before I forget. Would you round up two tickets to the Sonics game for next Wednesday? I discovered that our friend Walt's a basketball fan.''

"But I thought you hated basketball.''

"I like basketball exactly as much as I like Walt Wiley.''

She giggled. "I see. Anything else?''

"Not right now, thanks. Oh, and, uh, about that Friday night you were asking me about? I'll see what I can manage, but I'm not sure yet if Adele's definitely going to be out of town. You know how she is about making decisions.'' Barclay shrugged.

Nancy frowned, looked as if she wanted to say something, then changed her mind and turned to leave. As Barclay watched her go, a ray of sunlight fell on her hair, bringing out the golden highlights. He remembered what she'd looked like playing tennis, her long brown legs in a short white skirt. She'd practically danced on the court. Despite the difference in their ages he'd beaten her in all three sets.

Once Nancy was out of the room, he slipped on the reading glasses he never wore in public and turned toward his overflowing in-basket. The top item was another memo about the law firm's annual dinner-dance on Saturday night. Now that was something he wished he could get out of. Those damned parties were always boring as hell, and it was going to be on that blasted boat again—impossible to leave early. But he couldn't skip out, not after having made such a fuss about trying to hire Annie MacPherson. She and her partner were supposed to be there to meet the executive committee. No sense in taking chances now after weeks of laying the groundwork. The partners would be voting at the meeting on Wednesday, and it was imperative that they approve this merger. If MacPherson got out of his grasp, his entire plan could go down the toilet.

Barclay's face betrayed no emotion when he saw the next

item in his correspondence. Like the other notes he'd received, it was in a sealed envelope, on office stationery, with his name neatly typed in the center. Below it the words EXTREMELY PERSONAL AND CONFIDENTIAL were highlighted in blue.

As he reached for the envelope, Barclay's pulse quickened and he felt his face grow warm. He slashed it open with a letter opener. Inside was a single sheet of paper that looked just like the others. He skimmed it quickly:

> TO: GORDON BARCLAY
>
> FROM: AN INTERESTED PARTY
>
> RE: YOUR FUTURE, ASSHOLE
>
> IT'S ME AGAIN, BIG GUY. THE ONE WHO KNOWS
> *EVERYTHING.* YOU AIN'T IN PARADISE
> ANYMORE, TOTO.
>
> ARE YOU GONNA COME CLEAN AND TAKE IT LIKE
> A MAN, OR AM I GONNA HAVE TO
> > HUNT
> > > YOU
> > > > DOWN?

Barclay shuddered. He didn't need to read the note a second time. He unlocked his personal filing cabinet and shoved the paper and envelope in next to the others. Then, eyes closed, he took several deep breaths, fighting the urge to do something rash.

When he could feel his heart beating normally again, he buzzed Nancy and asked for some tea.

Chapter 2

Knifelike jabs of pain throbbed in Annie's arches and jolted up her calves as she walked across the terminal building to the restroom. The overly bright fluorescent lights in the ladies' lounge gave her freckled skin a bluish cast and turned her red-gold hair the color of kelp. She wondered if it was too late to bolt.

She felt absurd. Even though the invitation said semiformal, the strapless black dress and the Italian instruments of torture masquerading as shoes were totally out of character for her. She tugged at the top of her dress and prayed it would stay in the right place all evening.

Combing her hair, Annie took several deep breaths and tried to get into the right frame of mind for this party. All week Joel Feinstein, her law partner, had been reminding her how important it was that they make a good impression tonight. After several years of struggling, their two-person partnership was about to self-destruct. It was no one's fault. Sure, Annie felt guilty about having taken a three-month leave of absence, but the real blow had come when Joel's largest client, a local savings and loan, had been bought out by a California bank. They might have squeaked by if their professional liability carrier hadn't picked that moment to double their malpractice insurance premium. What had been a minor blowup at the beginning of the year had, by April, escalated into a financial Chernobyl.

That was when Kemble, Laughton, Mercer, and Duff had called to propose a merger. KLMD was one of the Northwest's largest law firms; it had seemed like a gift from the gods. But mega-law firms didn't merge with small partnerships without first taking a good, hard look. Annie and Joel had been subjected to endless hours of interviews. The books had been pored over, accounts receivable tallied, client names run through the computer to check for conflicts of interest.

Now all that remained was to see if the big fish liked the small fish enough to gobble it up. And Annie MacPherson felt just like a mackerel about to be fed to Moby Dick.

Joel and his wife, Maria, were waiting for Annie outside. The Kemble, Laughton party was being held on the *Alki Lady*, a vintage ferryboat from the 1920s specially refurbished for such elegant affairs. As soon as all of the guests were aboard, they'd begin a nighttime cruise around Seattle's Elliott Bay.

"Do you realize we're going to be trapped on a boat with over two hundred lawyers with no means of escape?" Annie asked.

"You can always jump," said Joel. "That dress of yours has almost as much fabric as a swimsuit."

"Knock it off, Feinstein, before I tell you what you look like in that monkey suit."

Formally dressed couples ranging in age from their late twenties to their midsixties were heading for the docked boat. Annie was greatly relieved to see that hers wasn't the only strapless dress in the crowd.

"I feel so dowdy all of a sudden," said Maria, looking around at the sequins and plunging necklines. "But what could I do? They don't make sexy evening gowns in my size." Joel's wife stood barely five feet tall and normally weighed about a hundred pounds. In her tasteful black maternity dress she bore a striking resemblance to an olive on a toothpick. "And forget what Joel says. I think your dress looks fantastic. I wish I had the guts to wear something like that!"

"So do I," Annie replied.

For a fleeting moment she wondered what David Courtney would think if he could see her right now. For the three months she'd spent on his sailboat in the South Pacific she'd worn nothing but shorts, swimsuits, and a lot of sunscreen, with her biggest decision being what to fix for lunch. But that had all ended when she'd left the boat in February, Annie reminded herself. It no longer mattered what David Courtney thought.

"Now remember, Annie," said Joel nervously, "tonight's our last chance to make this deal work. I don't need to tell you what bankruptcy can do to a lawyer's reputation."

"You already have, Joel. About four times."

"Don't fret so much, honey," said Maria. "You're starting to sound like your mother."

"That world-class worrier? No way. I'm strictly an amateur."

"Practice makes perfect," said Annie.

"You two sure know how to gang up on a guy. Now listen. I'm going to spend my time with the corporate folks, and you've got to try to meet the guy who heads up the insurance defense group, right? What was his name again?"

"Oh, damn. I'm drawing a blank." She caught Joel's anxious glance. "I can do this, I really can."

Joel scowled.

One of the senior partners, a genial man in a plaid cummerbund and matching bow tie, was playing host and ushering the crowd up the stairs to the deck where drinks were being served. He beamed when he saw Annie and Joel, shook their hands, got their names wrong, and assured them he would catch up later to see how they were doing.

"Now don't you be intimidated," he chortled, "we're quite a *wild* bunch when we get going."

"Oh, I'm sure of that," said Annie.

He thrust out a hip and snapped his fingers. "Party down, as the kids say!"

Annie smiled feebly in response and didn't resist as the surging crowd carried her into the salon. She gave a last look at Joel, easy to spot since he towered a good head above the crowd. He flashed her a thumbs-up and then she was on her own.

A score of waitresses circled the crowd taking drink orders. After Annie ordered a glass of white wine, she took a moment to survey the crowd. Barclay. Gordon Barclay. How could she have forgotten one of the most prominent trial attorneys in the state? If the merger went through, she'd be working in his insurance defense group, and his vote at the upcoming partners' meeting would be crucial. She wasn't quite sure where to start looking for him.

"So the rumors are true after all." The voice behind her sounded vaguely familiar. Annie turned. "Jed Delacourt? What are you doing here?"

"You obviously don't read your alumni newsletter. I work here. It'll be six years next week. Fabulous dress by the way."

"Thanks."

With his fair hair and boyish good looks John Edward Delacourt III looked no older to Annie than he had ten years earlier when they had graduated together from the University of Washington Law School. They hadn't been close friends. Jed, newly arrived from Boston smelling of old money, had had little to do with anyone who wasn't on Law Review, wealthy, or both. Annie had been neither.

"I thought you went to work for the public defender's office after law school?"

"Mm-hmm," he said, grabbing a prawn from a passing tray and popping it into his mouth. He wiped a touch of cocktail sauce from the side of his mouth. "Foolish me, thinking I'd be happier helping the poor than making money for myself. It only took me a few years to wise up. Kemble, Laughton made me an offer I couldn't refuse. Now I get paid a shameful amount of money to push paper, seek out experts whose job it is to create chaos out of clarity, and generally be a pain in the you-know-what." Annie looked confused. "Otherwise known as civil litigation."

She smiled and nodded politely while trying to think of a

way to extricate herself from Jed and his pomposity. Her feet had begun to throb again, and she wondered how long she would have to stand before dinner. "What practice group are you in?" she asked.

"Insurance defense."

"Oh? That's the section I'd be going into if this all works out. In fact, I'm supposed to introduce myself to—"

Jed raised his eyebrows. "The infamous Gordon Barclay?"

Annie nodded.

"The interviews went that badly, huh?"

"What do you mean?"

Jed sighed. "No one warned you then. The big guy thinks associates are a disposable product. Use a few times for dirty work, then toss in the nearest receptacle." He tried to demonstrate by lobbing his cocktail napkin into a potted plant but missed. "Rumor has it I'm next."

Annie was about to ask him to elaborate, but the waitress appeared with her wine.

"But that's another story, for another time and place," Jed boomed, a little too heartily. He quickly drained his drink and set the glass on the waitress's tray. "Not only is my glass empty, but I'm afraid I've misplaced my date!"

"Can't have that, son. This is a party." They had been joined by an elderly gentleman whose tuxedo looked to be the same vintage as the *Alki Lady*. He carried, but didn't seem to need, an antique ivory-handled cane. Despite his age his bearing was ramrod straight.

"Annie," said Jed, "this is the man who can tell you everything you would ever need to know about Kemble, Laughton, Mercer, and Duff. Meet Fred W. Duff, the firm's most 'senior' senior partner."

Amid a new rush of people Annie found herself standing next to the dapper gentleman as she watched the back of Jed's head disappear into the crowd.

"That must be a polite way of saying I'm the oldest dinosaur in the room," Fred Duff said. "Last of an era. Jack Kemble's dead, Ed Mercer's in a retirement home in Sequim, and Elmo Laughton was last seen in Malibu in the company of a twenty-two-year-old aerobics instructor. The fools had the poor sense to leave me here running the shop. Now I won't tell you how old I am, but I was too young for the First World War and too old for the Second." He chuckled as Annie tried to do the math in her head and then winked. "I lied about my age and joined up, anyway. I'll be eighty in July, but my wife says I don't look a day over seventy-three."

Annie smiled. Fred was a cross between Fred Astaire and William Powell, with a touch of Jimmy Stewart thrown in. Her reply was interrupted by Plaid Cummerbund circling through, announcing dinner.

"And here we haven't even had a chance to talk," Fred said, his disappointment obvious. "You'll probably be looking for your husband now."

"No, as a matter of fact, I came alone."

The old man's eyes lit up. "Excellent. So did I. My wife, Vivian, couldn't make it. Her sister's in the hospital and she didn't think she could have a good time. Would you do me the honor of being my dinner companion?"

"I'd be delighted," said Annie, taking his arm.

The middle deck had been set up as a dining room. There must have been twenty-five to thirty round tables for eight, each covered in a white linen tablecloth with a centerpiece of fresh flowers. Coming from a law practice where even the paper clips had been rationed, Annie was boggled by the lavish display. Fred Duff led her over to a table near the center. "What do you say we join Mr. Delacourt and his party?"

"Uh, fine," Annie mumbled, unable to think of a polite way to decline.

"Well, how about it? You think you young folks can make room for another couple?"

"Always room for you, Fred," said a young man who introduced himself as Steve, "though I don't expect dinner to be as good as your hamburgers. It's a tradition," he explained to

Annie, "all new attorneys get invited to Fred's house for a barbecue. It's worth taking the job just for those burgers."

"I have no doubt Annie will be able to test that theory for herself in the very near future," said Fred ceremoniously.

After she sat down, Annie surreptitiously slipped off her spike heels under the table and breathed an inward sigh of relief. Fred patted the back of her hand. "Thank you so much for keeping an old man company, my dear."

"I don't know about this, Fred," Steve teased. "Looks like you and Annie are violating 'The Rule.' We may have to refer this to the ethics committee." To Annie's confusion, his comment brought general laughter around the table.

"The firm is concerned about our morals," said the woman on Fred's left. "It's an unwritten but well-understood rule that KLMD employees aren't to get too familiar with one another. I think they call it 'fraternization.' " From the bitter edge to her voice, Annie wondered if the woman had been a victim of "The Rule" herself.

"I think management's afraid that if we actually had personal lives we might not bill as many hours," said Steve.

"Someone ought to remind a certain senior partner about the damned Rule," Jed Delacourt interjected sloppily. From the difficulty he had getting his words to line up correctly, Annie assumed that Jed had refilled his empty glass more than a few times during the cocktail hour.

Fred Duff quickly changed the subject by continuing with the introductions. Jed's date, no longer lost, was a bored-looking brunette named Chandler with a baby-doll mouth and a Barbie-doll figure complete with emerald satin evening gown. Her overly made-up eyes kept searching the room as if looking for the emergency exit. Next to Chandler was Steve, who turned out to be a first-year associate, and his rabbitlike wife, who managed to make it through the entire dinner without saying a word.

The woman on Fred's left was named Deborah Silver, a senior associate in the insurance defense group. She was alone but didn't look like the type who'd have trouble getting a date. Her red crepe dress was molded onto her slender figure and her jet-black hair was pulled back in an elaborate chignon. When they had sat down, Deborah had smiled and greeted Fred Duff with a kiss on the cheek but had ignored Annie. When Annie was introduced, she cocked her head.

"Well, what a pleasure to finally meet the girl wonder. The last few weeks Gordon's talked of practically nothing else."

"Gordon? You mean Gordon Barclay?"

"You look surprised."

"It's just that I've never met him. I wouldn't think that he'd even heard of me." She had heard of him, of course. Barclay had a reputation as one of the hottest litigators in the state. Just learning that he was appearing for the defense caused some cases to be settled on the spot. The addition of one more associate to his fifty-lawyer department shouldn't have ranked very high on his agenda.

Deborah looked puzzled. "That's odd. From the way he raved I'd assumed you were an old family friend or something."

Fred Duff interjected, "Gordon's been saying some very good things. We were all quite enthused when he proposed the idea of a merger with MacPherson and Feinstein. I must say, Gordon's quite anxious to get you on board. Yes, indeed."

Annie's eyes widened. She and Joel had been perplexed when they received a call out of the blue from the KLMD hiring committee, but they'd assumed the firm was primarily after Joel, who'd published a number of articles on real estate matters.

"And the rest of the partners were behind him all the way once we found out more about the two of you. That was a very nice article about you in the *Bar News*, by the way."

As the waiters began serving crab cocktails, Annie hoped someone would change the subject. Her wish was granted when Steve asked Deborah about her recent jury trial and she enthusiastically launched into a moment-by-moment recap, all the while pushing the food around on her plate as if by doing so she might make it less fattening. Every once in a while she took a minuscule bite.

Jed's date, more bored than ever, was amusing herself by making eyes at the waiter. Jed was too sloshed to notice, but the waiter wasn't. The rest of the evening Chandler got served first.

Fred Duff then livened the conversation by launching into a hilarious story of a lawsuit involving a bachelor party, three belly dancers, and a herniated lumbar disk. By the time the chocolate terrine with raspberry sauce arrived, they all had tears of laughter running down their faces.

Annie was sorry when the others began to leave to mingle elsewhere and Fred Duff excused himself to go out on the deck for a cigar. The last thing she wanted to do was to force her shoes back on and rejoin the rest of the party, but she still had to meet the elusive Gordon Barclay.

After locating her shoes, she glanced up and saw that she was alone at the table with Deborah Silver, who had slipped a compact out of her purse and was touching up her carnelian lipstick. Deborah slid over into Fred's vacated chair.

"I'm so *glad* they're thinking of hiring another woman." Deborah's words were friendly, but her voice was less than sincere. "Would you believe, out of eighty-nine partners, only *six* are women. I think they're afraid of us, you know. We women are so good at networking among ourselves without all that *competition* that men seem so driven by." Taking on the tone of a big sister, Deborah skipped the formalities and got right to the point. "Have they offered you partnership track or contract status?" Then, as if to point out that *she* wasn't driven by competition, Deborah added, "You have to make sure they give you what you deserve."

Annie wasn't fooled. Sisterhood had its place, but Deborah was hardly a shining example of female camaraderie. "No offer's been made yet, but we've been discussing eligibility for full partnership after one year's probation."

Deborah raised one eyebrow. "I see. Well, isn't that wonderful. Good work. I'm sure we'll be *such* good friends, if you come to work here." Deborah smiled thinly, revealing flawless white teeth. "Are you coming up to the dance floor? I hear they actually hired a decent band this year." Annie muttered a reply to Deborah's departing figure, secretly glad she didn't have to continue "networking."

Shaking her head, Annie wondered if she could really tolerate such co-workers. But she wouldn't even have the chance to find out unless she got her act in gear and found Gordon Barclay. Plaid Cummerbund told her he'd last been seen heading for the dance floor.

She climbed the stairs to the glassed-in upper deck where the band was warming up. Couples strolled around the perimeter of the room enjoying the view. It was a sparkling evening: spring rains earlier in the day had cleansed the air. The geometric patterns of the night-lit cityscape were dazzling.

Annie saw Maria Feinstein standing at the window and walked toward her.

"Look at that skyline! From here it pretends to be such a big city, don't you think?" Maria still spoke with the rhythm of her Puerto Rican heritage, though she'd lived in the United States for twenty years. "It's so different from when we lived in New York. I still can't get accustomed to the sight of Joel wearing a Gore-Tex jacket and Eddie Bauer boots with his pin-striped suit."

Annie laughed. "Seattle can't make up its mind whether it wants to be a big city or a small town. We want it all: sailing, skiing, and mountain climbing close by; all the cultural amenities of a major metropolis; and no crime, traffic, or urban sprawl. And we think we'd have all that if we could just convince the Californians to stay home."

Maria looked skeptical. "Wait, aren't you from California?"

"I lived there until I started high school, but don't tell anyone."

"Which building is Kemble, Laughton in?"

"The Nisqually Tower. It's the tall one, over there." The jagged spire Annie pointed to rose like an icicle above its surrounding buildings. "KLMD has four floors near the top."

Maria sniffed to show she wasn't impressed. "I like the office you have now in Pioneer Square better."

"I do, too."

Annie surveyed the crowd. She didn't want to be judgmental, but she couldn't help feeling as if she was surrounded by conservative, middle-aged white men making inane comments about sports. *How 'bout them Mariners—think they'll pull it off this season?* A cluster of women she guessed were senior partners' wives stood in one corner. They could have been clones of one another, with their ash-blond pageboys, simple black dresses, and throaty cigarette laughs.

Maria touched her arm. "Isn't that Senator Quinn over there?"

Annie looked. Maria was right. Washington's senior senator was standing near the dance floor talking with a slender, fiftyish woman in a black silk pantsuit. There was something that set her apart from the other partners' wives, a certain lack of social graces. Her pantsuit was several seasons out of date, and she'd made little effort to style her shoulder-length gray-blond hair. As she sipped her drink, she seemed to be listening with only half an ear to the senator. Either she didn't know who he was or didn't care.

Joel joined them, carrying a seltzer for Maria and a glass of champagne. "Here, Annie, take my glass. I'll go back for another."

"No, I can get it."

"I insist. There's a guy over at the bar looking for you who is incredibly drunk. Blond, Boston accent? I figured the state he's in, you'd just as soon avoid him."

"That has to be Jed Delacourt. Thanks. I don't need that right now. I came up here looking for Gordon Barclay."

"You mean you still haven't met him? Come on, Annie, his is the crucial vote. . . ."

Maria put her hand on Joel's arm. "Calm down, hon."

"It's okay, Joel. I know how important this deal is. You think I want to see your kids selling carnations on street corners? Believe me, I won't screw it up. I just need someone to point him out to me. I was told he came up here."

They wandered over toward the dance floor. The combo was playing big-band-style music, and the couples on the floor were doing their best to imitate 1940s dance styles. Only one couple was succeeding. A tall man, in his late fifties or early sixties, was deftly leading Deborah Silver through the steps. They made an incredibly handsome couple. He had a full head of snow-white hair set off by the kind of tan that Seattleites only get on vacation. His graceful moves and athletic physique made Annie think of the men who went to work carrying duffel bags and worked out at their clubs on their lunch hours. Deborah didn't seem to know the dance moves but was doing an able job of following his lead.

Suddenly there was Jed Delacourt, a drink in one hand, too smashed to even see straight. He grabbed Annie's hand and jerked her toward the dance floor, singing "Gotta Dance!" at the top of his lungs. The spike heel of her left pump snapped, sending Annie sprawling forward. The rhinestone clip flew from her hair, sending a mass of red curls in every direction. When she stood up and got her bearings, the dance floor was quiet, all eyes on her. One black stocking had a gaping hole in the knee, the other had a huge run up the back. Pushing her hair out of her face, she looked up at the tall, elegant dancer and saw her champagne dripping from the front of his tuxedo.

Breaking the silence was Jed's voice, saying, "Annie Mac-Pherson, I'd like you to meet Gordon Barclay."

Chapter 3

"Joel, would you please stop pacing? You're driving me nuts!"
The offices of MacPherson and Feinstein were so tiny that Annie hardly had to raise her voice. It was Wednesday morning, and for almost an hour Joel had been striding up and down the short hallway that divided the two attorneys' offices from the front room where Val O'Hara was busy typing.

"Sorry, I can't help it. It's almost noon. Don't you think the partners' meeting should be over by now?" He didn't need to remind her that the merger vote was first on the Kemble, Laughton agenda.

Letting Joel worry enough for them both, Annie started to feel nostalgic as she glanced around the cluttered office she'd called home for the past four years. While the best features of the cramped space were its low rent and proximity to the King County courthouse, Annie knew she'd miss the clunking radiator, threadbare carpet, and colorful characters who called the streets of Pioneer Square home. Not to mention Val O'Hara, who had notified the attorneys that she intended to retire to spend more time with her grandchildren. She'd even started planning her own retirement party.

The phone rang at 11:50. Val answered on the first ring and put the call on hold.

"It's Fred Duff on line one. He asked for either of you."

"You take it, Joel. I'm too nervous after my Saturday-night fiasco."

"Okay, if you say so." Joel picked up the call while Annie and Val listened from the doorway.

"Yes, Mr. Duff. . . . Thank you, sir. Yes, we had a very good time. . . . Uh-huh. . . . Could you hold on a minute?" Joel cupped his hand over the receiver to block out the din as a fire engine roared out of the station next door. "All right, I'm back. . . . I've got no problem with that. . . . Yes, we've discussed it, neither of us would have any objection. . . . I'm sure that can be arranged. All right, sir." He slowly placed the receiver back in the cradle but didn't say a word.

"Well?" said Annie.

"Come on, out with it," said Val impatiently.

He grinned, infuriating the two women.

"Tell us!" they exclaimed in unison.

"We start next Monday. They approved the starting salaries we asked for. Full partnership to be negotiated after a one-year probationary period."

Eyes closed, Annie let out the breath she hadn't known she'd been holding. She cracked open one eyelid. "You're not kidding, are you? This would not be a good time for a joke."

"Annie, the last time I told a joke was twelve years ago at my brother's bar mitzvah and it sank like the *Titanic*. No, Annie, I am not joking." He rushed to the refrigerator and came back carrying a bottle of Dom Pérignon and three mugs. He filled the mugs, then raised his in a toast. "To the greatest law-firm merger in the history of the world. MacPherson and Feinstein—meet Kemble, Laughton, Mercer, and Duff."

"Why does that sound like Bambi meets Godzilla?" Annie raised her glass and sipped. "Hey, Feinstein, this is good stuff. I wasn't sure you'd ever trust me with a glass of champagne again."

"I probably shouldn't. We still have to get through our probationary period, you know. Maybe it's just dance floors and senior partners I need to keep you away from."

"I still can't believe you threw champagne all over your new boss!" said Val, chuckling. "He must have been furious."

"Not at all," said Joel. "Annie was the only one who was upset."

"That was mainly because all I could think about was whether my dress had stayed where it was supposed to."

"Barclay was a perfect gentleman, stood there dripping wet and offered Annie a hand up as if nothing had happened—"

"—which of course made me even more embarrassed."

"Especially when *he* apologized to *Annie* because he had to excuse himself and couldn't stay to get acquainted," said Joel. "But the best part was when he promised to take Annie to lunch on our first day at work. The way he said it, I just knew we were in."

Val looked skeptical. "So all that pacing just now—that was for exercise?"

"Of course."

The year-old Nisqually Tower, with 106 stories, was for the moment the tallest building in Seattle's skyline. Annie had never liked it, with its steel-blue exterior and shape evocative of a futuristic ray gun. At its base it covered an entire city block, with a postmodern shopping mall occupying the first four floors. Inside, one could find everything from Thai fast food to Italian handbags to a "relaxation center" complete with flotation tanks and Shiatsu massage. It always reminded Annie of Fritz Lang's *Metropolis*: thousands of androids living and working underground without ever seeing natural sunlight.

Although Annie had been inside many times, she'd never quite mastered the labyrinthine geography. Snaking escalators surrounded by white marble carried pale-faced office workers to dozens of unknown destinations. A security guard in a powder-blue coat pointed her toward the elevators that would take her to the eighty-eighth floor. Maneuvering through the surging crowd, Annie was glad she didn't have a fear of heights.

The talking elevator announced her floor. She stepped out to face a circular reception desk, where three pretty young women with headsets were rapidly dispatching incoming calls at a computer panel worthy of NASA. Finally, when there was a lull, Annie jumped in.

"Hi, I'm Annie MacPherson. I'm starting work today, and I'm afraid I don't know where my office is."

"Thank-you-just-one-moment-please." The woman's sugary monotone sounded exactly like the talking elevator's. Annie watched, fascinated, as the receptionist handled a dozen more calls, the firm's name rolling effortlessly off her tongue. Annie looked closely to see if the woman was breathing. Maybe her earlier suspicion about androids had been truer than she thought.

At last the woman looked up and smiled. "Thank-you-for-waiting-Mr.-Barclay's-secretary-will-be-here-shortly-please-have-a-seat," she said, then calmly went back to her blinking lights.

Within a few moments a woman appeared from one of the side corridors. She was slender, about twenty-five, with honey-blond hair pulled back in a French braid. The cameo brooch at her throat gave Annie the impression of a demure, Victorian schoolgirl rather than a legal secretary. No android here. She held out her hand.

"Annie? Hi, I'm Nancy Gulliver. I'm Gordon Barclay's secretary, and I guess I'll be working for you, too, now. Come on, I'll show you where your office is. The movers delivered your furniture this morning, but I'm afraid it's rather a mess."

Annie followed the young woman down what seemed like an endless maze of corridors. She had a lilting walk that caused her silky skirt to swing back and forth.

"Should I drop bread crumbs so I'll be able to find my way back?"

Nancy laughed. "It's not so bad once you know the way. Just bear right until you see the green rest room signs, go left at the ladies' room, then right at the computers, and left at Central Filing. Right—left—right—left."

Right, thought Annie. Young lawyer last seen alive making a wrong turn at Central Filing.

"Here you go. There's a southern exposure, which means you get to see Mount Rainier on a clear day, but it also tends to get hot in the summertime. My desk is down at the end of the corridor, right outside Mr. Barclay's office. That reminds me, Mr. Barclay would like you to stop by his office at twelve today to go to lunch. Is that okay?"

"Sounds fine."

"I'll give you a few minutes to get settled in here and then I'll buzz the office manager. She'll take you on a complete tour of the office and fill you in on procedures, then get your picture taken for the firm brochure."

"Picture?" Annie asked with trepidation. Even though she'd worn her best summer suit in honor of starting her new job, having her picture taken always seemed like a trip to the dentist.

"Uh-huh. We have to keep the firm marketing brochure up-to-date for the clients. Your copy should be in the packet of materials on your desk. If there's anything you need, just let me know."

"Thanks, Nancy." After she left, Annie looked around at the sterile office with its bare white walls and teal carpeting plush enough to leave footprints in. Quite a step up from water-stained walls and scratched hardwood floors. At least her desk and credenza were familiar old friends. With their square corners and rough-grained blond wood reminiscent of old-fashioned library tables, they weren't anything special. But they had been her father's, left to her when he died, and she'd used them at every job she'd held since law school.

Annie thought back on those times when, as a child, she'd visited her father in his office. Her parents had separated when she was only five, divorced when Annie was six. Since she'd lived with her mother in California, Annie's visits to her father had been limited to Christmas, Easter, and three weeks during the summer.

He rarely had time to entertain her when she came to the office, but she remembered one time when he'd allowed her to make-believe she was a client. Annie had sat in the big leather chair across from his desk, drinking cocoa from a china cup and imperiously dictating which doll or teddy bear was to go to which playmate in her will. It was the only time she could remember playing a game with her father that didn't have a winner and a loser.

Now Annie sat in the big chair behind the desk. She ran her hand along the surface of the desk, ink-stained and scarred from years of use. It seemed like the one anchor of stability in an otherwise chaotic life. The private practice she'd worked so hard to build was gone now, and as for her personal life—well, she'd certainly mucked that up, hadn't she? Ahead she had a single year to prove herself to the firm, establish her worth as an attorney. Not that long ago the prospect wouldn't have frightened her at all. She'd always welcomed new challenges. But now things were different. Annie not only knew what it felt like to fail but what it felt like to run away.

Chapter 4

Gordon Barclay's corner office was at least twice as large as Annie's and practically had a one-hundred-and-eighty-degree view. The morning fog had lifted, and as Annie waited for Barclay she could see Queen Anne Hill and the Space Needle to the north and west across the sound to the Olympic Mountains. Down below, commuter ferries on their way to Vashon and Bainbridge islands etched curving white wakes in the water behind them. The snow-covered volcanic cone of Mount Rainier dominated the view to the south, towering above the surrounding Cascade range. Due to frequent low clouds, the great mountain made only rare cameo appearances, leading even native Northwesterners to point and stare as if they'd spotted a celebrity.

Even though he was on the telephone when she appeared at his office door at noon, Barclay had waved her in, gesturing that he was almost through. She tried to relax and keep her nervousness to a minimum. She could still hardly believe she was going to be working with Barclay, one of the superstars of the Washington bar, a man whose trials made the front page of the *Times*. He'd even been mentioned in a *Newsweek* article about the nation's top attorneys, along with F. Lee Bailey and Melvin Belli.

After checking out the view, Annie took a seat and looked around. Barclay's decorator must have been influenced at an early age by Horatio Hornblower novels, for the office held

enough brass to plate a battleship and the walls were covered
with Old World charts and stormy seascapes. Every surface
contained at least one nautical knickknack: a sextant, a pair of
antique running lights, a telescoping spyglass. At exactly twelve
noon the chronometer on the wall behind her chimed eight
bells. The only items that seemed out of place—and probably
the only things that actually reflected the real Gordon Barclay—were the graphite putter leaning against one wall and a
photograph of a smiling, sunburned Barclay in climbing gear
on a snow-covered peak.

"Ah, Annie. Sorry to keep you waiting. I'm so glad you could
join me for lunch." Gordon Barclay strode across the room
with the same air of confidence he'd shown on the dance floor.
Instead of the typical lawyer's navy-blue suit and rep tie, Barclay dressed with flair. His suit was of a gray-green nubby fabric that could have been silk and his tie, a floral pattern in
muted earth tones, was the up-to-the-minute fashion. He
wore a heavy gold and onyx ring on his right hand, but Annie
noticed that he didn't wear a wedding ring.

"I see you've found my pride and joy," he said of the photograph. "That was taken last summer the day Alex Guiterrez—
he's one of your fellow associates—and I climbed Rainier. God,
what a glorious experience!"

Annie was impressed. While the 14,000-foot peak didn't re-
quire a great deal of real mountain-climbing experience, it did
demand tremendous physical stamina. For Barclay to have
accomplished it at his age proved what kind of condition he
was in.

He perched casually on the edge of his desk. "Before I forget, I wanted to be sure to tell you that my tuxedo came back
from the dry cleaner's in flawless condition." His smile, worthy of Robert Redford, made Annie even more embarrassed.

Her face reddened. "I really need to apologize . . ."

He held up a hand. "No, I won't hear of it. It clearly wasn't
your fault. That was Jed Delacourt at his finest. I have to admit,
Annie, we've had our eye on that boy for some time now. That

party wasn't the first time he's shown . . . well, a certain lack of appropriate behavior. It's a problem that will most likely be wrapped up in the near future. But enough of that," he said, glancing at his watch. "We're here to talk about *you*. This will give me a chance to get to know you before I start piling on the work." He chuckled. "Everyone jokes about the awful hours we put in around here, but you'll find it's not that bad. In fact, we received a memo recently that slavery had been abolished and have adjusted our billing requirements accordingly. Shall we go?"

As they rode down in the elevator, Annie wondered what it was really going to be like to work for Barclay. Jed Delacourt's opinion was negative, but that could be explained by his precarious standing at the firm. According to his bio in the firm marketing brochure, the senior partner was purely a local product: B.A. from Seattle University, J.D. from the University of Washington, graduating summa cum laude from both. He'd been at the UW law school one year behind Annie's father, both of them returning to school after a stint in the military. She wasn't surprised to see that Barclay's tour of duty in the marines had earned him a Silver Star for bravery in action.

Annie hoped her disappointment wasn't too obvious when she saw that Barclay was taking her to the Cascade Club across the street. Even though Seattle's oldest men's club had been admitting women for the past two years, it had yet to rid itself of its stuffy conservatism and thinly veiled chauvinistic air.

The maitre d' showed them to a table in the East Room. The mauve-flowered wallpaper and chintz upholstery were holdovers from the time, not that long ago, when it had been the Ladies Dining Salon, the only place in the club where members could bring female companions. In those days women entered through a side door.

Their waitress, an ancient crone in black taffeta, set a basket of sticky buns on the table, another club tradition Annie had never been able to fathom. Her name tag, partially obscured by reading glasses on a fake pearl chain, read MILLIE.

"Need menus?" she snarled in a tone that implied she disapproved of the club's newfangled trend of admitting women.

"Yes, please, Millie." Turning to Annie, Barclay said, "The crab and avocado melt is one of my favorites, and on Mondays the soup is broccoli-cheddar."

"I take it you eat here often?" Annie was unable to keep the judgmental tone out of her voice. For years it had rankled her that male attorneys would come to the club to hobnob with clients—they still did in the segregated men's bar—to the exclusion of their female competition.

He smiled. "You don't approve, do you? Well, neither do most of your sister attorneys in the firm, I'm afraid. But they serve a good lunch at a fair price here, and it's quiet enough to have a private conversation. In most restaurants they put the tables so close together you can't hear yourself think. Besides, I bring women here in an attempt to change the atmosphere." He winked. "Don't worry. We'll break down the barriers eventually."

As they talked about work, Annie began to relax. She could understand why Barclay was so successful as a rainmaker. His ability to charm was almost overpowering. Annie tried to put her finger on it. Was it the eye contact, the way he listened attentively, or the way he managed to zero in on what she was thinking? The mere fact that a man as important as Barclay would take time out for a private lunch with a new associate was very flattering.

Millie returned for their orders. While Annie ordered a spinach salad, no bacon, light dressing on the side, she almost detected a sneer from Millie. Barclay's order of London broil with fried potatoes was more to her liking. Barclay persuaded Annie to join him in a glass of wine.

"So," he said when their drinks arrived. "You've been with the firm . . . what? four, five hours? How's it feel so far?"

"It's a little daunting. Last week I was in a three-person firm and KLMD has . . . what, about four hundred employees in all? That's a little bit of a change. But as much as I loved working in a small firm and being my own boss, the idea of not having to worry about drumming up business in a slow economy, meeting payroll, and collecting from recalcitrant clients is starting to sound pretty good."

"I'm glad to hear that. I think you'll like being part of our, uh, little family."

They paused while Millie set down their meals. Annie decided not to complain that her salad was generously laced with bacon and smothered in rich salad dressing, Millie's way of making a statement.

"I still have to make it through probation, of course."

"That's true. I'm not going to lie to you," Barclay said seriously. "Working at KLMD is no piece of cake. The hours are long, the expectations are high. Many of the young attorneys we hire simply don't make the cut. Your friend Delacourt, for example." He gestured with his knife and Annie got the point. "But trust me on this one. There's a special place for you in this firm, Annie."

His overly friendly tone, or maybe his attentive eye contact, made Annie shift in her chair. Then she decided she was being silly, that Barclay was just trying to make her feel welcome.

He leaned back. "You know, now that I see you in person, I can see the family resemblance."

"Family resemblance?"

"I was good friends with your father, you know. It's more than just the red hair. You're a regular chip off the old block, as they say."

"My father was a handsome man, so I'll take that as a compliment."

"It was intended as such. I knew George in law school, although we weren't in the same class. We were at the U-Dub together—first met as opponents in a moot-court competition. Your father won, though to this day I'll swear I gave the better argument. That was the beginning of a long and friendly rivalry, you might say. Always competing over this or that, you know how young men are." He laughed, stabbing a little too violently into his steak. "Young women, too, these days, I guess. So what about it? Did you inherit your father's competitive streak? You're smiling, so I'll take that as a yes."

"I wonder sometimes if it's a benefit or a curse."

"Both, of course. But we competitive types, Annie, we've got a leg up on the rest of the world. Everyone knows that life's a game, but we play to win. As some general said, there's no second prize for runner-up." Setting down his knife and fork, Barclay pushed his plate away and sighed. "George MacPherson. Old George. It's been a while since I've thought about him. Brilliant legal mind. We were hired by KLMD the same year, you know. He'd worked as a prosecutor for a while, just like you did, and I was straight out of law school. We were like this"—he crossed two fingers—"for five years. I always felt bad that we more or less lost touch after he left the firm. Such a shock when I heard he'd died. His heart, wasn't it?"

"Yes."

"And how old was he?"

"Only forty-six."

"Damn, that's young." Barclay took a gulp of water, as if to wash away a bitter taste. "But he probably saved my life, now that I think about it. Back then we didn't know all this stuff about fat and cholesterol, stress and high blood pressure. After your father passed away, quite a few of us started taking notice of our health. Before that I never exercised, can you believe it?" He looked down at his plate. "I usually eat right, too, but today was a *special* occasion."

Again Annie got that niggling feeling that Barclay was coming on a bit too familiarly, but perhaps that was just his style. She pushed the thought aside.

"I understand you're doing an article on George? Is that what I read in the *Bar News*?"

"Yes, well, research for part of a book, really. A friend of mine at the university is editing a book on Washington attorneys and their landmark cases. I was honored that she wanted to include a short piece on my father, and she asked me if I'd pull together the research."

"Interesting. And how's it coming? You'll be focusing on one or two major cases, I take it? He did some civil rights cases, didn't he?"

"He did, and that will be mentioned, but actually my friend wants more of a biographical piece, a personal study. She's interested in what types of people choose law as a career and succeed at it. I'm nowhere near organized yet. I just recently got all of his papers out of storage and will have to start putting them in order."

"You have much to work with, after all this time?"

"Surprisingly, yes. My father was very meticulous."

Barclay laughed. " 'Meticulous.' I remember the way his desk always looked, not a paper out of place. Those of us who weren't quite as organized as old George used to wonder how he did it. Did you inherit that trait as well?"

Annie smiled. "Unfortunately, no. I can't seem to work unless I'm surrounded by piles threatening to topple at any moment." They were interrupted by the apologetic maitre d'.

"Mr. Barclay, I hate to disturb you, but there's a Mr. Guiterrez in the lobby. He apologizes but says he must speak to you regarding an emergency."

Barclay looked displeased. Both he and Annie were only halfway through their meals. "All right. Send him in." To Annie he said, "Terribly sorry about this, but Alex would never interrupt unless it was important."

The maitre d' returned, followed by a man in his late twenties. His skin was fair, but he had Hispanic features and dark, intense eyes. Built like a bantamweight boxer, he seemed as nervous as if he were about to step into the ring. The maitre d' pulled another chair up to the table.

"Annie, this is Alex Guiterrez. He's one of our newer associates and an invaluable member of our insurance defense team. Alex is what you might call my right-hand man. I used to call him my boy wonder, but I guess I'll have to stop that when Alex turns thirty this July. Right, guy?''

"You better, Gordon." Annie shook the hand he extended but noticed that Alex Guiterrez didn't return her smile. His black eyes were unreadable.

"So, Alex. What's this emergency?''

Alex glanced at Annie, as if uncomfortable about delivering his news in front of an audience. "It's Walt Wiley over at Trans-Pacific Casualty. About the, uh, upcoming plans. He's . . . concerned about some of the details. I sensed that he might be wavering.''

Barclay frowned. "Not good. This could delay things terribly. I'd better get over there right away and smooth things over." Slapping Alex on the back, he said, "You made the right call coming over here. I feel terrible about having to run off like this, Annie. Alex, why don't you stay with Annie while she finishes her lunch? Have some coffee and dessert. I'll take care of the check on my way out." Without waiting for a reply, Barclay strode toward the door.

Alex twisted in his chair, drumming a nervous rhythm on the armrest. He clearly didn't appreciate the order he'd just been given.

"So," said Annie, wishing she could eat faster and conclude the meal, "how long have you been with KLMD?''

"Four years." Somehow he made the simple reply sound like a threat. She could see the tension in his neck muscles. He looked away.

"Are you from around here?''

His head snapped back. "Look," Alex said brusquely, "you may be charming the pants off of Gordon, but don't try your act with me. It was Gordon who wanted you here, nobody else. But in this place what Gordon wants, Gordon gets.''

Annie set her fork down and took a deep breath. Alex's snide outburst had a ring of jealousy to it. She remembered Deborah Silver's reference to her as the "girl wonder." Perhaps Alex felt his role as Gordon's right-hand man was being threatened.

Keeping her voice low, she said, "I'm sure you have other things to do besides stay here with me, Mr. Guiterrez. Why don't you feel free to go do whatever it is I'm keeping you from, and we'll get better acquainted some other time. My feeling is, since we're going to be working together in the same department, we might as well make an effort to get along. What do you say?"

There was no friendliness in Alex's thin smile. "There's a lot you have to learn, Annie MacPherson. Personally, I don't think we're going to be working together for very long."

Chapter 5

At eight o'clock that Friday night most of the KLMD offices were dark, their occupants gone to a health club, a bar, or home to the family for dinner. With his shirtsleeves rolled up and his tie loosened, Gordon Barclay pored over the spread sheets with the intensity he normally reserved for trial work. He jumped when he heard the sharp rap on the door, then quickly covered the papers on his desk.

"Who is it?"

The door opened a crack. "It's just me, Gordon."

Barclay's muscles relaxed. "Oh, Alex. Come on in." The overhead lights were switched off; the office was illuminated only by the yellowish glow of Barclay's desk lamp and the green of his humming computer terminal. Alex Guiterrez entered and pulled the door shut behind him. The lamp cast a huge, hulking shadow of the small man on the wall.

Alex gestured at the spread sheets. "How're we looking?"

Barclay leaned back in his chair and grinned slyly. He pulled a bottle of Glendullan single-malt whiskey and two snifters out of his credenza and poured them each a drink. "I had a very satisfactory chat with Walt Wiley late this afternoon."

Alex's expression was that of a shoplifter who's just seen the security guard go into the alley for a cigarette break. "He's decided not to back out, then?"

"He was feeling pretty shaky on Monday—the day you talked to him—but I managed to get him calmed down. Now that he's had a few more days to think about it, he's with us one hundred percent. He told me that the day we pull out of Kemble, Laughton he'll fax over a blanket authorization to send *all* of his files with us."

"All of them? You're kidding. Including the cases for Spectrum Defense International? They've been Fred Duff's client for years. That's enough business to keep fifteen attorneys busy full-time."

Barclay nodded. "It's far more than I expected. If we'd gotten only forty percent of Walt's business, we'd have had it locked up."

"Spectrum Defense! How on earth . . ." He paused, then looked Barclay in the eye. "Senator Quinn?"

Barclay picked up his snifter and twirled it in his hand, watching the amber liquid cling to the sides of the glass. "A few words in the right ears."

Alex tossed his drink back in one swallow. "A man has to be careful when he owes favors to the devil."

"Quinn knows what he's getting out of the deal."

Alex gave Barclay a questioning look, but the older man said no more. "So," said Alex. "Where does this put us?"

"Here. Take a look. We've got solid commitments from Physician's Fund and the Apex Group. With the attorneys coming over from Bemville, Couchet, that'll bring the business from Canadian Fidelity and the Heritage Mutual. And if Bill Flores joins us, he's assured me he can bring the FNA Indemnity business. I'd say we are in a comfortable position to control the insurance defense business in Seattle."

"Control?" Alex chuckled, tapping a rhythm on his thigh. "Shit, Gordon. We're going to *dominate* this town."

Barclay smiled. "I know. I can't wait to see the look on Fred Duff's face when I give him the news. The old bugger will have a stroke on the spot."

"And you're sure the financing works out? With my partnership contribution coming out of my draw rather than up front?"

"I told you, Alex. I'm taking care of the financing. It's solid, believe me." And the less you know about the details, the better, Barclay thought. As a protégé Alex Guiterrez had exceeded all of Barclay's expectations. He was loyal and ruthless, and he and Barclay seemed to think alike on so many levels. The senior lawyer had found that he could trust Alex Guiterrez with practically anything. But not this.

"What about associates? Have you made any decisions? I still think Deborah Silver is the logical choice."

Barclay stiffened. "I know you do, and it makes me question your otherwise sound judgment. Her writing is adequate at best, her image is unprofessional, and her billings are sloppy."

"The clients like her."

"The clients like her because they think they've got a shot at sleeping with her, which probably isn't too far off the mark. Now I don't want you bringing up her name again. Like I told you before, I'd rather hire new grads we can train as we like. They also don't cost as much." He paused. "But I am planning to make a partnership offer to MacPherson." Barclay watched Alex's face to gauge his reaction. There was none. If Alex was angry at being put in his place, he didn't show it. But then, Barclay thought, Alex rarely revealed his emotions.

The two men leaned over the spread sheets. The first page was the profit-and-loss projection Barclay had prepared for the new law firm. The estimated start-up date was three weeks away.

"It looks good, Gordon, but do you think we can make it by then?"

"We'll have to." He looked up and watched Alex closely. "I have reason to believe that there may have been a leak."

"What?" Alex exclaimed, nearly jumping out of his chair. "Somebody knows we're planning to split off from the firm?"

"It's possible. I've been getting some very disturbing anonymous letters lately from someone who says he 'knows everything.' I can't think what else he'd be referring to. We may have to move up the date, get the files over to the new office space before anyone at KLMD can do anything to stop us."

"But how could there be a leak? We have to do something about this. You think it was one of the guys coming over from the other firms?"

"Calm down. You're getting too worked up about this. I don't think it's one of the other attorneys—they're all trustworthy. After all, it's as important to them as it is to us that we make a clean break."

"Well, what did the letters say?"

"Here, I'll show you." Barclay unlocked his personal filing cabinet, located the most recent letter, and handed it to Alex. "They're all pretty much the same. I got this one a little over a week ago."

"A week ago? Shit, the news could be all over the firm by now. What about your wife? Could she have told someone?"

"Adele? Don't be ridiculous. She's as lost in the ozone as ever. She wouldn't notice if I were planning a trip on the space shuttle. No, I'm convinced it has to be someone inside the firm. The letters have come through the inter-office mail, on KLMD stationery."

"Nancy?" Alex asked slowly. Barclay's secretary seemed like innocence itself. Yet it was hard to ignore the fact that she was the only other person at KLMD who knew about the move. The fact that the entire office knew Barclay was having an affair with her didn't help matters.

Barclay frowned. "I'd hate to think so, but nothing's impossible. She's known about the plan since the beginning."

"Could she have found out she's not going to come with you when you start the new firm?"

A bitter smile crept onto Gordon Barclay's face as he refilled their glasses. "I'm not sure she'd even want to anymore, my friend."

"What do you mean?"

"What I mean is that the girl's thrown me over. Dumped me flat. I guess she got tired of dating an old married man."

"What? For chrissakes, when did this happen?"

"Just this morning. She read me the riot act, then didn't come back after lunch today. What d'ya think of that, Alex?"

The younger man sat back in the shadows. What Alex thought was that he'd discovered the source of their leak.

Nancy Gulliver threw another damp wad of Kleenex toward the growing pile at her feet, startling Groucho. The huge black-and-white tomcat, reacting to her sobs, had been trying for an hour to crawl into her lap but kept getting ignored. Her tiny basement apartment, usually so neat, was strewn with clothes and papers. A half-empty bottle of white zinfandel was starting to leave a ring on the coffee table. Hardly the way she'd imagined spending this special Friday night.

Tonight would have been their one-year anniversary. She had wanted so much to spend the evening with Gordon. He'd said his wife had gone out of town after all, so he could have stayed the entire night for once. But then it had all exploded, all this rage she hadn't even known she was holding in.

Nancy walked into the bathroom in search of another box of Kleenex. She pulled her hair into a ponytail and splashed cold water on her face in an attempt to wash away her smeared makeup and make herself presentable. Desperate for someone to talk to, she'd called her sister, Suzy. Ever dependable, Suzy had said she'd be right over. Nancy dried her face, then grimaced when she saw her reflection in the mirror. Her hazel eyes, ordinarily her prettiest feature, had swollen to puffy slits, and her cheeks were mottled with ugly red splotches.

A light tap, then a key turned in the outside door.

"Suzy, is that you?" Nancy called from the bathroom.

"Yeah, Nance, sorry it took me so long to get here." Suzy Gulliver walked over and embraced her sister with a warm hug, patting her on the back. "Hey, kiddo, it's gonna be okay. You know you did the right thing. Now I'm here, you can tell me all about it."

For sisters, they didn't look much alike. Where Nancy was
slender, almost fragile-looking, Suzy Gulliver was short and
stocky, her well-muscled body giving evidence of her passion
for aerobics and working out with weights. She kept her curly
dark hair cropped short for convenience, unwilling to spend
hours in the bathroom with hair dryers and curling irons as
Nancy did.

Nancy noticed that her sister still had the spare door key in
her hand. "Here, I need to put that back."

"Oh, I forgot. I'll do it." Suzy opened the outside door and
returned the key to its hiding place under a pot of geraniums.
"But I still think you should find someplace else to put your
spare key. Everybody knows to look under the flowerpot. It's
not safe, especially with the folks upstairs on vacation."

This comment brought forth a new burst of tears.

"Did I say something wrong?"

Nancy sniffed. "It was Gordon's idea. I kept it there for
him."

"Well, then. That settles it. You can find a new place for it,
now that that stinker's out of your life." Suzy grabbed a wine-
glass from the kitchen, poured herself some of the zinfandel,
and refilled Nancy's glass.

"Okay, start at the beginning. What happened?"

"Well," Nancy said, "the last month or so has been really
weird. Gordon's been so moody lately. Remember I told you
he's been getting these anonymous letters? About one a week
for the last month or so. They were really ugly and threatening.
They all talked about him 'coming clean' about something. I
told him I could help him figure out what they were about, I
even gave him my ideas, but he said he didn't want my help."

"Typical."

"But then, a few weeks ago, he needed me to do some private correspondence. He told me he was planning to split off
from the law firm, he and Alex Guiterrez. They're going to start
a new firm with some other lawyers in town."

"Wow, that's big news. This could really stir things up, huh?"

Nancy nodded. "I guess it would be kind of bad for the other lawyers at Kemble, Laughton, huh?"

"No shit, Sherlock. From what you tell me, Barclay's one of their biggest guns. It might even wreck the firm."

"I guess that must be what those awful notes were about, then."

"Uh-huh," Suzy said. The cat, having given up on Nancy, sprawled across Suzy's lap. She scratched him behind the ears as he purred loudly. "So, what happened today to set things off?"

Nancy sighed. "I've been bugging him for weeks about tonight. It's our anniversary of seeing each other for a year. I really wanted to do something special, fix him a nice romantic dinner, have him spend the night. The timing was perfect. His wife was going to be out of town at some decorating convention or craft show or something. I kept asking him about it, and finally last week he said yes."

She poured more wine into her glass, spilling some on the carpet. "Oh, damn."

"It's all right. We'll clean it up in a minute. Then what happened?"

"Okay, so this week he started, like, ignoring me. On Monday, we were supposed to sneak out at lunchtime and maybe go to the Four Seasons Hotel, you know? We've done that before—it's so elegant. He orders room service and stuff. But he told me at the last minute that he was taking that new associate, Annie MacPherson, out to lunch. And then on Tuesday I swear he didn't say a single word to me."

The look on Suzy's face implied that she was struggling to hold back her opinion.

Nancy continued. "I decided to write him a note. I told him that I didn't like the way he was treating me and that I needed more from him. I put it on his desk on Wednesday. He must

have seen it; but can you believe it, he didn't even say a word
to me until today. And even then he didn't mention the note.
He just breezed into the office, talking real fast, really manic,
and blurted out, 'Come on, we need to get out of here.'
'Where?' I said, and he goes, 'The hotel. Now!' Just like that.
Like an order, telling me, not asking me.''

"The bastard.''

"I reminded him about tonight and asked him what time he
was coming over, you know?''

"What did he say?''

"He just said he couldn't. He'd *forgotten*.'' Nancy sniffed
and Suzy handed her another Kleenex. '' 'Sorry' and all that,
he says, 'but gee, you know how it goes.' Well, I told him I
didn't know and I thought we'd had plans.''

"And?''

"He said . . . he said he had to work late because everything
was coming together so fast. He planned to stay at the office
all night.''

"All night at the office? How come?''

"I don't know. Something about this new law firm, I guess.
He just tried to brush me off, said it couldn't be helped. So I
got real mad. I mean, I was really looking forward to this. He's
never spent the whole night here before. I even got raspberry
croissants and his favorite tea for breakfast. And then he comes
in and treats me like that. I couldn't take it anymore. I don't
know where I got the courage, but I told him, 'We have to
talk,' and I sat down.''

"And then what? How did he take that?''

"Lousy. He slammed the door, hardly let me say anything,
just got all upset, saying it was my job to understand, how I
had an *obligation*. . . .''

"How *you* had an obligation?''

"Yeah, can you believe that? So I told him off. Right then
and there. I said, 'I'm not your whore—' ''

"You said *that*?''

Nancy nodded, unable to choke back a new flood of tears,

as her sister reached over and squeezed her hand. "I said, 'You don't pay me that much. And if this is how much you care for me, then it's over,' and I just walked out. I grabbed my purse and got to the elevator before he could stop me. I was . . . I was going to go back after lunch, but I just couldn't. I got so scared and . . ."

Shoving the massive cat off her lap, Suzy leaned over and wrapped Nancy in her arms. "Oh, baby, don't cry. It's not your fault." Nancy let herself be cradled, feeling better now that she had Suzy's shoulder to lean against. "It's gonna be okay, kid. Everything gets better with time. That's it. Now, come on, let's get cleaned up and go to a movie, okay? You want to do that? Just you and me?"

Nancy sniffed and then nodded. "I guess so. Just as long as it's not a . . . a love story with a happy ending."

"Sure, kid. Anything you want."

It was almost midnight when they got back to Nancy's place. Suzy got out to open the garage door while Nancy backed her Toyota down the steep driveway. After Suzy padlocked the garage door from the inside, they went through the adjoining door to the apartment.

"You sure you're going to be okay?" Suzy asked. "Tomorrow's Saturday. I could stay over if you like."

Nancy reached down and hefted Groucho, all sixteen pounds of him, into her arms. "No. Really, I'll be fine. But thanks for everything. It's helped just to talk it out."

"I'll come by in the morning then. We'll go shopping or something. And you'll call me tonight if you need me?"

"Yeah. Don't worry, I'm just going to go to bed. And thanks again."

Nancy watched Suzy go, then turned the dead bolt on the outside door. With Suzy gone, she felt the tears were ready to start again. If only she could get a good night's sleep, everything would surely look better in the morning.

She remembered the sleeping pills she had left over from her wisdom-tooth surgery and went to the bathroom to search for them. The dose was one pill, but as there were only two left in the bottle, she figured taking them both wouldn't hurt. She swallowed them one at a time, then tossed the empty bottle into the wastebasket. After one last trip around the one-room apartment to make sure all the windows were closed and locked, Nancy settled into bed with Groucho curled up at her feet. It didn't take long for her to fall asleep.

Dead to the world, Nancy Gulliver didn't hear the key turn in the dead bolt for the second time that night or see the gloved hand slip it back under the flowerpot.

Inside, the basement apartment was dark but for a strip of amber from a streetlight creeping in through a crack in the curtains. There was just enough light to illuminate the outline of Nancy's sleeping form in the rumpled Hide-A-Bed, the empty wine bottle, the papers and clothes strewn uncharacteristically about. And enough to see that no windows were open.

The figure surveyed the room, mentally measuring it. The low ceilings would help—less air space. Moving silently, the figure searched for Nancy's handbag, finally spotting it on the kitchen counter. The visitor ran a gloved hand along the spotless white surface, impressed that it was so clean, not a speck of grease.

Next to the handbag was Nancy's set of keys, which were picked up without a noise. The figure took the most important item from its plastic bag and propped it against a canister, where it was in full view. Now for the difficult part.

Through the adjoining door into the one-car garage, closing the door behind to muffle the noise. Good, the length of hose the visitor brought would be more than enough. A hand attached the hose to the tailpipe with duct tape.

The figure opened the car door and sat inside, taking a deep breath. It was an older-model car, likely to be noisy. If the plan was going to fail, this would be the time. The gloved hand turned the key. The motor started. There was no noise from the apartment.

Moving quickly now, the trespasser opened the adjoining door and looked inside. Nancy wasn't stirring. The visitor took the hose and led it into the apartment. Excellent, it reached within a few feet of the bed.

Then, satisfied with the job, the figure departed. After the click of the key relocking the outside door, the basement was still, except for the soft hum of the Toyota's engine.

Chapter 6

Spring weather in Seattle is a lottery. One day the sky is the color of asphalt, and the mist is heavy enough to make moss grow on the north side of one's shoes. The next day the colors are as crisp and clear as Dorothy's entrance into a Technicolor Oz. Annie was lucky. After a grueling first week at Kemble, Laughton, Mercer, and Duff, her first Saturday was easily worth five stars.

The second-story deck at Copacabana, a Bolivian restaurant near the Pike Place Market, was packed. Every available table had been moved from the inside out onto the narrow, triangular patio. From where she sat Annie could look over the window boxes bursting with red and yellow tulips to the street below, where tourists were busy stalking the wild souvenir, a sticky cinnamon bun in one hand, a Space Needle pencil sharpener in the other. Did the little man at the Asian vegetable stall ever sell any of those jumping paper snakes? Across the way, under the big clock, an entire family decked out in "Emerald City" T-shirts was posing for a photograph with the life-size bronze pig. The pig statue had appeared a few years back— Annie never really did understand why.

Despite the touristy aspects, locals still came to the market in droves to buy in bulk spices and teas, at the Market Spice Shop, fresh fruits and vegetables at the family-owned stalls, and the best salmon and Dungeness crab available in the city. Annie could hear the guys at the Pike Place Fish Market putting on their typical show, hawking their wares and slinging twenty-pound fish to each other as they rapidly filled orders. Down on the sidewalk a familiar street performer was charming a group of children with his raspy-voiced rendition of the "Teddy Bears' Picnic," making them giggle as he shook his bushy gray beard. While she waited for her friend to show up, Annie got out her dark glasses and the *Seattle Weekly* and settled in for some intensive sun therapy.

A little before noon Annie spotted Ellen O'Neill turning the corner onto the alley that runs through the public market, moving at a brisk pace. Everything about the tiny woman was designed for speed, from her functional blunt-cut hair to her brightly colored cotton shorts and T-shirt. Even her voice raced at an accelerated tempo, like a record album accidentally set at 45 rpm. Ellen waved to Annie from the street below and sprinted up the steel-grated stairs.

"Good, you got a table already," she said, not even slightly out of breath. "As usual, I am utterly famished!"

"With everything else in my life so uncertain, I'm glad to hear that some things at least are constant."

"Hey, there are three things you can always count on. Death, taxes, and Ellen O'Neill's appetite. I need some serious food."

As if on cue, the waitress arrived with menus. The women each ordered a Corona and then looked over their choices. When the waitress returned with their beers, Ellen ordered a large bowl of shrimp soup, paella, and corn bread with extra butter. Annie opted for the *ensalada chola*, a light chicken salad with slices of avocado.

"I take it you're still running marathons?" Annie asked. She could almost feel her own metabolism speeding up just by sitting next to Ellen.

"Yup. I do fifteen miles a day for training and at least one race a month. I couldn't stop now if I wanted to. I'd probably keep the same eating habits and balloon up to three hundred pounds overnight. And I imagine you're still addicted to caffeine?"

"It's my only vice."

"Right, you expect me to believe that one. Can you think how zingy I'd be if I drank coffee? I wouldn't need to run—I'd just *fly* everywhere." Ellen leaned back and looked Annie straight in the eye. "Now down to business. I know I invited you out to lunch to celebrate this new job of yours, but that's not what I want to hear about. You've been back from your 'vacation' since February, and I have yet to hear one word about New Zealand. Or David Courtney."

Annie looked around for the waitress. She should have known when Ellen asked her to lunch that she'd want to know what happened. She couldn't avoid the subject forever. "But there's really not much to say. We had a great time." The waitress arrived with their orders and had to juggle plates to find enough room for everything on the tiny table.

"The strangest thing happened at work yesterday . . ." Annie continued.

"Uh-uh, not so fast. You're changing the subject. I'm not going to let you get away with that."

"Ellen . . ."

"Ellen nothing. Look, you surprise the world by taking a leave of absence from your law practice to go halfway around the world for a trip with a man you'd known for all of . . . what? Two weeks? Completely out of character—we all think space aliens from the party planet Pismo have come down and inhabited the body of the workaholic we all know and love. Fine. Then you show up here again after three months with nothing but a sunburn and the clothes on your back, and you refuse to talk about it?"

"I didn't say that."

"I know. You didn't say *anything*. Oh, except for that one postcard. What did it say again? 'The weather is here, wish you were beautiful'?"

Annie laughed. "That's not what it said!"

"Okay, you're right. It said 'Having the time of my life with Mr. Right, we're going to get married and have fourteen kids

and live on a South Sea island and drink mango juice. . . .'
Or did it say 'David is the most wonderful, exciting, passion-
ate . . .' ' "

"All right. Stop. Do I have to tell you my life story just to
get you to shut up?"

"Yes. Or at least the Cliffs Notes synopsis—intense, thirtyish
attorney meets romantic mystery man in the San Juan Islands,
agrees to fly down and meet him on his sailboat in the South
Seas. . . . And then the plot thickens." Ellen paused to dig into
her food.

"Enough already. But it really isn't all that dramatic. I flew
to Auckland in late November. David met me and took me to
where his boat was moored. We spent three months sailing,
fishing, lying in the sun, and drinking mango juice. Except for
the mango juice, which I really wasn't crazy about, the vacation was wonderful. The boat was wonderful. David was wonderful."

"And?"

Annie shrugged. "And I decided to come back."

"Time out. I'm confused."

So was I, thought Annie. That was the problem.

"I don't know. I guess I missed the structure. Getting up
and going to work every day. Accomplishing something. For
David it's enough just to exist, live for the moment and all that.
I'm not wired that way."

"What did he say when you told him you were coming
back?"

Annie took a large bite of salad, then poured the rest of her
beer into her glass. Signaling to the waitress that she needed
more water, Annie debated whether to tell Ellen the truth.

"Not much, really."

"Hmm." Ellen stared skeptically, fork suspended in midbite.
"So what's next?"

Annie shrugged. "I'm going to work. He's going to finish his
trip. . . ."

"How long will that take?"

"Who knows? He didn't have any specific plans, just sailing until his money ran out. I assume I'll hear from him when he gets back to the West Coast. He's got friends in San Francisco he wanted to see. That's all I know."

"Do you miss him?" Ellen asked between spoonfuls of shrimp soup.

Annie paused, then nodded. "Yes."

Ellen's look said she knew there was more to the story, but she was smart enough not to push the issue. They were both quiet for a moment and quickly consented when the waitress asked if they each wanted another beer.

"So," said Ellen, trying to lighten the mood. "Moving to the next item on the agenda of 'catching up.' You may now tell me how the new job's working out. Is it weird not working in your little three-person office anymore?"

Annie savored her last slice of avocado. "It's bizarre. The secretary they assigned to me is this sweet young thing in her twenties who tries really hard, but I've got to take the time to explain everything to her. With Val it was the other way around—she told *me* what to do." She grabbed a piece of bread before Ellen ate it all. "And Joel's on a different floor now. It's so strange to call him on the phone instead of shouting down the hall."

"How does he like it?"

"He's in heaven. He's always hated doing the run-of-the-mill kinds of cases you get in a small practice, things like wills and guardianships. Now he's doing only complex real-estate cases and estate planning and loving it. He's the type of person who thrives on minutiae."

"And what about you?"

"I think I'll have to tell you after I've recovered. The first week was thoroughly and completely overwhelming, convincing me I'm going to collapse from the stress. Other than that, I guess I like it all right."

Ellen mopped up the last of her paella with a piece of bread. "Stress? You think you've got stress?" She started counting on one hand. "This past week the hospital budget was due, and my secretary left three weeks early for her maternity leave, saying she just didn't feel like working anymore. The nurses were threatening to strike, the water was off for four hours on Tuesday when some construction workers sliced through a water main downtown. . . . Should I go on?"

"I take it you'll have no sympathy when I tell you that they assigned to me seventy-seven major insurance files that practically nothing's been done on, that next week I have to prepare for seven depositions and two summary judgment motions, answer three sets of interrogatories, and write a trial brief and jury instructions for a federal court case that is scheduled to go out a week from Tuesday?"

Ellen downed the last of her beer. "Sounds like a piece of cake to me."

"Well, how about the fact that I have to go spend the rest of my Saturday, and probably Sunday, at the office just to get organized enough so that I can find my files? Or that I'll be expected to bill an average of two hundred hours a month, not counting time spent on administrative work, committee participation, *pro bono* cases, and entertaining clients?"

"No sympathy here."

"You're no fun."

"Nope. There's only one answer for stress like that."

"What?"

"Industrial-strength chocolate. When we're through here, we'll hit the Dilettante for dessert."

An overweight man with a very large gun stood in the doorway of Annie's office, casting a shadow over the papers on her desk. On his uniformed hip a radio squawked and buzzed.

" 'Scuse me, ma'am?" He spoke with the slow drawl often heard in the more rural parts of Washington. He probably pronounced Washington with an *r*—*Worshingt'n*.

"Uh, fine, Officer."

Squinting at the new brass nameplate on her door, he asked, "Are you A. MacPherson?"

"Yes."

"Name's not on the list."

"Excuse me?"

"Th'authorized sign-in list. To work in this building on Saturday. Cain't be in here unless you're on the list." He hooked his thumbs in a belt that already hung several inches too low and said in an overbearing tone, "I think I may just have to ask you to leave, young lady."

Annie sighed. If she didn't get her desk organized, she'd be hopelessly behind on Monday. "Look. I can give you all the ID you want. They gave me a code to work the elevator, but I wasn't told about any list—"

The guard shook his head. "No can do. I want you outta here in five minutes or I call my buddies down at the security desk to help me out."

"Oh, for all the—" Annie started stacking her papers.

"She's all right, Bob. I'll vouch for her." Gordon Barclay, looking crisp in khaki slacks and a Ralph Lauren Polo shirt, appeared behind the guard and slapped him on the shoulder. "Bob, this is Annie MacPherson, our newest associate. Her name should have been placed on the supplemental employees list. I'll personally check the list on Monday and take all responsibility for her being here. Annie, you'll find that the security in this building is superb. The guards make regular rounds in the evenings and on Saturdays and get to know who's supposed to be here. They do a good job of keeping out the riffraff. If you plan to spend much time here at night or on weekends, Bob's a good person to get to know."

Satisfied that Annie wasn't a trespasser, the large man touched his hat and winked. "Some folks have even been known to bring me doughnuts. My favorite is the kind with those little colored sprinkles on top."

At their old firm Annie and Joel would hardly have been able to afford the doughnuts, much less a security guard. And in Pioneer Square, with its homeless population, work release centers, and high crime rate, a little security would have come in handy. She recalled one time when, while Val was at lunch, someone had come through and grabbed Annie's purse and Joel's laptop computer. Or that other time, when an unhappy husband of one of Annie's divorce clients had barged in waving a loaded shotgun and shouting pseudoreligious curses having to do with vengeance and hellfire. Annie decided to ignore Bob's earlier brusqueness and put doughnuts (colored-sprinkle variety) on her shopping list.

"I'll recognize you next time, ma'am—never forget a face. You have a nice day now." Mumbling into his radio, Bob ambled heavily down the hall toward the next lighted office.

"He may not be fast on his feet, but Bob does a good job," Barclay said. "As you can see, he takes his work extremely seriously. How's everyone treating you so far?"

"Couldn't be nicer. Several of the associates took me to lunch last week, and Joel and I are going to Fred Duff's for dinner tomorrow night."

"Ah, the famous Sunday-night hamburgers. You'll love Mrs. Duff; she's just as charming as Fred. Other than that . . . We're not working you too hard on your first week, are we?"

"Oh, no, the work load's fine," Annie lied. "I just thought I'd come in and sort through some of this paperwork." Annie gestured to the rainbow assortment of papers on her desk. "I swear this place has more forms than the IRS. There's the time sheet, where I have to divide my day into six-minute segments. Then there's the sheet for keeping track of time spent entertaining clients, as opposed to the form for office administration and committee participation. There's a computer log-on form, the computerized docket printout showing the precise location of all two hundred and fifty attorneys at any given moment.

The word processing priority request, fax log, travel voucher, expense-account reimbursement form, computer-entry data slip. How do you keep it all straight?"

Barclay chuckled. "It'll be second nature in no time. My wife thinks I'm crazy—whenever I answer the phone at home, I automatically reach for a time sheet in case it's a business call."

Annie noted that it was the first time Barclay had mentioned a wife. "I don't know," she said. "I think I'll be filling out my retirement papers in triplicate before this stuff comes naturally. If you have a few minutes later on, I've got some questions on the files you gave me. I need to get a feel for priorities, which matters you'd like me to work on first."

"Sure, I'll be in most of the afternoon. My tee time isn't until—"

Hearing a commotion out by the elevators, they both stopped and looked up. The security guard's voice carried down the hallway.

"Stop! You cain't come up here. Now you hold it right there, miss."

"God damn it, let go of me!"

"Ouch! Hey, you little bitch . . . You *bit* me, for cryin' out loud. Come back here."

"No!"

A small woman with closely cropped brown hair came hurtling around the corner, with Bob huffing along several paces behind her.

"Where is he?" she shouted. "Where is that bastard Gordon Barclay?"

Stunned, Barclay didn't budge but just stared in amazement at the small woman.

She threw a brown-paper shopping bag at his feet and lunged for Barclay's neck. He stopped her in midflight and struggled to hold her at arm's length by both shoulders. Despite her small size she had the muscles of an athlete. "God damn you, god damn you, god damn you," she yelled, head flailing, hot tears streaming down her face.

The security guard finally caught up just as she succeeded in spitting at Barclay. Placing one hand over the woman's mouth, the other circling her waist, the guard pulled her away while she kicked and thrashed.

"What the hell's going on here?" Barclay asked, outraged.

"You mean you don't know this woman?" Bob asked, out of breath.

"I've never seen her before in my life."

Slowly she stopped kicking. The guard set her feet down on the floor. "Now, look here, miss, I'm gonna uncover your mouth so's you can tell us what's going on. Calmly now."

He gestured with his eyes for Annie to pick up the paper bag the woman had tossed on the floor. Annie was surprised to feel how heavy it was. Bob uncovered the woman's mouth and slowly loosened his grip on her waist. Immediately she lunged for Barclay again, tearing at his shirt with her fingernails until Bob got her back in his grasp. "Now that's not what I asked you to do, little lady." They could hear her trying to speak under his hand. "If I uncover your mouth, will you talk to us nice and ladylike?" She struggled to nod.

"All right now."

Her mouth uncovered, she licked her lips and glared at Barclay. She jerked her head at the bag. "That's for you, you goddamned son of a bitch."

"What?" Barclay asked, taking the bag from Annie. "Good God, child. What on earth?" The bag fell from his hands. When it hit the floor, the stiff tail of a dead black-and-white cat fell out.

"Don't you recognize poor old Groucho? I brought him as a little token of your 'romantic interlude.' But you probably didn't see it that way. You probably thought my sister was just another little slut you could have some fun with, then toss in the garbage."

"Young lady, that's enough. I'll talk to you in private."

"Uh-uh. You're not getting off that easy. I want witnesses to what I have to say." She looked at Annie and the guard. "They both stay."

A few minutes later they were all seated stiffly in Barclay's office. After placing the dead cat out of sight, the security guard stood in the doorway with one hand resting on the butt of his gun. Annie and the young woman sat on the sofa, with Barclay sitting on the edge of his desk.

"All right, young lady," said Barclay. "We'd all like to know what this nonsense is about."

"I'd like to know how in heck you got in here," Bob interjected, still red in the face from his vigorous encounter.

She turned to look at him. "It was easy. I signed my sister's name in the log and punched her code into the elevator. I've done it lots of times to pick things up for her, since I live close to downtown."

Bob was still breathing heavily, perhaps less from exertion than from a wounded ego, because someone had so easily breached his fortress. He was about to inquire further when Barclay cut in.

"I don't care how you got in here. I want to know who you are, and what in God's name are you doing here with a dead cat?"

"I'm Suzy Gulliver, your ex-lover's sister." She enunciated the words slowly and carefully for maximum effect. "Didn't you recognize the cat? I know you've been to Nancy's apartment because she kept a special key for you under the flowerpot."

Looking at the tightly wound woman on the sofa, Annie found it hard to connect her to Barclay's secretary. Although both women had the same heart-shaped face and wide-set hazel eyes, this little powerhouse seemed to have little in common with the willowy secretary. She had a toughness that Annie would have been surprised to observe in her quiet sister.

At the mention of Nancy's name, Barclay blanched. When he spoke again, the harsh edge was gone from his voice. "Why are you here? Is Nancy all right?"

"No, Barclay. She's not all right. I found her this morning. You remember her little basement apartment? Hardly enough room to turn around in? Well, this morning I opened the door on a small, stuffy room filled with exhaust fumes. I practically passed out myself getting to her. She's dead, Barclay. I found my only sister dead with a damned dead cat curled up on her bed." Silent tears ran down the woman's face. She refused to acknowledge their presence by wiping them away. Through wet eyes she stared unblinkingly at Barclay.

"Was it . . . an accident?"

She shook her head. "No, this was no accident, Barclay. Does this sound like an accident to you? There was a length of hose running from the tail pipe of her car into the middle of the bedroom. The car was out of gas, and the keys were in the ignition. There was an empty bottle of sleeping pills in her wastebasket and a damned suicide note in the kitchen propped up so it's the first thing you see. My . . . sister . . . killed . . . herself, Barclay. And it's your fucking fault."

She paused. When she continued, her voice was soft, almost as if she was talking to herself. "I was with her most of the night last night. She was depressed. We talked about a lot of things, but mostly about you, about the fight you had, about how she still loved you in spite of the way you treated her. In her mind you were such a big man, Barclay. She thought you ran the world single-handedly and still had time for a round of golf. Well, all I can say is, if you're so damned important, couldn't you manage to keep your hands off the people who work for you, ordinary people who look up to you and respect you?"

Barclay shook his head. "I never thought—"

"Exactly. Men like you never think."

"Why did you come here? What do you want from me?"

Standing up, she spoke with calm deliberation. "What do I want? What do I *want*? Besides your burning in hell? Besides your living with the guilt of my little sister's innocent death for the rest of your natural life? Nothing, Barclay. I don't want a goddamned thing from you. I just wanted you to hear it from me." The woman turned and walked away, leaving a claustrophobic stillness in the room behind her.

Chapter 7

"Ouch, not so hard."

"Sorry, I thought you liked my back rubs," said Deborah Silver, pulling her hands away. She sat back on her heels and caught her reflection in the mirror over his dresser. The afternoon sunlight filtering through the miniblinds made a tigerlike pattern on her naked skin. She liked the way it looked.

"I do," her partner replied. "I just don't like to be kneaded like bread dough."

For that he got a jab in the ribs. "I don't *need* anyone, buster, and don't you forget it. Hey, what are you—"

Before she could get the words out, Alex Guiterrez had rolled and lunged, flipping her over and pinning her shoulders to the mattress. Despite his small stature, the muscles of his upper body were well developed. The bristly hair on his chest made Deborah want to tickle him, but the way he held her, she couldn't budge.

Smiling, Alex said, "I think I've changed my mind. I don't want a back rub anymore."

"What do you want?" she asked with a smirk, holding herself perfectly still. When he released the pressure on her shoulders, she seized the moment and rolled to the edge of the bed, but Alex managed to spank her as she jumped to the floor. He crouched in the middle of the bed as she moved around the room, planning her next move. They kept their eyes locked, like two animals circling before a fight.

She grabbed a pillow that had fallen to the floor and swung it at him as hard as she could. He grabbed the end and pulled her onto the bed, immobilizing her beneath him.

"Truce, truce," she called, laughing and gasping for breath. "It's no fair, you're a wrestler."

"But I never tangled with anyone like *you* in the ring." Alex rolled onto his back, pulling Deborah on top of him.

"I'm sure that would have been against the rules," she said, leaning down and brushing his chest with her nipples, then pushing herself away.

"Only because you don't fight fair," he said, grabbing a handful of black hair and using it to pull her down again.

"What's the fun if you don't cheat?"

"What time is it?" Alex asked sometime later. "You want something to eat? I've got some leftover shish kebabs."

"Lamb? Do you know how much fat there is in red meat? Besides, I ate like a pig yesterday. I don't want to eat for a week." A lazy hand fumbled for the clock on Alex's bedside table. "Five P.M.? Do you realize we've stayed in bed *all day*?"

"We're so decadent," he said.

"Decadent? Hell, I'm putting this on my time sheet. 'Consultation with counsel regarding . . .' We must have some case together, don't we?" said Deborah slyly.

"You're terrible."

"What? You don't actually *work* all the hours you bill, do you?"

"Sure. Don't you?"

"No comment." She rolled out of bed and headed for the bathroom. When she came back, she was wrapped in Alex's silk bathrobe, her hair pulled up in a loose knot on the top of her head. She sat down on the edge of the bed and looked him in the eye. "Since we're talking business, Counselor, I think it's time you told me what Barclay said when you talked to him about associates for the new firm. When am I getting my offer?"

Alex rolled away from her. He stood up and pulled on a pair of boxer shorts. "Come on, let's see what's in the fridge."

"Alex . . ."

She followed him to the kitchen, where he was taking items out of the refrigerator and lining them up on the counter. "I've got a couple of skewers left—oh, I forgot, you don't eat meat. A bunch of salad . . ."

"It's got dressing on it."

"Sorry, your highness, that's the way real men eat salad. We could cut open this pineapple. Fruit? You eat fruit, don't you?"

"Alex, stop changing the subject. This is important to me."

"Look, you're not even supposed to know about this deal. If Gordon ever found out . . ."

"Well, I do know. Can I help it if Gordon's wimpy little secretary can't keep a secret? All I did was ask her to schedule something on Gordon's calendar a month from now and she flipped out—started getting all teary-eyed. So I took her to lunch."

"You kissed up to her and then pumped her for information, is what you did."

"I didn't pump her, I just asked her a few questions about what was bothering her, the way any concerned person would."

"Thank you, Dr. Joyce Brothers."

"Alex, that's all beside the point. The thing is, I do know about the plan to split off from KLMD, and I need some answers. It's bad enough that you didn't trust me enough to tell me."

He put an arm around her and drew her close. "Come on, you know I couldn't. Barclay's a madman. If he found out I betrayed a secret, God knows what he'd do. Hey"—he put his hand under her chin—"look at me. You know I love you, right?"

Deborah nodded. "I know. But I'm just a neurotic wreck over this whole thing. What if Barclay doesn't make me an offer? What will I do then? He'll leave and take all the files with insurance-coverage issues and that's the only thing I've got any experience at. I'll either get laid off or I'll get stuck in some other department where I don't know what I'm doing, I won't get any jury trials—"

"Come on, you're getting too worked up about this."

"Worked up? I can't lose my job right now, Alex. My house payment's eleven hundred a month, and then there's my student loans, and my car's four twenty-five a month, not counting the insurance—"

"You didn't have to buy a brand-new Lexus, you know."

"Don't lecture me about my life-style, Alex. The point is, I couldn't even last a month without a paycheck, okay? Of course I'm feeling scared. You would be, too, in my position."

"Listen, Debbie, honey—"

She kicked him in the shin. "Don't ever call me Debbie."

"All right, Deb-o-rah. I did what I could. I recommended you, I told him I thought you were the best choice."

"And?"

"He hasn't made up his mind yet." Alex moved quickly around the kitchen, putting the shish kebabs in the microwave and moving dirty dishes into the sink.

"You're lying. I bet he told you he won't consider me. I ought to talk to him myself, explain what—"

"Now, wait a sec—"

"So what's he *really* gonna do, *kill me*? My career's going to be ruined by this as it is. What can I lose? Maybe I just need to remind Gordon of my strengths." Deborah turned to face Alex and let the silk robe slip open.

Alex closed it and retied the sash. "I think Gordon's fully aware of your strengths . . . and your weaknesses."

Deborah let that one pass. Carrying the pineapple over to the butcher-block island in the center of the kitchen, she drew the largest carving knife out of the knife rack. "I could let him know that because I'm so upset that he hasn't considered me, I might just happen to say the wrong thing the next time I'm talking to Fred Duff. . . ." With both hands she leaned hard on the knife. The top of the pineapple fell to the floor with a *clunk*.

Alex walked over and took the knife from her hands. "Trust me on this one, Deb. That would definitely *not* be a good idea."

They were interrupted by the telephone. Deborah reached for it.

"Wait," said Alex, pulling her hand away from the receiver. "It could be someone from the office."

She frowned at the ringing phone. "Goddamn that stupid 'Rule.' It's petty and cruel. I hate sneaking around."

"Yeah, well, we won't have to worry about it for much longer. The new firm won't have any such rules." Alex wiped his hands on a towel and picked up the receiver. "Hello? Oh, hi, Gordon."

Deborah stuck her tongue out at the phone.

"Oh, my God, that's horrible. When did it happen? . . . Uh-huh. . . . How? Wait, you mean it wasn't an accident? Jesus, that's awful. . . . No, it's okay, I'll come right over." He slowly placed the receiver back in its cradle, his face ashen.

"What is it?"

"Gordon's secretary, Nancy Gulliver. She killed herself last night."

Gordon Barclay hung up the portable telephone and tried to tune out everything but the calming sound of water hitting tile. The garden patio of his Capitol Hill home was his sanctuary, the place he went to when he needed to unwind and think. Large cherry trees, as old as the house, blocked out most of the late-afternoon sun. His wife, Adele, took care of the gardening, and the place looked like a showcase. But Barclay's favorite was the fountain, added soon after they moved into the house. The handmade tiles and four carved granite lions had been imported from Mexico—it reminded Barclay of the Alhambra in Spain. He could listen to the sound of cascading water and picture himself far away from the worries and hassles of his law practice.

But today being alone in his sanctuary didn't help. This thing with Nancy Gulliver—it was simply too much. He'd left the office shortly after his unpleasant encounter with her sister. What a hellion, that one. How dare she blame Nancy's death on him, in front of witnesses, like that. Barclay made a mental note to speak to Bill Johanson in commercial litigation, find out if he could bring a libel action.

Barclay closed his eyes and tried again to shut out the world. Thank God Adele wasn't gardening this afternoon and he could have the place to himself. She was inside, busy on one of her other worthless projects. At least it kept her out of his hair.

After a few moments he opened his eyes. Time to get ready for his strategy session; Alex would be here at any moment. He tried to think rationally. There was no reason why Nancy's death by itself should have any impact on their plans. She wasn't an important player. On the contrary, it was a relief to have her out of the way, no longer pestering him with her silly demands.

But the reaction of Nancy's sister . . . Now that had been a complete surprise. He hoped Alex would have a plan for how to deal with that little bitch.

Barclay walked into the kitchen to boil some water for a pot of tea. The pungent smell of airplane glue hit him the moment he entered the room. He crossed to the sink and opened the window. "Adele, I've told you before, you need to have adequate ventilation when you work with that stuff."

"Oh, is it bad? I hadn't noticed."

Barclay stifled a reply. The kitchen table, protected by several layers of newspapers (some of which Barclay hadn't read yet, he noticed unhappily), was littered with tiny twigs, wood chips, and bits of straw. Adele Barclay's head was bent over a small wooden box to which she was meticulously gluing a row of sticks in a vertical pattern. A *Sunset* magazine was open to an article entitled "Backyard Birds Will Enjoy These Lovely Abodes for Years to Come!" His wife had apparently chosen the "country French" birdhouse, a miniature half-timbered house with a thatched roof and window boxes complete with tiny artificial geraniums.

Barclay silently filled the kettle and set it on the stove. He'd stopped trying to understand his wife's various "projects" years ago, thankful that they at least kept her occupied. They had had no children and of course Adele didn't work. She had to have something to occupy her time. He'd even gotten used to the extra bedroom being crammed with past diversions: the needlework tapestry of a medieval unicorn, a papier-mâché piñata for a "Mexican" party they never held, enough Christmas gewgaws to supply an entire church bazaar. Her things weren't bad actually. She was good with her hands and had a certain artistic flair. They were just useless.

He looked at her with distaste. Her small eyes with those pale lashes appeared smaller behind oversized glasses. Her hair, blond shot through with gray, was pulled back into a limp ponytail and fastened with the blue rubber band she'd taken off the afternoon paper. At fifty-one she still could have made herself attractive, had she cared. Once he'd thought her hands were lovely, with those long, tapered fingers. Now just the sight of those fingers, stained with glue and ink, cuticles dry and peeling, made him nauseous.

God knows, he thought, he gave her enough money. She could spend some of it getting a manicure or touching up her gray hair. He'd even tried to get one of those personal shoppers at Nordstrom to help her pick out clothes, something new and stylish, but she couldn't have cared less.

The kettle whistled. Barclay prepared two small pots of tea— it was easier than asking Adele if she wanted any, thus risking getting stuck in a conversation. He quietly set one down at her elbow. Adele looked up. "You're making tea? Thank you, dear." She went back to her gluing, and Barclay thought he'd be able to make his escape without actually interacting with her. He was wrong.

"Where do you want to put the hives, dear?"

"The what?"

"The beehives. Don't you remember? The seminar I went to last night in Port Townsend. Tending your own beehives and things to do with the beeswax. It was fabulous."

Barclay didn't need to ask Adele if she was serious. She was always serious when it came to a new project.

"Anywhere you like, dear. As long as it doesn't block my view of the fountain."

"Of course not. I think by the lilac bush would be nice." Her inane smile made him want to run from the room.

He was saved by the ringing telephone. "I'll take it in my study, dear. It's probably Alex." But when he picked it up, the line was strangely silent.

"Hello?" Nothing. "Is this some kind of prank? Hello? Is someone there?"

"You've really gone and done it now," a low, hoarse voice whispered. It was barely audible; he couldn't even tell if it was a man or a woman.

"Who is this?"

"Is this history repeating itself, Gordon? Just another day in Paradise? You got away with it once, didn't you? But this time . . . This time you're going to get what's coming to you."

"What? Listen, whoever you are, I'm calling the police—"

But the line was dead.

Chapter 8

The street numbers on South Lake Washington Avenue were so well camouflaged that Annie had to slow to about five miles per hour to search for the Duffs' house, infuriating a black sports car behind her that was trying to pass on the narrow, winding street. It was Sunday evening, Annie's night for the famous barbecued hamburgers with the managing partner. As friendly as Fred Duff had been at the KLMD party, she wasn't entirely looking forward to the evening. The stress of her first week on the job had been bad enough, but the encounter at the office following Nancy Gulliver's death had been wrenching. It would be hard to make small talk as if nothing had happened.

On the right were large brick homes designed to take full advantage of the view of the lake. But to the left, where Duff's home was supposed to be, there were only tall hedges and imposing brick walls. With the land sloping sharply to the water, the lakefront homes were obscured from view.

Annie wondered what kind of mansion to expect. A senior partner in one of the Northwest's most successful law firms could certainly afford just about anything in the city.

When she spotted Joel Feinstein's mustard-colored Volvo, she knew she was close and finally located the house number discreetly hidden by ivy. As she pulled over to park, the black sports car gunned its engine and whizzed past. Buried in the hedge below the street number was an intercom. She pushed the button.

"Annie?" was Fred Duff's unmistakable bellow in response to her buzz. "Good job. Most people are at least half an hour late finding the place. Come in through the gate and down the steps."

When she heard the buzzer, she pushed open the gate to find herself at the top of a brick stairway that curved, among shrubs and rock gardens, a good two hundred and fifty feet down toward the water. The Duffs' house was a tiny blue and white Cape Cod bungalow, which seemed dwarfed by the expanse of lawn. Fred appeared on the porch and waved her down.

"This way, this way. Everyone's inside. Vivian's looking forward to meeting you." Fred relieved Annie of the bottle of wine she carried and herded her inside. Maria Feinstein, looking like she was hiding a basketball under her stretchy knit top, was helping Mrs. Duff in the kitchen. She greeted Annie and said, "We may have lost Joel for the evening." She rolled her eyes. "Mr. Duff is showing him his baseball card collection in the den."

Annie knew what an avid fan Joel was. If Fred Duff was the same way, she and Maria would have to try hard to keep the conversation on other topics.

"So glad you could make it, dear," said Vivian Duff, wiping her plump hands on a dishtowel, then reaching out to give Annie's hands a squeeze. The image of a powder puff came to mind. Soft white hair framed Vivian's almost perfectly round face, and a pink angora cardigan and white slacks did little to slenderize Vivian's short, round figure. She smelled of rosewater and freshly baked chocolate chip cookies. Meeting Vivian, Annie felt a pang of regret that she'd never known either of her own grandmothers.

Fred reemerged from the den with Joel in tow. "You wouldn't believe his collection, Annie. He's got cards that haven't shown up on the market in thirty years!"

"No, really?" Annie said in false amazement. She'd been giving Joel a hard time about his baseball fetish for years.

"I always love meeting the new lawyers, especially the women," said Vivian, ignoring the baseball talk. "I'm just so darned proud of all of you girls, going to law school and all. I had a cousin who went to law school. Graduated in 1911, can you believe that? I wish I'd had that much gumption." She crinkled her eyes. "Duff still thinks I should give it a go!"

"Been telling her that for forty-four years. Why should I stop now?"

"That man. He's nuttier than a tin-roof sundae. Duff? Why don't you get Annie something to drink?"

Fred Duff winked as he sidled into the kitchen. "She runs this place with an iron fist, you know. What can I get you? Beer, wine, a cocktail?"

"A beer would be nice."

"Beer it is. Goes best with hamburgers." He opened a Heineken and poured it into a pilsner glass for her.

"I've been hearing all about the lovely time you had at the dance. I was so sorry I couldn't go. My sister, the one that was in the hospital, is doing much better by the way. Do you like hamburgers, dear?"

"I love them."

"Oh, good. That last girl that we invited, Debbie something?"

"Deborah Silver," said Fred.

"That's right, Debbie Silver. Vegetarian she was, can you believe it? I felt so bad. Here I'd made nice fat hamburgers and all she'd eat was a little salad. And she wouldn't even put dressing on that. How about you all? You're not like that, are you?"

"Not me. I love to eat," Annie replied. Looking at Vivian's rounded figure, Annie guessed she wasn't alone.

"Even ice cream?" Fred's wife asked with a conspiratorial twinkle in her eye.

Maria beamed. "For eight months I've wanted nothing but ice cream. And Joel will eat two hamburgers at least."

"Well, well." Vivian beamed. "I like these kids, Duff! You should hire more like them. Now, Maria, you can stay and keep me company, but I'm going to shoo all you lawyers out while I finish in the kitchen."

"Are you sure you don't need us to help?" Annie asked.

"She's sure," said Fred. "Hates to have anyone stand over her shoulder when she's cooking, especially me. Says I steal her recipes."

They moved out to the deck on the lake side of the house. A path ran down to the water's edge, where a small wooden sailboat in need of a coat of paint was tied up to an equally peeling dock.

"Let's go down by the water. Cooler down there." Fred picked up two webbed lawn chairs and ambled down the path. Joel grabbed a third chair and followed. Even in casual slacks and a golf sweater Fred cut an impressive figure with his proud bearing and neatly trimmed white mustache. It wasn't hard to picture how dashing he must have looked in an army uniform in 1945.

They set up the chairs on the lawn. A cool breeze blew off the lake, the only sound from a single speedboat pulling a water-skier. It felt good to relax. Amid the whirlwind of Vivian's enthusiasm and Fred's graciousness, Annie had almost forgotten the uncomfortable encounter at the office the day before with Nancy Gulliver's sister. She wondered if Fred knew about the suicide or if she should tell him. He answered her question once they were out of Vivian's earshot.

"Gordon called me last evening and told me all about Nancy and that awful scene with her sister that you had to witness. I've filled Joel in. Terrible thing it was."

"I didn't know her very well," said Joel. "Other than to see her at her desk when I came up to visit you. But she seemed a pleasant sort of girl."

"She was," Annie replied. "And she was so young and seemed happy enough. It's hard to imagine what depressed her enough that she would want to kill herself."

"I just hope it wasn't the pressure of the job that got to her," Fred said, looking grim. "I called the sister. Apparently there's no other family. I said the firm would take care of the funeral expenses. It's simply shocking what such things cost these days. It'll be tomorrow, by the way, at St. Matthew's Presbyterian in Auburn."

"That was very kind of you."

"Well, I may be a dinosaur, Annie, but I still believe that a law firm has got to be like a family. Viv and I were never blessed with children, so maybe that's why I feel so close to my employees. To me, every single one is equally important, and as long as I'm managing partner, they'll be treated like kin."

Kin. What a nice old-fashioned word, Annie thought.

"That's a pretty rare attitude these days," said Joel.

Fred laughed. "One of the advantages of getting old, son. You can ignore progress when it doesn't suit you."

Annie looked out at the water, enjoying the view. "What a wonderful spot."

"Yes," said Fred, looking back toward the little bungalow. "It is fun, isn't it? The house was built in 1917, someone's summer cottage. Two bedrooms, no frills. We bought the place back in the early seventies during the Boeing slump. Lakefront property was pretty easy to pick up in those days. Everyone thought we'd tear down the cottage and put up some big fancy house. Lord, you should see some of the places the other senior partners live in. 'Conspicuous consumption' is the modern phrase for it, but Viv and I call it 'just plain showin' off.' After we'd lived here about six months, we realized it was perfect for us, as is. Viv has her garden and I can go out and sail around the lake—I even pretend to fish every now and then. We wouldn't have it any other way. Our little paradise in the city."

"Duff, honey?" Vivian called from the porch. "Are your coals about ready?"

Fred stood up. "Well, I think I'm being summoned to do something productive around here. Come on, you can help my wife tell me what to do."

As predicted, Vivian closely supervised Fred's barbecuing, while Annie, Joel, and Maria carried trays of dishes and condiments out to the redwood table on the deck. As they ate, the smell of the citronella candle and the taste of corn on the cob gave Annie glimpses of a "Leave It to Beaver" childhood she'd never known. Maybe with a grandmother like Vivian, Annie would have learned how to do more in the kitchen than microwave frozen dinners.

"So," said Vivian, wiping a touch of catsup off her chin, "Duff tells me that your father used to work at the firm."

"From what I understand. I really don't know much about that time. I was pretty young, and living with my mother down in California. I only visited at holidays."

"Yes," said Fred. "Heavens, that must have been . . . what, twenty-five or thirty years ago? Things were pretty different then, I can tell you. KLMD only had about twenty-five attorneys."

"Can you imagine?" asked Vivian. "Now it's almost two hundred and fifty. I can hardly keep track. We used to have picnics in the park and I actually knew everyone's name."

"But I remember George," said Fred. "Hell, I was the one that hired him. Knew right from the first interview he'd make a damned good attorney. He had that same bright red hair that you've got and was skinny as a bean pole. I could always tell them apart, but a lot of the other partners back then confused him with Gordon Barclay."

"Gordon told me they'd been close."

"Oh, my, yes. Practically inseparable, those two. Gordon and your father both came to us from the University of Washington. Your dad might have been a year ahead, I think. But they paired up right away. George and Gordon—the G-men they called themselves—did just about everything together. Offices next door to each other, even went on double dates."

Vivian looked thoughtful. "Duff, didn't they both work with that pretty secretary? The one with the gorgeous dark hair?"

"No," Fred said gruffly, almost snapping. More calmly he said, "I think you're thinking of someone else, dear."

"Wait. I think I met my father's secretary once," said Annie. "When I was visiting the office one Christmas when I was just a child. She had really long dark hair, almost down to her waist, and big brown eyes?"

"That's the one. Lucy something or other. Lovely girl. Tiny little thing, couldn't have been over five feet."

Annie tried to think back. "I did meet her, I'm sure of it. I must have been about six, because it was the first Christmas my parents had lived apart. I'd started first grade down in California, but I'd come up to spend Christmas with Dad. The firm was having a Christmas party where everyone brought their children. I remember I sat on her lap while we sang Christmas carols, and I thought she looked like a princess in a fairy tale. Isn't it strange the things we remember?"

"Oh, I always remember Christmases," said Vivian. "Every one's been special in some way. Does anyone need seconds? There's plenty more. Joel? You look like you need another hamburger."

"No, thanks. I couldn't eat another bite."

"Then is everyone ready for ice cream? Duff got me this cute little ice-cream machine for Christmas. It's Italian. I get such a kick out of it!" Vivian returned from the kitchen carrying a small blue and white contraption with a handle on top. She gave it to Fred, who started dishing up fresh peach ice cream, and came back a moment later with a plate of cookies.

As she sat down, Annie caught the glance Fred gave his wife of over forty years. His expression could have been that of a sixteen-year-old with his first crush. "She's right, every single night it's a different flavor. I'm upset because I don't get to bring home Fratelli's anymore. I have to make do with her crazy concoctions."

"Oh, Duff. You just get out of here. You know I make vanilla for you at least once a week." She reached over and slapped him playfully on the knee. Across the table Joel had his arm around his diminutive wife, who leaned a tired head against his shoulder.

What was their secret? Annie wondered. Her own parents, like so many couples she had known, hadn't managed to stay married for more than a few years. And Annie's own history of relationships certainly wouldn't set any records for longevity. Yet here was one couple, perfectly in sync, ready to add to their growing family, and another couple still obviously in love after almost half a century. Maybe it was possible after all.

After dessert it was clear that Maria was fading fast, and she and Joel said their good-byes. Annie made a valiant attempt to help Vivian with the dishes, but she wouldn't hear of it, insisting that she and Fred "get out of her hair" and go down to the lake while she puttered.

A cool breeze ruffled the lake's surface. The ski boats had all gone in for the day, but there were still several sailboats out for a twilight cruise, pushed along lazily by the light wind. A huge bird circled overhead.

"That's not a bald eagle, is it?" Annie asked, incredulous.

"Yep, crazy old bird. Must not know he's in a city. He lives over there in Seward Park, to the south of us. Dusk is his favorite time to come hunting. Viv gets so worried, she keeps her cat inside till after dark." They watched his slow arcs for a while, enjoying the long spring twilight.

Annie turned to Fred Duff. "Can I ask why my father left KLMD? All I can remember about that time was my mother being terribly upset. They were in the midst of getting divorced—it was pretty messy, in fact. I learned later that there was a horrible custody battle. Right in the middle of everything, my father left his job and started his own practice. My mother was furious because for a few years the child-support checks were practically nonexistent. Looking back, it just seems like such odd timing."

Fred looked uncomfortable, like it was a subject he'd rather not talk about. "It's hard to say, Annie. I know your dad enjoyed starting his own firm. I dealt with him from time to time over the years, and he always seemed happy with his decision. As for the timing, I think he just felt it was time to move on. For personal reasons."

"Did Gordon Barclay have anything to do with it?"

"Barclay?" Fred shifted in his chair. "Why do you ask?"

"I was just curious. It sounds like they were such good friends when they worked together. Then they completely lost touch. I can't recall my father ever even mentioning Gordon's name."

Fred stared fixedly at the water. "I'm sure it's just old history, nothing important. These things happen between the best of friends." He looked back at Annie and patted her on the arm. "And it certainly hasn't affected Gordon's opinion of *you*. My God, he talks like you're the greatest thing to happen to the practice of law since the Post-it note."

So, thought Annie, she wasn't the only one to notice Barclay's inordinate interest in her. Still, he was probably attentive to all his new associates until they got settled in.

They sat for a long time watching the light slowly fade, listening to quiet water sounds, before Fred said, "You seemed a little distant during dinner. Is there something on your mind?"

"I guess I was just wondering why some people can find so much happiness in their lives and others . . ."

"You're still thinking about that poor girl's suicide?"

Annie nodded.

"Yes, anytime a young person dies it's tragic, no matter what the circumstances. And suicide, well, one can hardly help thinking that it could've been stopped." Fred paused. "You're thinking that Gordon pushed her to it?"

Annie looked over, surprised. "How much did he tell you?"

"No, it's not what he told me, which wasn't much. It's just a reasonable guess under the circumstances."

"You knew about . . ."

"Their affair? Oh, my heavens, yes. Gordon thought he was hiding it so well, but everyone down to the kids in the mailroom knew. I don't condone gossip myself, but it's a fact of life that gossip flies through an office faster than morning glories will take over a garden."

"Do you think he had anything to do with her wanting to kill herself?"

"That's hard to judge, not knowing the girl. But I have every intention of sitting down with Gordon, after all this is over, and having a long chat with him about his penchant for the ladies. And I'm sure I don't have to warn you to be careful around him."

Thinking back on Barclay's charming manner, Annie felt vaguely uneasy. "Have there, um, been problems in the past?"

Fred frowned. "For someone who has good judgment when it comes to everything else, that man is plain nuts when it comes to women. He's going to get himself into a hell of a bind one of these days—maybe he has already—and it's the firm that'll suffer."

"Look, I may be out of line in asking, but why does the firm tolerate Barclay's behavior? Surely as managing partner . . ."

"I wish it were that easy, Annie. But, unfortunately, Gordon Barclay's just too important to this firm."

"Because of his clients?"

A look of worry crossed Fred's face. "Gordon is personally responsible for bringing in over half of the insurance business that this firm handles—we're talking about a fifty-attorney department here. And the clients are devoted to him. Walt Wiley at Trans-Pacific Casualty thinks the man walks on water. And Gordon's close standing with Senator Quinn has certainly brought business to the firm. But it goes further than that. You have to understand how fragile a structure a law firm is, Annie. This is a highly competitive business, and every year the legal market becomes more and more saturated. Dog eat dog doesn't even begin to describe it. Confidence in the solidity of the firm is a major factor to both clients and the attorneys who work here. Young lawyers these days are nervous. The larger firms are merging right and left, they divide, go out of business. What good does it do if an associate slaves away ten or fifteen years of his life, waiting for the big payoff when he gets to be a senior partner, if the firm collapses? All that groundwork is meaningless."

Annie began to see what he was getting at. "So if the associates perceive that a firm's stability is shaky, they'll bail out?"

"Like rats from a sinking frigate. The loss of a key figure like Barclay could start a domino effect. Whole departments could split off, major clients could get jittery and bail out. Ultimately, Annie, if we lost Barclay, it could mean the end of Kemble, Laughton, Mercer, and Duff."

Annie pondered this for a moment. It made working with Gordon Barclay a dangerous game. If they ended up having a "personality conflict," it sure wouldn't be Barclay who got the boot.

"But there isn't any indication that Barclay would leave the firm, is there?"

Fred looked at her through the deepening twilight and sighed. "I was about to ask you the same question, my dear."

Chapter 9

The Presbyterian church in Auburn where Nancy Gulliver's funeral was being held was an unpretentious edifice, a square box with plain, frosted amber windows. Besides the flowers on the altar, fabric banners that looked like they'd been made by the second-grade Sunday-school class were the only decorations. Annie had never been much of a churchgoer, but there had been a few times during her childhood when her mother, thinking the experience would be beneficial, had taken her to an Episcopalian service. Hearing Bach played on the powerful pipe organ, along with the silvery prose of the Episcopalian liturgy, had seemed awe-inspiring, even to a nonbeliever, and Annie had enjoyed her limited exposure to religion. In contrast, the down-to-earth, unadorned austerity of most Protestant services just never seemed to evoke much of a religious mood.

The funeral service for Nancy was no exception. The minister, a balding man in his late fifties with thick glasses and a lisp, appeared uncomfortable delivering the eulogy. It was clear from his flowery generalizations that he had never met the deceased. As he mumbled on about the "beautiful child whom God has chosen to call to His side," extolling what he imagined her virtues to have been, he skirted the unmentionable subject of suicide with careful, mincing words.

The casket, open for viewing before the service, was now

closed. Annie focused on the photograph of Nancy that had been placed on a small easel near the casket, a shot of the laughing young woman cradling her black-and-white cat in her arms.

Most of the firm's support staff was present and a fair proportion of the lawyers. But from the small number of other friends in attendance, Annie surmised that Nancy Gulliver's life had revolved almost entirely around her work at the office. Not to mention Gordon Barclay, who was conspicuously absent.

As the group seated to her left stood to leave, Annie noticed with a start that the service had ended. The minister moved down to greet Suzy, the only family member present, and was no doubt uttering bland phrases meant to be comforting. Annie rose and joined the crowd wandering into the church hall for the reception. She was thankful that there wasn't going to be one of those dreadful trips to the cemetery, as the body was to be cremated later that day.

Suzy Gulliver, dressed unseasonably in a black wool skirt and cardigan, stood near the buffet table looking like the victim of repeated shock treatments. Her eyes were barely focusing as she greeted those who had come to offer condolences. Annie wished she could say something that would help, but she knew her words would be as empty as the others'. Having only met Suzy that one time in the office, the afternoon Barclay had been confronted with the news of Nancy's death, she couldn't think of what she could say that wouldn't remind Suzy of that dreadful day.

Wondering how long she should stay, Annie picked up a cup of coffee and moved away from the food to the corner where Jed Delacourt was standing alone. His eyes darted around the room, taking in the scene.

"So where do you think our illustrious boss is today? Out looking for a replacement now that playmate number one is gone?"

Annie smelled alcohol on his breath. "Jed, if you have to

make crude comments, please stay away from the woman in
the black skirt and sweater. That's Nancy's sister, and I'm sure
she wouldn't appreciate your sparkling commentary.''

"Oh, sweet Sue and I have already met. I'm sure that's why
Barclay didn't show up. He didn't want sister Suzy throwing
hot coffee down his crotch.''

Annie cringed and looked for a means of escape. She muttered something about offering to help with the food and
started to move away, when Jed placed his hand on her arm.
"I'm sorry, Annie, I was being bad again. I didn't mean it. It's
just that I'm not feeling too generous toward Gordon right
now."

A softness in his expression, like a puppy who knows he's
chewed the wrong slipper, made Annie pause.

"Why? Has something happened?''

"Oh, he's just acquired one more piece of ammunition in
his battle to get rid of me." Jed squared his shoulders and tried
to look nonchalant. He didn't succeed. "I don't know how he
found out—I thought the records had been expunged.''

"Something criminal?''

"Annie, it was a long time ago. Really. I was only eighteen,
a freshman in college. I was caught selling a minuscule amount
of cocaine. I wasn't a dealer or anything. It was just once. Anyway, my dad's pretty well connected. He made some calls, got
a deal where I'd plead guilty but get the sentence deferred. I
had to pay a stiff fine and do a hundred hours of community
service, but if I kept my nose clean—no pun intended—for a
year, the record would be expunged. No more conviction.
That's what I was sure had happened.''

It was a common-enough scenario for first offenses, but from
Jed's expression Annie could tell there was more to the story.
"What's this got to do with Barclay?''

"Somehow he got hold of a certified copy of the criminal
record, only it didn't show the deferred sentencing. From the
copy he had it looked like I'd pled guilty to a felony and been
sentenced to a year in jail.''

"The firm wouldn't fire you just for that. It was over ten years ago, in another state; it was before you were a lawyer. I'm sure if you explain the circumstances . . ."

Jed was shaking his head. "That would be fine if we were dealing with the firm's personnel committee. But Barclay's smarter than that. He said he hasn't made up his mind what to do about it, but he said if the state bar got hold of it, I could lose my license to practice."

"What?"

"Failure to disclose the conviction on my application to be admitted in Washington. I don't know what I'm going to do. . . . It was hard enough for me to get this job. It's not like I was top of my class at Harvard and Stanford Law and editor in chief of the Law Review like Barclay's little pet, Guiterrez, was. I'm just a rich white male with mediocre grades in an overcrowded market."

Annie had to feel a degree of sympathy for Jed. It certainly sounded like Barclay was riding him awfully hard for an error that occurred in his youth. On the other hand, if Barclay didn't believe Jed's story about the deferred sentencing, perhaps he was just doing what he thought was in the firm's best interest. It could be read both ways. Barclay's behavior seemed less sinister than whoever it was who had provided him with Jed's criminal record.

"So," said Jed, squaring his shoulders with an air of bravado, "John Edward Delacourt the Third, the older and wiser associate, shall give the new kid some advice, and you may quote me on this: Whenever you're dealing with the big guy, keep your head down, your rear covered, and mumble when they ask your name." Jed laughed at his own joke, but Annie knew he was having difficulty finding humor in the situation.

"Well, Jed. Interesting seeing you here. I'm surprised you could afford to take the afternoon off." They had been joined by Deborah Silver, neatly turned out in a black linen suit and a white blouse. She was actually one of the few people who'd worn black to the funeral. Turning to Annie, she said, "Jed's always notoriously behind in his billables. He refuses to take my advice."

"Which is?"

"Always stay *at least* twenty percent above your quota. That way, when something like this comes up, you can afford to take the time. I always work my tail off in January and February stockpiling billable hours."

Jed rolled his eyes. "Excuse me if I'm not in the mood for a lecture about climbing the legal ladder of success. Annie, I'll talk to you later."

Without another word to Deborah, Jed turned and left. From the corner of her eye Annie could see him speaking to Suzy Gulliver. She hoped, for Suzy's sake, that he would stay on his good behavior and not say anything crass.

Deborah continued, unruffled by Jed's parting shot, "You know, Annie, may I give you a little suggestion?"

Annie wondered if someone had placed an invisible sign around her neck saying "Advice wanted—no reasonable suggestion turned down."

Deborah glanced around, then lowered her voice. "I'm sure you're aware of this, but, uh, KLMD is rather a, uh, political place."

"Uh-hmm."

"And it's important early on to—how should I put this?—associate oneself with the proper faction so to speak."

Annie was starting to catch her drift. "And Jed Delacourt's part of the wrong faction, is that it?" She made a note to call Jed for lunch the following week. Someplace public.

Deborah just smiled. "I'm not saying this to be mean. It's just that I thought you might not know. Not that it really makes any difference. My grapevine tells me he's on his way out, anyway."

Pretty fast grapevine, Annie thought, wondering how good Deborah was at doing criminal background checks. "And did your grapevine tell you why?" Annie asked pointedly.

Deborah looked as smug as a teacher's pet who's just been

appointed hall monitor. "Let's just say that the way to get ahead in this job is to know how to get information, how to use it once you've got it, and how to make sure no one else knows as much as you do. Just like a good reporter, never reveal your source."

Annie contemplated how thin Deborah's neck was and wondered why no one had gotten around to wringing it yet. If this was her way of making friends, Annie didn't want to be around when she was making enemies.

Deborah took a delicate sip from her cup. "It was very thoughtful of them to serve chamomile tea. It's so calming, especially in trying situations. Usually, at affairs like this, all they have are horrid things with *caffeine* in them." She shivered in distaste, as if she were talking about a toxic chemical. Annie took another sip of weak coffee and wished it was Italian-roast espresso.

"Did you know Nancy well?" Annie asked.

"Nancy?" For a moment Deborah looked confused. "Oh, you mean . . ." She nodded in the direction of the church, suddenly remembering that the funeral was more than an opportunity to network. "No, not as well as I would have liked. Although we did have lunch once or twice. When the dear thing needed a shoulder to cry on."

They were certainly broad enough, given the shoulder pads Deborah wore, Annie thought sarcastically, as Deborah rattled on. "Such a horrible waste." Under her breath she muttered, "Is he ever going to get here?"

Annie got the feeling that her colleague was not terribly crushed by the loss. Suddenly Deborah tensed, and as Annie glanced out of the corner of her eye, she could see the source of Deborah's discomfort. Alex Guiterrez stood in the doorway and was beckoning to Deborah.

"If you'll excuse me, Annie, I really should be getting back to the office now. I, um, I've got so much to do before my deposition tomorrow. But let's do lunch next week, hmm?" The woman left in such a fluster, Annie was afraid she was

going to take her teacup with her. She remembered to deposit
the cup on a table near the exit, but Annie noted with interest
that it wasn't the exit where Alex was standing. He stood where
he was, watching her bolt with a look of bewilderment on his
face.

Funerals were such odd occasions, Annie thought. Those
close to the deceased were affected by the sense of grief; everyone else just muddled through it. She decided it was time
to leave.

In the covered walkway leading to the parking lot she was
stopped by a tall, thin woman with gray-blond hair carrying an
enormous wreath. "Am I too late?" The woman glanced around
nervously. Her glasses were so large and the lenses so thick
that Annie wondered if she was nearly blind. "I ran from the
parking lot. I was afraid they'd all be gone."

"Are you looking for the funeral reception? For Nancy Gulliver?"

"Yes, Nancy. That was her name. Uh-huh." The woman focused her pale eyes on Annie. Apparently she could see well
enough. Annie noticed that her strange gaze was accentuated
by eyelashes that were completely blond.

"Here, let me help you carry that wreath."

"Oh, thanks. I am out of breath." They walked back across
the flagstones, the woman's high heels making clicking sounds
on the pavement. When they entered the church hall, the
woman looked around, somewhat confused. She whispered to
Annie, "Where's the casket?"

Annie whispered back, "I think it's still in the church. I
thought you'd want to give this to Nancy's sister."

"Her sister? No . . . I think I should put it on the casket."

"Would you like some help?" The poor woman seemed so
out of it, it was the least Annie could offer.

"Thank you, if it's not too much trouble."

The church was empty. There were no other flowers except
for the two bouquets of gladiolus next to the altar. Annie helped
the woman place the wreath on top of the casket. It was a

lovely piece, decorated with irises and rubrum lilies and heavily scented with freesias. The woman stepped back to admire it, then sat, exhausted, in the first pew. Annie joined her, worried that she might need more assistance.

"She was very pretty, wasn't she?" the woman asked, referring to the photograph. Annie nodded. "Yes, I can see why she was so special. And is that her cat?"

"Yes."

"I've always liked cats."

"Are you from the florist?" Annie inquired. The woman hadn't seemed to recognize anyone in the hall, yet she was dressed as if for church in a navy-blue shirtdress with green piping, years out of date, and matching green pumps.

"Oh, no. No. I . . . my husband, actually . . . knew her. I've been working on the wreath all morning. I was so afraid I wouldn't get it done in time."

"It's beautiful."

"Thank you. All of the flowers are from my own garden." She went on to describe each one. "Do you garden?"

"No, unless you count geraniums in a window box."

"You should try gardening. It's very relaxing. They have classes at the arboretum, you know. Tuesdays and Thursdays. I never miss. It's very easy to learn. I think I've got a brochure here." She rummaged in a voluminous shoulder bag and brought out a crumpled map of the arboretum. "I thought I had the flyer on the classes, but all I've got is this. But the phone number's on there; you could call and find out."

Annie nodded and put the crumpled map in her purse. She didn't have the heart to tell this woman she lived in an apartment. The window box was all the dirt she had. Now the question was how to get away gracefully. The woman seemed to have caught her breath but still wanted to talk.

"Would you like some tea, coffee? There's a reception . . ."

"Are you a relative?" the woman asked, apropos of nothing.

"No. Just a co-worker. I just started at the firm a week ago, and Nancy was my secretary."

"Oh, really. She was my husband's secretary, too. I'm sorry,
I didn't introduce myself. I'm Adele Barclay."

The name took Annie by surprise. This inelegant-looking
woman was hardly whom Annie would have expected as Gordon Barclay's wife. Annie suddenly remembered that she'd seen
the woman before, at the KLMD dance talking to Senator
Quinn. There was something almost childlike about her man-
nerisms. Yet the wreath she'd constructed was of professional
quality.

"Pleased to meet you, Mrs. Barclay. I'm Annie MacPherson.
I'm working in your husband's department. He's been very
kind to me so far."

Adele's eyes widened and she gave Annie a long, evaluating
look. "I've heard about you," she said but didn't explain her
comment. Turning to stare at the coffin, Adele said, "She was
his mistress, you know."

Annie didn't reply.

"He always thought I didn't know, but I did. I've known
about all of them. It's not that hard to figure out."

"I imagine it's been hard on you," Annie said softly.

"Hard on *me*?" She laughed, a high-pitched girlish giggle.
"Hard on him, more likely. I don't know where he gets the
energy. You've never been married, have you?" she asked with
a gentle smile.

"No, I haven't."

"That's why you don't understand then. The best a woman
can hope for out of marriage is just to be left alone to pursue
her own interests." Adele sighed. "Gordon takes good care of
me and lets me do what I want. That's all I ask."

It was a painfully small amount to ask for, Annie thought
bitterly. Annie was about to comment when she heard footsteps in the back of the church. Turning around, she saw Jed
Delacourt leading Suzy Gulliver into the church. Thinking it
might not be a good idea for Suzy and Adele to meet, Annie
excused herself and walked to the back of the church. There

was an awkward silence as Suzy recognized Annie from the day at the office.

"I'm sorry about Nancy."

Suzy smiled and nodded. "I know, thanks. And I'm sorry you had to see me like that the other day. I'm normally not . . . you know."

"Of course not," said Annie. "If there's anything I can do . . . ?"

Looking toward the front of the church, Suzy noticed that the casket was closed and tears began to form in her eyes. She took a deep breath, then sank down onto a pew. "Now what am I going to do with this?" In her hand was a small square of paper with writing on it. "I was going to put it in the casket, but I forgot. . . ." She relaxed her hand and the paper fell to the floor at Annie's feet.

"It's the note," Jed said quietly. "From Nancy's apartment."

Annie reached down to pick it up.

"You can read it," Suzy said, in a daze. "I don't understand it."

Annie looked at the note. Its shape was bizarre. It was a piece of stiff paper, about five inches across and two inches deep, the top edge slightly crooked. Near the top was writing in a curved, feminine script:

If this is the way it has to be, then I can't stand it anymore.

Love forever and ever,
Nancy

"It was on the kitchen sink, next to the gas range," she said, her voice cracking. "We had a couple of drinks that night after the movie. And when they did the autopsy, they found barbiturates. Sleeping pills. I never even knew she had them." She looked at Jed. "I should have known. I should have stayed there that night."

Even though she barely knew the woman, Annie wanted to

reach out and take her hand, but her attention was drawn by a noise in the front of the church. In the first pew, staring at the photograph of Nancy Gulliver, Adele Barclay was softly crying.

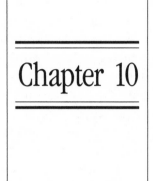

Chapter 10

The sky was a leaden gray as Annie drove out of the church parking lot. As soon as she pulled onto I-5, Annie realized that she should have put up the top of her convertible.

She knew better than to take a chance with Seattle's changeable weather, but it was nearly seven, and after a draining afternoon at the funeral, all Annie could think about was a warm tub, a quick microwaved dinner, and sleep.

She turned on the radio just in time to hear the KIRO weatherman telling her about the 90 percent chance of rain. The mist was now heavy enough to congeal into tiny droplets on the windshield. Cursing, Annie reached over to the glove compartment, pulled out a crumpled sailing hat, and plopped it on her head. It was easier to endure a few minutes of dampness than to take the time to stop on the shoulder of the freeway to put the top up. Nineteen seventy-two Fiat Spiders didn't come equipped with remote-controlled ragtops.

Her plan sounded reasonable and would have worked if it hadn't been for the jackknifed semi blocking three lanes of traffic just south of Boeing Field. The few minutes of dampness escalated into three quarters of an hour of hard drizzle in bumper-to-bumper traffic. Stuck in the middle lane with no way to get to the shoulder, Annie struggled into the parka she kept stashed in the backseat while listening to the KIRO traffic watcher telling her to avoid I-5 northbound at Boeing Field. The drizzle turned into a hard, pelting rain.

As soon as she was clear of the accident, Annie pulled onto the shoulder and struggled with the cartop. It took longer than usual; the left clasp that normally stuck a little was adamantly refusing to lock. Annie tried to think of creative ways to murder Jurgen, her auto mechanic, who had assured her the last time the car was in the shop that all the clasp needed was a little three-in-one oil.

When she got back in the car, the interior immediately fogged up. Jurgen was also supposed to have fixed the defroster, which was now blowing nothing but cold air out of two of the three vents. Annie pictured herself setting Jurgen afloat in Puget Sound on an overturned VW with nothing but a lube gun for company.

It was almost eight-thirty when she finally pulled into her parking lot. An hour and a half to go fifteen miles—a new record. Luckily her building was one of the few on Capitol Hill with off-street parking, for which Annie was eternally grateful. She sprinted around the side of the five-story brick building to the front door, the only one not secured with a dead bolt after six. If she'd entered through the side door, as she usually did, she would have missed him.

He was seated on the stone bench by the front door, legs pulled up out of the rain, reading a paperback by the yellow light of the porch lamp.

"David?" Annie was surprised that her voice sounded normal. Her stomach was turning triple back-flips, and her legs had turned to Jell-O.

David Courtney looked up, pocketed his book, and rotated a shoulder. "So I do have the right address, eh? I was starting to worry." From his demeanor one would have thought they'd been apart a few hours rather than a few months.

"Come in and get dry," she stammered, rummaging nervously for her keys, which had disappeared in the black hole she called a purse. After searching unsuccessfully for several minutes, she finally had to empty the entire contents out on the bench. The keys, of course, were on the bottom.

Inside the bright lobby Annie struggled out of her rain parka and took a good look at the man she'd spent three months on a boat with. He was dressed, as always, in faded Levi's, a T-shirt, and Top-Siders without socks. Part of her automatically expected to see the warm twinkle in his eyes and that familiar lopsided grin. But, not surprisingly, the warmth was gone, replaced by wariness. He'd lost a little weight; the slight paunch he'd had when she first met him was gone. His sandy hair was longer, and his bushy beard could have used a trim.

"I would have called first, but this friend of mine's a charter pilot. He was making a run to Seattle and asked if I wanted to ride along. I didn't have time to let you know." After a pause he said, "You're not angry, are you?"

Angry. As if she would have any right to be angry at him after what she had done. Annie shook her head. "Of course not. Come on. My place is upstairs."

She led the way up a carpeted stairway and down a hall.

"Pretty fancy place here."

"Well, they're small. In 1922 these were 'bachelor' apartments." Annie felt as if she was babbling, needing to fill the void of silence. "A developer bought it a few years back and renovated it. It's not much, but it's all I need." She pushed open the door into the small one-bedroom unit. David looked around, taking in the hardwood floors, coved ceilings, and brass light fixtures. The furniture, almost antiques, had mostly been acquired from relatives or quality used-furniture stores. The Chinese rug in the living room had been a present from Annie's mother after she'd married the L.A. film producer with postmodern taste.

Annie had never thought of her life-style as extravagant, but seeing the apartment through David's eyes, a man who lived on his boat and only got a job when he ran out of money, made her feel uncomfortably pretentious.

"Here, let me take your jacket." She took her own dripping parka and David's Helly Hansen out to the kitchen and hung them over the backs of chairs.

"You call this a kitchen?" David asked, following her to the four-by-four-foot area containing a small refrigerator, a two-burner gas range, and a microwave. "I've got more room in the galley of my boat."

Annie shrugged. "It's enough space for someone who never cooks."

"I guess." He opened the refrigerator. It was empty except for two bottles of Talking Rain seltzer, half a lemon, a quart of nonfat milk, one egg, and three bottles of Ballard Bitter.

"I . . . don't eat at home that often. Things spoil," Annie said apologetically, then told herself to get a grip. She didn't need to apologize to David for her life-style. They were different. Wasn't that part of the problem? "Would you like something to drink? A beer?"

"Yeah, I would, actually. Join me?" She nodded, and he pulled two beers out of the near-empty fridge.

"What happened to you, by the way? You look like a drowned rat."

"Oh, well, my car . . ."

"You're not still driving that damned convertible?" He laughed, almost like old times. Somehow it made her more uncomfortable than his wariness had.

"Make yourself comfortable. I need to get out of these wet things."

"Sure."

Annie escaped to her bedroom and shut the door. The excuse gave her time to compose her thoughts. David was going to want an explanation. That was obviously why he was here, and she didn't have the faintest idea what she was going to say.

After changing into jeans and a sweatshirt, she joined him in the living room, took the beer he handed her, and sat in the chair across from the sofa.

"Just so you know," he said. "I'm going back to San Francisco tonight. This friend of mine with the charter plane—I'm meeting him at Paine Field at eleven to fly back."

Annie nodded, still finding it hard to speak. "Your boat's in San Francisco?"

"Uh-huh. I got there a few days ago. The engine started having some problems off Santa Cruz. Nothing serious, but she'll be laid up there a few days while I work on it."

"And where will you be going after that?"

"I don't know. I might stay there a while. Not in the city, of course. Maybe down on the peninsula. I know some folks in Carmel that run a private school. I've taught sailing for them before. Or I might just spend the summer cruising. Go down to Baja."

Another pause. He was being so damned nice, as if nothing had happened. It would be so much easier if he would just demand some answers from her. But that wasn't his way. Annie marshaled her courage. "I'm sorry, David. I shouldn't have—"

"I didn't come here for an apology."

"But you want to know why." He didn't say anything. It was hard for her to look at him directly, so instead she studied the pattern in the rug. "I wanted to explain to you what I was feeling, but I didn't know how. I'm not sure I knew myself." She looked up. "More than anything, I didn't want to hurt you."

She could see his grip tighten on the beer. In the entire time they'd been together on his boat, she had never seen David Courtney angry. She needed him to be angry with her now.

"You didn't want to hurt me?" he asked, his voice taut with strain. "What, you didn't think I'd be hurt when I woke up and found you'd taken off? Like a dumb fool, I thought you'd bicycled into town for groceries or gone for a walk. I was worried sick until that kid from town brought me your note, the one that didn't say anything except that you'd taken a taxi to the airstrip and were flying home. Christ, Annie, if this is the way you *don't* hurt a guy, I never want to be around when you're feeling vindictive."

He strode over to the French doors and out onto the tiny balcony. The wet wind whipped into the room, billowing the drapes. Annie pulled her legs up onto the chair and hugged her knees, as if trying to make herself smaller. She wanted to shrink until she disappeared. How could she make him understand her panic? For that's what it had been, a fear that she couldn't explain, coming from who knows where, like a stranglehold whenever he tried to get too close. Now, seeing him again, she still felt the pressure of that fear. After a few moments he came back into the room, wiping the drops of rain from his face. He stood with his back to the wall.

"Sure, I knew something was wrong. I'm not blind. I just don't . . . Look, I know I'm not your Mr. Right. I picture you with . . . what, another yuppie lawyer maybe. Banker, politician. How about a nice, uptight CPA? No way do I see you with a forty-year-old beach bum who's never held a job longer than three months. No MBA, no IRA, no BMW.''

"It's not you, David.'' Annie spoke so softly, she wasn't sure he'd heard.

But after a pause he replied. "What do you mean, it wasn't me? Who else was out there? It was just you and me, and it should have worked.'' He crouched next to her chair and forced her to look at him. "I loved you, Annie. Love—it's a verb, remember? *To love.* It's not a state of being that falls from the sky. Couldn't you at least have *tried* to love me back?''

"I wanted to, David. I did try.'' She reached out for his hand. It was calloused and rough, with engine oil under the fingernails. But he pulled it away. *I got scared,* was what she wanted to say. *I was afraid of losing myself in you, afraid of losing control, afraid of being engulfed by you. Here you are, so confident, knowing exactly who you are and what you want out of life. You know how to enjoy every moment. Since I don't know who I am, or what I want, how do I know I'll still exist, if I'm with you?*

But Annie couldn't say any of those things. "I just don't

know how to make it work, David. Maybe I could have tried harder, but, right now, I think I need to be here. Get my own life sorted out."

He pushed himself into a standing position. "You really don't know what you want, do you?"

Annie looked up at him standing there and wondered if she'd ever be as sure of her needs and desires as David appeared to be. "Can you ever forgive me?"

He crouched in front of her chair again, taking her hands in his. "Are you kidding? You could drive a stake through my heart and I'd still think you're the best thing that ever happened to me."

She squeezed his hands. "Think we're going to laugh about this someday?"

For the first time since he'd arrived, David broke into his big, crooked smile. "Yeah, when I tell our grandchildren how hard it was to get you to fall in love with me." He stood up, pulled Annie out of her chair, and wrapped her in a big hug. For a moment, leaning her head against his chest, Annie almost felt safe.

Almost.

He lifted her chin and kissed her softly. It was easy to remember why she'd agreed to go away with him.

"Now I'm not trying to pressure you or anything," he said, pushing her hair out of her face. "I didn't come here"—he kissed her forehead—"to try to win you back."

She smiled up at him, glad to see the familiar twinkle in his blue eyes. "I admire your restraint."

"Yeah, no one ever said I wasn't a gentleman. But I think I understand what you need," he said softly, before giving her a long, lingering kiss.

"What's that?" she whispered, feeling almost ready to agree to anything he asked.

"Time," he replied. "To think. About life, what you want," he smiled, "about how much you miss me. So I'm going to go now."

That wasn't what she'd wanted him to say, but she knew he
was right.

"Can I drive you to the airport?"

He laughed. "In that little death trap you drive? No way! No,
I'll make my own way out there. Get a bite to eat, do a little
thinking of my own. We solitary sailors do that now and then."
He winked. "Wait, I just had an idea." Pulling a penny out of
his pocket, David opened the French doors and walked out on
the balcony. Curious, Annie followed and watched as he threw
the penny into the street, where it landed with a *plop* in a
puddle. "An old seafaring tradition. Whenever you leave a port
of call, if you throw a coin into the water, it means you'll come
back someday." He shrugged. "I have no idea if it works. I've
lost a hell of a lot of pennies that way. You take care now."
He grabbed his jacket and was gone.

Annie stared at the door, the apartment's emptiness ringing
in her ears. She was amazed that David Courtney had done it
to her again. She'd gotten what she'd asked for, he'd left her
alone to sort out her life, but all she could think about was
how good it had felt when he'd held her. She remembered the
first time he'd kissed her, sitting on top of Mount Constitution
on Orcas Island watching the sunset. She'd known virtually
nothing about him then, but the magic had been there from
the start. The kind of magic that didn't happen to sensible lawyers with sensible jobs. The kind of magic that had never, in
thirty-some years, struck Annie MacPherson with such an up-
percut to the solar plexus.

She'd almost missed her chance then, and here she was,
blowing it again. Out of her need to remain in control, her fear
of letting anyone else into her life, she'd let him slip away. He'd
said he'd be back, but how could she know she wouldn't push
him away again?

Maybe it was genetic, Annie thought bitterly. Her mother was
on her third marriage, and that one looked shaky. And her father?
He'd never remarried and, to Annie's knowledge, hadn't even
dated anyone since the divorce. During the years she'd lived with

him when she was in high school, there had been no one special in his life. Maybe she'd just never been taught how to love.

The jangling telephone made Annie jump. She looked around, searching for the extension she tended to carry from room to room on its long cord, and finally found it in the bedroom under a pile of laundry.

"Hello?"

"Annie, babe. You're home. Tha's great." The words were slurred, almost incomprehensible, but the voice was all too recognizable.

"Jed. Where are you calling from?" And why, Annie wanted to know.

"I'm really close to your place, at Bigelow's on Broadway."

Swell. Just happened to be in the neighborhood. "Why are you calling me, Jed?"

" 'Cause she took 'em." The pay phone must have been near the bar. It was hard to hear him over the din.

"Who took what?" Annie made no attempt to keep the frustration out of her voice.

"Suzy. I told her I'd give her a ride, but she took my keys. I think she stole my car." Annie didn't have to ask why. It was obvious from the sound of Jed's voice that he had no business driving. Suzy Gulliver had probably done the only appropriate thing to keep Jed off the streets.

"Do you have enough money for a cab?"

"Wha'?" Jed had probably been drinking steadily since the funeral.

"A cab. Have the bartender call you a cab."

"Can't. Lost my wallet."

Damn, thought Annie, wondering how he'd gotten her number. "All right. Stay where you are. I'll come get you."

"You're a peach, Annie. A regular Florida peach."

This guy is drunker than I thought, Annie surmised, pulling on her coat.

———

Seattle is not famous for its nightlife. They don't exactly roll up the sidewalks, but if you're looking for action on a week-night, you have to look pretty hard. Nevertheless, at 10:00 that Monday night, Bigelow's on Broadway was just starting to warm up. Annie pushed open the heavy brass-trimmed door into a sea of faces and noise. Cigarette smoke stung her eyes. She scanned the crowd in the lounge for a comatose Jed, hop-ing to scoop him up and make a fast getaway.

Magazine columnists allege that yuppies are passé—an out-dated trend from the Reagan years—but from what Annie could see, the species was far from extinct. Bigelow's was probably on the protected list of endangered habitats. The place was jammed with women with briefcases and men in striped shirts and suspenders downing martinis as if they were mineral wa-ters. Annie pictured them all talking about adjustable-rate mort-gages, foreign films, and safe sex.

Jed Delacourt was enthroned at a corner table with a trio of young women who were guzzling margaritas and gesturing with their Virginia Slims.

"I hate to be the one to break up the party, ladies, but it's past Jed's bedtime."

"Annie?" His eyes couldn't quite focus on her face. "What are you doing here?" Annie rolled her eyes.

"Is this your wife?" one of the women taunted, blowing smoke over her shoulder and brushing it away with a wave of her hand.

Annie, not terribly anxious to enter the conversation, grabbed Jed's elbow and tried to help him up. "No, I'm the head nurse at Western State. It's my job to retrieve the psychi-atric patients when they go AWOL." This brought a round of giggles. Annie hoped Charlie's Angels weren't going to be driv-ing, either.

"Okay," Jed replied meekly, putting some wadded-up bills on the table. Annie saw they were all ones, not nearly enough to cover his tab. Since none of the women had noticed, she decided to keep this information to herself. Jed turned back to the blonde and whispered loudly, "I gotta go now, Wesley. You unnerstand. But I'll call you tomorrow."

"Yeah, you do that, sweetheart. I really do want to go for that ride in your plane." Annie could hear the threesome roaring with laughter as she hauled her charge out into the damp air.

Annie wasn't in the mood for games. After unlocking the passenger door for Jed, she commanded him to get in. "All right, Jed, listen to me. I'm only going to say this once. If you're going to throw up, tell me and I'll stop the car."

He burped. "Got it."

"Now, where are we going?" Jed looked perplexed. "Come on, the questions get harder after this. Give me your address."

"But she took my keys."

"I know Suzy took your car keys. She probably didn't want you to drive."

"But she took the whole ring."

"Your house key, too?"

"Uh-huh."

"And you don't have another way to get into your house?"

"Nuh-uh." Annie felt like she was dealing with a fifth-grader.

"Damn it, Jed!" Annie banged her hand on the steering wheel, causing the horn to tweet. "You mean I came all the way down here to get you and you can't even get into your own house?"

Jed probably would have answered, but his head had fallen back and was lolling against the passenger door. The only sound he made was a cross between a hiccup and a snore. Well, at least he was less likely to throw up in the car.

Somehow she managed to get him up the stairs to her apartment. After opening the door, she shoved him toward the sofa, where he landed with a thud. The blow woke him up. "Where am I?"

"You're at my place, and if you have any will to live, you'll avoid making speeches. Anything you say can and will be used against you in the morning."

Annie returned from the hall with an armload of linens. "Here's a towel, a sheet, and a blanket. The bathroom's down the hall. If you make a mess, I'll kill you. This sofa does not conceal a Hide-A-Bed. What you see is what you get. It's lumpy and too short for anyone over five-six to sleep on comfortably, but it's the closest thing to a guest room I've got. I'm leaving for work at seven-thirty. I'll wake you up before I go. Any questions?"

"You're upset, aren't you?"

Annie sighed. "Any *intelligent* questions?"

Jed blew his nose loudly on what looked like a handkerchief. "I'm sorry, Annie, I shouldn't have called you."

"That's true. Plenty of people spend the night on Broadway, and most of them survive till morning. But right now I'm not in the mood for a debate. We'll talk about it in the morning."

"I lost my job."

"What?"

Jed looked up at her with eyes as bloodshot and pitiful as a lame hunting dog's. "I went back to the office after the funeral. The letter was on my desk. They gave me a month's severance pay and told me to have my office cleaned out by tomorrow."

Annie sat down on the edge of the couch. "I'm sorry, Jed. That's a rotten deal."

He closed his eyes and nodded. "I know. You know anyone that would be interested in a used Beemer, leather interior, great sound system?" He glanced down at his Brooks Brothers suit, now rumpled, and his Giorgio Armani tie stained with guacamole and picante sauce. "Hey, I could sell my clothes. They're worth a fortune. Got any boyfriends who wear a size thirty-six?"

"Not anymore. Look, Jed, take it easy. You'll find another job. We can talk about this in the morning."

"Yeah, okay. Hey, if you think of any good voodoo curses for Barclay, write them down. Right now . . . I have to be sick."

At seven the next morning Annie touched Jed on the shoulder. He groaned, then spoke without opening his eyes. "Do I look as bad as I feel?"

"If it were Halloween, you wouldn't need makeup."

"That good, huh? I'm doing better than I thought."

"How much of last night do you remember?"

Jed rubbed his eyes and sat up. "Most of it, unfortunately. Even the part where I told the blonde I flew fighter planes in the Persian Gulf and would take her up for a spin. For God's sake, do I look like a fighter pilot?"

"I don't think she believed you, anyway."

"I gotta call Suzy and get my keys." He stood up with the blanket wrapped around him and padded out to the kitchen. "Good thing you don't have a boyfriend who's likely to drop by. This could be difficult to explain."

"I'd be willing to take the risk."

"What?"

"Nothing."

Jed found Suzy Gulliver's number in the phone book and dialed. "Hi, yeah, I'm okay. I called Annie, and she brought me back to her place. . . . Because you had my keys. I couldn't go home. . . . What? You're kidding." He cupped his hand over the phone. "Annie, would you take a look in the left-hand pocket of my overcoat?" Annie didn't have to. When she picked up the Burberry, she could hear the jangling keys.

"Oops." Jed tried his best to look contrite. It didn't work. With his blond hair flopping into his eyes, he looked like a six-year-old who was used to getting away with murder without being spanked.

"No, I haven't talked to her about it. . . . I don't know. . . . Maybe." He covered the receiver again. "Suzy wants to know

if you'd like to get together for a drink tonight. She'd like to
talk to you about—"

"Nancy?"

He nodded.

"Sure, I guess so," Annie replied.

"All right. She says F. X. McRory's at six."

It turned out to be a bad choice for a Tuesday evening in May.
F. X. McRory's Steak, Chop, & Oysterhouse was across the
street from the Kingdome and was *the* spot for the sporting
crowd to congregate prior to baseball games. As it was still
early in the baseball season, the fans clung to the prospect that
the Mariners might, just this once, have a championship season.
There's always hope. That evening the game started at seven
and the bar was jammed. The raucous crowd mimicked the
colorful Leroy Neiman paintings that lined the walls.

Annie spotted Suzy and Jed at a window table across the
room and shoved her way through the crowd. Nancy's sister
was wearing a red sweatsuit with a sports club logo and her
short curly hair was damp. Annie felt a twinge of guilt as she
always did around people who exercised. Maybe tomorrow
she'd start jogging or something. A waitress came and took her
order for white wine.

"Annie, thanks for meeting us here. I guess I should have
looked at the baseball schedule. I didn't even know there was
a game tonight. I work at the health club down the street and
this is my break. I don't have a lot of time."

Jed and Suzy were seated close together on the wooden
bench against the wall. "Look," Annie said, "I hate to be slow
on the uptake. But you guys didn't meet at the funeral, right?"

Jed smiled. "I should have explained. Suzy and I are old
friends. I, uh, dated Nancy for a while when I first started at
the firm. She and Suzy were the only two people I knew in
Seattle for a while. But we hadn't seen each other for a while.
Since . . ."

"Since Gordon Barclay invaded my sister's life," Suzy interjected. The venom in her voice reminded Annie of that day in the office when Suzy had tried to attack Barclay. She might have calmed down since then, but the hatred was still there.

"That's why we both need to know."

"Need to know what?"

"I didn't believe Jed at first," Suzy said, a little timidly. "But the more I looked at that note, the more I began to question it."

"Annie, we don't think Nancy killed herself," said Jed.

"What?"

"The note's a fake, Annie. It has to be. Look." Suzy pulled a Ziploc bag out of her sports bag. The note was inside. She hadn't left it in Nancy's coffin after all. "Look at the shape and the type of paper. It's obviously cut from a card or some other kind of stationery."

"Do you think it's her writing?"

"Absolutely," Suzy replied. "I'd know it anywhere. And Nancy liked to write down her thoughts. She was kind of shy, so that was how she communicated when she had something really important to say. She'd put it in a letter. What I think is that this is part of another letter. Here, look at this." Suzy rummaged in her bag and pulled out a box of notecards. On the front was a Seurat print. "I got these cards at the art museum. One box for me and one for Nancy. I gave them to her in her stocking at Christmas. They're all Impressionist prints."

Annie compared the "suicide" note to the inside of the Seurat card. The size and type of paper seemed to be a match.

"Last night I remembered something that Nancy had told me the night she died. We were talking about Barclay and about her wanting to break off the affair. She said she wrote him a note telling him she was mad at him."

"And you think this is part of that note?"

"It seems pretty obvious to me."

Annie studied it for a few moments. The theory had a certain logic, but the implication was hard to swallow. "Are you saying you think Barclay . . . killed Nancy?"

Jed said, "We think that's pretty obvious, too."

Annie sat back and took a deep breath. There was no question that Barclay had his faults. He had a reputation for having affairs; his marriage was a sham. He was extremely demanding of the people who worked for him. Certainly he had handled the matter with Nancy badly. But a killer? It was inconceivable.

This business with the note seemed *too* obvious. Annie couldn't ignore the fact that the two people in the entire world who hated Gordon Barclay most were seated at this table.

With as much tact as possible, she told Jed and Suzy her reservations.

Suzy eyed Annie warily. "He's sucked you in, hasn't he? With his charming act? Nancy told me all about how engaging he could be." She took a sip of her Coke, then said, without looking at Annie, "Maybe he's found a replacement already."

Annie knew exactly what she was implying. "No" was all she said.

Jed sensed the hostility and intervened. "We're not saying we *know* he did it. We don't have any proof. We thought you could help us, maybe even rule out the possibility."

Annie considered this, then nodded. Given Suzy's state of mind, it would be better if she could let go of her anger at Barclay, come to grips with her sister's suicide.

"Well, for a start, you could give this to a document expert," said Annie. "I can give you the name of the one I've used on cases. I'm sure he could identify the type of paper and the handwriting as well. Possibly get fingerprints, although I'm sure a lot of people have handled the note by now."

Suzy smiled. "That would be great, Annie. And don't worry about the expense. Nancy had a life insurance policy through KLMD. I'll spend it all if it means catching her killer."

Annie wrote down the name of the document analyst. "Then you'd want to find out where Barclay was on Friday night."

Jed and Suzy exchanged looks. Jed was the one who finally spoke.

"Annie, neither of us can talk to him, for pretty obvious reasons."

She looked at them expectantly, not sure she wanted to hear what was coming. It was what she expected.

"You could talk to him easily. You wouldn't have to ask him anything directly, just sort of, well, bring up the subject. See if he accidentally lets something slip."

Annie started to say no, but Suzy said, "Don't you see? If Nancy was murdered, it had to be Barclay. She's just broken up with him. He was probably pissed."

"That hardly seems like enough reason to kill someone."

"Even if Nancy was pregnant?"

"Was she?"

Suzy shrugged. "We'll never know. But when I went through her apartment I found one of those pregnancy self-tests in the trash. It had been used, but I couldn't tell what the results were."

This was all sounding just too pat. Why hadn't Suzy brought up these concerns before now? She was the only one with access to Nancy's apartment, the only one who knew about Nancy's breaking up with Barclay. Maybe last night, over a few drinks, Suzy and Jed had cooked up a way to get back at Gordon Barclay.

"Will you do it, Annie? Just talk to him? Bring up her name? See how he reacts?"

Annie looked at Suzy and concluded that all the guts in the family had gone to the older sister. Her lips were set in a firm line of determination, holding back the rage still evident in her eyes. If this woman held a grudge against me, Annie thought, I'd watch out.

She knew that an alibi from Barclay, or some explanation of his relationship to Nancy, would be the best way to diffuse Suzy's anger.

"Look, I'm not going to promise anything. But Gordon's asked me to have lunch with him tomorrow. I think we're just going to be discussing cases. It's been so crazy at the office we haven't had a chance. But *if* the subject of Nancy comes up, and *if* he says anything that would confirm or deny your suspicions, I'll let you know. That's all I can do."

A smile played across Suzy's face. "Thanks, Annie." She turned to Jed and whispered, "We're gonna get him, Jed, I just know we're gonna get him."

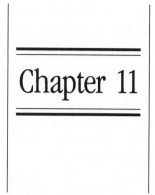

Chapter 11

In the quivering fluorescent light of the KLMD ladies' room Annie stared in dismay at the run in her panty hose that started at the top of her big toe and ended just above her knee. Any other day she might have pretended that she hadn't noticed it, but not on a day she was having lunch with Gordon Barclay. Whatever Jed and Suzy had to say, she was still in awe of her new boss's renown.

For a brief moment Annie pictured herself back in the old office with Joel and Val, where a ruined stocking wouldn't have merited a second glance. On days without court appearances or clients to meet, it had been perfectly acceptable to pad around the office in an old cardigan and bedroom slippers or to come to work in jeans and a T-shirt. No one had worried about what hours anyone else kept as long as the work got done. If Annie wanted to come in at noon or leave at three on a sunny day, she just did it.

But at Kemble, Laughton, Mercer, and Duff appearances counted. As everyone kept telling her, it didn't matter if you worked twelve-hour days unless someone *saw* you work twelve-hour days. A working Saturday was wasted unless a partner breezed by and observed you with your head buried in a file. Some associates even went out of their way to learn which partners were planning to come in on a weekend, just so they could arrange to be visible. Eight A.M. was an acceptable time to arrive at the office, but seven-fifteen was better. It wasn't going to be an easy adjustment.

"Oh, that is a bad one, isn't it?" Deborah Silver commented, pushing open the ladies' room door. Her eyes had gone immediately to Annie's run. Annie didn't appreciate the critique from someone who undoubtedly practiced power dressing in her sleep. "You must have an extra pair in your desk—let me run and get it for you."

Withholding a sarcastic retort, Annie glanced over at Deborah's size-six Geoffrey Beene pumps and size-five Liz Claiborne suit and realized that yes, this woman would keep emergency panty hose in her desk. "No, I'll just have to dash out to"—Annie stopped herself from saying Pay 'n Save. Deborah probably bought her hose at I. Magnin—"the store and get another pair."

"I would give you my spare pair, but—"

"Oh, I wouldn't dream . . ." Annie cut her off before Deborah had to apologize that *hers*, unfortunately, were extra petite.

Annie gave up on the stockings and decided to fix her hair. Perhaps if she looked smashing from the neck up no one would notice the run as she dashed down to the drugstore. Deborah joined her at the mirror. "Aren't the lights in here horrid? They make one look so *pale*."

"Mmm." The "one" she was referring to must have been Annie because Deborah's skin looked just as rich and creamy as it had in natural light, while Annie's was the color of skim milk. She fumbled in her purse in search of a blusher.

"I hear Gordon is just thrilled with your work so far."

"Oh, really?"

"Uh-huh, he was just going on and on about you last night, couldn't say enough nice things." Annie had attended a deposition with Barclay the previous afternoon that had lasted until after five o'clock. She wondered where Barclay and Deborah had conversed after that. Deborah didn't volunteer the information, and Annie muttered something suitably reciprocal about enjoying working with Barclay.

Using a fuchsia lip pencil to outline her lips, Deborah continued, "You know, I'm surprised that a man like Gordon, with his client base, has stayed at KLMD for so long. One would think he'd want to head his own firm. You know, strike out on his own. Don't you think?"

It was an odd question, and Annie suspected Deborah was fishing for information. "Well," Annie hedged, "I really don't know Gordon that well, but from my experience running your own practice means a lot of additional work and responsibility."

"Oh, well, I didn't mean *your* type of practice. I was picturing something of a more, uh, challenging nature."

Oh, my practice was challenging, all right, Annie wanted to say, as she pictured Deborah facing an interview with a gun-toting ex-husband or the habitual car thief who always said he'd "borrowed" the car from a "buddy."

Deborah took out a tiny brush and dabbed bright pink lipstick between the perfect pencil lines. Something about the delicate movements gave Annie the urge to jar her elbow.

"Would you ever consider going back to a smaller practice, if the right opportunity came along?" Deborah asked. Like a ventriloquist, she'd said it without moving her lips. The question sounded innocent, but the look that accompanied it wasn't. At that moment Annie wouldn't have trusted Deborah with plans for a surprise party, much less her career goals.

"I'm sure I'm going to be very happy at KLMD."

Deborah blotted her lips on a tissue. "I'm very sure you will, Annie. Did you hear the news about Jed?"

"Yes. And to tell you the truth, I think he got a rotten deal."

"Well, if you want to feel sorry for him go ahead. But it's good news for us."

"How so?"

"Well, we're all in the same year group, up for partnership

next year. I'm sure they explained the odds to you when you came on. Last year, out of a group of twenty-three associates, only two were made full partners."

"And the others?"

"Four more were given contracts to remain as non-equity partners. A decent salary and a secure job, but no hope of moving up the ladder. The rest have one year to find work elsewhere."

"I see." It hadn't been explained to Annie in quite those terms when she'd interviewed. She'd been told that after a year she'd be eligible for partnership, but she had assumed that if her work was satisfactory she would at least keep her job, partnership or not. She looked up to catch Deborah's chilly glance.

"So what you're saying is, without Jed, we have less competition to worry about."

Reaching over, Deborah lifted a red hair off of Annie's shoulder. "Personally, I can't say I'm sorry to see him go. If there are only a couple of open spots, I'd much rather see them go to us women. We have to stick together, you know. Good luck with that run."

Back in her office, Annie pondered the world she found herself thrown into. She and Joel had never been rivals—they had been teammates. Wasn't the practice of law adversarial enough without having to compete against your own co-workers? Why was she doing this, anyway?

She remembered one of the countless arguments she had had with her father about the practice of law. She could never understand how he could take a position for a client that he knew was in the wrong. How could he sleep at night knowing that he had gotten a guilty man acquitted or denied an injured person the recovery he or she was entitled to?

The *system*, he kept telling her. In order for the *system* to work, both sides were entitled to the best possible defense, the best arguments money could buy. Justice might not prevail in every individual case, but overall the *system* worked.

Years later Annie had heard herself repeat the same argument to nonlawyers who didn't understand. But she knew now what her father hadn't been able to explain to her. It wasn't the idea of helping people or preserving the integrity of the judicial process that kept lawyers going. The argument about the system was a convenient cliché. No, for those who stuck with it, it was the game that made it all worthwhile. The thrill of taking on the competition and beating them fair and square.

Every time Annie had stood in front of a jury ready to begin closing arguments, she had felt it. That rush of adrenaline, the belief that, at that moment, nothing mattered more than prevailing for your client. It was a feeling she didn't like to admit to.

After a quick outing to the drugstore to pick up a fresh pair of panty hose, Annie stopped by Barclay's office at noon, where she found him expertly sinking a twelve-foot putt into a glass in a corner. The surface of his desk was shiny and devoid of papers, making Annie wonder if the man actually practiced law or just came to the office to practice his golf stroke. Unintentionally, she found herself on edge after last night's chat with Jed and Suzy, wondering if perhaps she could be wrong about Gordon Barclay.

"Ah, there you are. Right on time. I wish you'd give my wife lessons in promptness. After thirty years she still hasn't figured out how to be on time. I thought we would head out to Shilshole, go to Ray's. How does that sound?"

"Great." In a town famous for its fresh seafood, Ray's Boathouse was the name most Seattleites came up with first when asked where to go for great fish. It could take weeks to get a reservation for a Saturday night, and the restaurant was always packed at lunchtime with the business crowd. Annie hadn't been there in years.

When they arrived, the hostess showed them to a window table with an excellent view of Shilshole Bay, looking out toward the lighthouse at West Point. If it had been clearer, they would have been able to see across Puget Sound to Bainbridge Island and the Olympic Mountains behind it, but the morning fog had given way to an overcast sky with low visibility. The interior of the restaurant was evocative of the inside of a sailboat: the smooth wooden paneling was the color of teak, every corner curved. On the walls were hand-tinted black-and-white photos of Ray's through the years, dating from the time it was just a fish shack on the end of a pier.

Their waitress—Kristen, according to her name tag— bounced up to the table. Slim and fit, with straight blond hair pulled back in a ponytail, she looked like she'd just stepped out of a light beer commercial. Annie noticed Barclay appraising her legs, which were long and tan in short white shorts.

"Run and see what the bartender has in single malts, would you, dear?"

"I'm sure he's got Glenlivet."

"Yes, I'm sure he does. See if he's got anything drinkable."

Annie stifled a laugh. When Kristen sprinted back, she read off the back of a napkin, having some difficulty pronouncing the names, "Glenlivet, Glenfiddich, Laphroaig, and Macallan."

"Macallan?" Barclay's eyes lit up. "Twelve or eighteen?"

"Years old? Eighteen. But I've got to warn you, that one is really expensive."

"As well it should be. Annie, you have to try this with me, it's the best single-malt whiskey you can get in Washington. Why are you smiling?"

"My grandfather was from Edinburgh and loved his single malts. He always said that drinking *usquebaugh*—blended whiskey—was like drinking sheep dip."

"Your grandfather was a smart man." Their drinks arrived in balloon snifters. Barclay swirled his, breathed in the bouquet, and, with his eyes closed, took a sip. "Ah, nothing better on the face of this earth." Although not much of a whiskey drinker, Annie had to agree. The Macallan was smooth, with an essence of cinnamon and sherry, resembling a fine cognac more than a typical scotch. Her grandfather had died before Annie had been old enough to drink with him, but it brought back pleasant memories nonetheless. She let the flavors linger on her tongue.

"There's one brand better than this. I'll have to pour it for you sometime. I always keep a bottle in the office for clients. It's called Glendullan, available only in London at Milroy's wine shop in Soho. I pick up a case every time I'm over there."

Kristen sprang up from nowhere, slightly out of breath as if she'd just run from the kitchen. "Ready to order yet?"

"No, no. Give us some time here. We're in no rush this afternoon." Barclay was obviously in an expansive mood, without the tension that Annie had observed on other occasions. Thinking back on the conversation at McRory's the night before, Annie had to wonder why Jed and Suzy had formed their antagonism for the man. After all, Barclay had never been anything but kind and helpful to her. She was actually starting to enjoy his company.

"So tell me, Annie, how is your research coming along?"

"My research?"

"The work you're doing. Regarding your father."

"Oh, that. It isn't, really."

"Problems?"

"No, it's just that I've been so swamped at work. I haven't really gotten around to it. I'll probably start sorting the papers this weekend."

"Well," said Barclay, picking up a menu. "There's never enough time to do everything, is there? If there is anything I can do to help, give you my recollections of old George, you just let me know. I've got some stories . . . Well, some of them are no doubt too risqué to tell a daughter, from when your dad and I were young and carefree . . . Those were the days, Annie. You know, the salmon is truly excellent here. Fresh, of course. I don't think Ray's has ever served a frozen piece of fish."

It still seemed odd, thinking of Barclay as such a close friend of her father's. As she watched him pore over his menu, she realized why it was so difficult. As fit as Barclay looked, he was still sixty, the same age her father would have been if he had lived. But she would always picture her father as he had been the last time she had seen him before he died, in his midforties. The two men didn't seem like contemporaries.

Perhaps the other thing that bothered her about thinking of Barclay as a peer of her father's was that despite her conversation with Jed and Suzy (or perhaps because of it?) she was acutely aware of Barclay's attractiveness. Not that she, herself, was attracted to him, of course. Just that she could understand how other women might be. More than just good looks; it was the sense of extreme self-confidence. Barclay was so sure of himself that he had no need to be arrogant.

When Kristen returned for their orders, Annie opted for the seared ling cod with roasted red-pepper aioli, while Barclay ordered the sautéed scallops, asking the waitress to be sure the chef didn't overcook them. When the salads arrived, she was surprised that it was Barclay who brought up the subject of Nancy Gulliver.

"I've been interviewing secretarial candidates today. Some acceptable, but none, I'm afraid, who will be as delightful to have around as Nancy." Annie noticed that Barclay ate in the British manner, with the knife in his right hand and the fork remaining in his left. An affectation, she assumed, knowing that he'd been born and raised in the Pacific Northwest.

"How long had she worked for you?"

"Hmm, let's see. She started with the firm three or four years ago, in the word processing department. Then she took over as my secretary last year."

The bread in the basket at the center of the table gave off the warm aroma of sourdough. Annie tore off a piece.

"I'm sorry I didn't get a chance to know her better."

Barclay took the last sip of his drink, savoring it, then said, "I'm going to miss her, Annie. I shall truly miss her."

A vague sense of doubt nagged at Annie. She tried to be open-minded and not be influenced by the negative comments of the previous night. But still she felt compelled to ask, "Why does her sister think you caused Nancy's death?"

Barclay set down his knife and fork, dabbed a spot of dressing from his mouth. "That woman . . . I wished you hadn't seen that, Annie. The way she barged into the office that day, her rudeness . . . It's all because she thinks I used Nancy, that I toyed with her. She's wrong about me. Oh, I know what you're thinking. An old man like me. That I needed her youth to prop up an aging male ego, that the affair was all to my selfish benefit." He shook his head. "It wasn't like that. I can honestly say that I was good for Nancy. I taught her about love. I wouldn't go so far as to say I loved her—I think she realized that I didn't. But I cherished her, Annie. So many young men these days, they have no idea how to treat a woman. How to respect her, and I do mean respect. I taught Nancy what to expect from a man, and I hoped that after our affair came to an end, she'd move on with pride in herself and the self-confidence that she deserved. It was never my intention to hurt her in any way."

Barclay was speaking so openly, Annie felt encouraged to draw him out even more, follow up on what Suzy had said about their last fight. "But she was upset with you. Was she expecting something more from you?"

"Oh, no, nothing like that. We'd had a little spat about how to spend the evening. She'd planned something special, a dinner or some such, and I'd had to cancel at the last minute. No more than any couple goes through. Remember how emotional one is at that age, every little thing is a crisis? As to the future, we both knew from the beginning our affair wasn't going to last forever, we'd talked about it many times. I'm sure she wouldn't have married me if I'd asked. I think what was really happening was that she was ready to move on, find someone her own age. It was hard for her to come to that realization. But I wouldn't have stood in her way." Looking down, Barclay seemed to realize with some embarrassment that he had closed his hand around a piece of sourdough. He brushed away the crumbs as he regained his composure.

"How's your salad? Need anything?" he asked her.

"No, no. Everything's fine."

"Good, good. And you, Annie. Is there a special love in your life? You know, it's so frustrating now that we're not allowed to ask anything personal during the job interviews. Can't even ask if someone is married, for chrissakes."

And a good thing, too, Annie thought, feeling suddenly uncomfortable. She wondered if her discomfort came from the idea that Barclay was expressing a personal interest in her or from the fact that she felt flattered by his attention. "No, no one right now" was all she said, looking down at her plate. Not anymore.

Barclay smiled and nodded, as if filing this bit of information away for future use. "Don't get the wrong impression, Annie. The purpose of this lunch is purely . . . business."

The way he said it, Annie immediately knew he meant the contrary. She tried for a light tone. "Let's see, you're either making me a partner already or I'm being fired."

He chuckled. "Neither, but you're right. It does involve your job, Annie, and I think it's time I got to the point. I know you enjoyed working in a small firm. How would you like to do so again?" The question was almost a carbon copy of the one Deborah had put to her earlier that morning.

"I thought you just said I wasn't being fired?" she joked.

"You're not. You're being solicited. I'm sure you understand that what I'm about to say is strictly confidential." She nodded. "I'm leaving KLMD, Annie. Effective next Monday. I'll be starting my own firm, and I'd like you to come with me."

Annie gulped. So this was the reason for Barclay's expansive mood, Fred Duff's suspicions, and Deborah's prying questions. She remembered what Fred had said about the domino effect, how the departure of someone like Barclay could cause the entire firm to crumble. "Does Fred Duff know yet?"

"Of course not. He would do everything in his power to stop it if he did. He founded KLMD—the firm means more to him than his own life."

"But the risk? I would think the security of a large firm—"

"Security. Security is for old geezers like Duff, Annie, who have lost their ability to try cases, who are scared to put it on the line. A life without risk is boring. Don't you think I know it's unusual for a man my age, a senior partner in a major law firm, to strike off on his own? That's why I want to do it, to show them I still have the right stuff."

Annie forced down a swallow of salad. "Why me?" She now knew that Deborah had been pumping her to see if she'd gotten such an offer. She wondered whether Deborah had.

"I need someone with a general practice background to round out the firm. Someone with good trial experience. And I'll be blunt. I wanted a woman to balance the rowdy crew I've already lined up. I've been on the lookout and I suspected that you were the woman I needed, but I wanted a little more time to get to know you to be sure. That's why I made sure that KLMD grabbed you before you found something else."

His reasoning didn't sound entirely persuasive, but Annie was unable to detect what his real motives might be.

"How many attorneys are we talking about?"

"Six in all, Alex Guiterrez and myself, and three attorneys from other firms in town. All young, all aggressive, all fighters. I've seen your trial work, Annie. You're good. Lots of fire. Lots of competitive spirit, just like your father. And you'll be the only woman on the letterhead."

Annie took a sip of water. "What does 'on the letterhead' mean?"

Barclay smiled. "I like a woman who gets right to the bottom line. It means a partnership, Annie. I've set up a two-tiered system. I'll be a senior partner, based on an additional capital investment and, as a result, for the first five years, I'll get a higher percentage of the profits of the firm. The other attorneys, you included, I hope, will be junior partners, with your

capital investment coming out of your draw—no up-front
money required.''

"Maybe I like working at KLMD.''

Barclay laughed loudly enough to turn heads at the neigh-
boring table. "You don't fit in, Annie, and you know it. Associates struggling over each other to get to the top, the
bureaucratic chaos, the political backbiting. You're a litigator,
Annie. Just like me. All you want to do is just get on with the
practice of law. And the more time in court, the better, am I
right? But unlike your little firm, this would be the big league,
Annie. I'm talking a six-figure salary, with year-end bonuses on
top of that. And the kind of trials that get national news cov-
erage.''

Annie tried to suppress a gasp. Almost against her will she
found herself envisioning what it would be like. A small firm,
important jury trials, Gordon Barclay's prime client base. An
escape from the political morass of the huge firm. She couldn't
deny that it was an attractive offer. And Barclay knew it—the
smug expression on his face said it all. Nevertheless, he continued his pitch.

"You mentioned security, but it's really not as big a gamble
as it might look. I've already gotten commitments from most
of my major insurance clients—including the carrier for Spectrum Defense International—and with the attorneys who'll be
joining me from the other firms, we'll pick up even more accounts. The way it looks right now, it's going to be the legal
coup of the decade. We'll have insurance defense in this town
virtually locked up.''

Gordon paused while Kristen trotted over to clear the plates.
"Dessert, Annie? They have a wonderful chocolate decadence
here.''

"No, just coffee. Black.''

Barclay lowered his voice. "And if you aren't convinced yet,
I could always spell out what your chances will be if you de-
cide to stay at KLMD.'' He said it with a smile, but Annie knew
Barclay wasn't joking.

She looked down at the tablecloth as Fred Duff's face came to mind. "I understand. Your leaving will decimate KLMD's insurance practice, could impact the entire firm. As a newly hired associate, still on probation, I'd be one of the first to go."

"You're quick, Annie. I knew that from the start."

Kristen set down her coffee and Barclay's tea, barely pausing before bounding off in another direction. Annie ran through the pros and cons again. Alex Guiterrez was definitely on the negative side of the ledger. Since their first awkward meeting at the Cascade Club, he had gone out of his way to avoid her, to the point of walking in the other direction when he saw her approaching in the hall. She wasn't sure she would be able to work with the man. On the other hand, her co-workers at KLMD weren't exactly the most congenial group she'd ever met.

Annie paused, sipping her coffee. "When do you need an answer?"

"The sooner the better. By this weekend at the latest." He looked her in the eye. "I already know what your answer is, but I'm going to humor you and give you some time to sleep on it. It's a big decision, after all."

The check arrived and Barclay slipped his American Express card into the leather folder without bothering to look at the total. Knowing that she had to make a decision about her future, and soon, Annie suddenly felt very cold, as if a winter draft was blowing through the room. What if she was wrong about Barclay? What if Jed and Suzy were right? No, she thought. Whatever else Barclay was up to, he wasn't a murderer.

Barclay's voice cut through her foggy-minded wanderings. "I know I can trust you to be discreet, Annie."

"What?"

"Trust you not to breathe a word to anyone. No one knows about this, of course. Except for Alex and the other attorneys involved. Nancy Gulliver was the only other soul who knew."

His words went through her like an icy bullet. Nancy's name, hanging there in the air, sounded vaguely like a threat. Had Nancy died because someone was worried she couldn't keep a secret? Or was Annie just letting her morbid imaginings get the better of her?

Barclay held the door and Annie walked outside into the fresh air. A parking valet in khaki shorts and a striped rugby shirt materialized and took Barclay's ticket. "Car, sir?"

"Mercedes sedan."

"Yes, sir." The valet jogged off around the corner.

The valet soon pulled up, and as Barclay walked around to the driver's side and handed the young man a tip, the sun emerged from behind a cloud and reflected sharply off the shiny black hood. Annie blinked, shielding her eyes.

"Wait, Gordon, my sunglasses. I think I left them on the table. I'll be right back." Annie turned back in the direction of the restaurant.

She had only taken a step or two when it happened. First there was a sharp crack, then two more. A woman somewhere was screaming. She heard Barclay's voice, rising above the others, but couldn't make out the words. What was wrong, why were there so many people? Then she felt the stinging. Sharp, hot, a thousand needles. Terrible pain. Someone pulled Annie to the ground and shielded her body.

Chapter 12

Suddenly the entryway was jammed with people, all shouting at once. Annie felt her body being shoved, almost carried, back toward the restaurant. She felt removed, as if it were all happening to someone else.

"She's bleeding!"

"Get a doctor, damn it."

A body jostled Annie's arm, and she cried out with the intense, searing pain. Pulling away the bar towel that someone had pressed against her right biceps, she saw a gash in the white linen sleeve like a lipstick-smeared mouth. Later she remembered thinking how red the blood was, almost glowing in its intensity.

"I'm a doctor. Bring her over here." A dozen arms guided her in the direction of the voice. "Here you go, sit down right here. That's right. It's okay now, you'll be okay." The doctor could have been a pediatrician or a vet, so soothing was his bedside manner.

Annie's head was swimming. Voices were mumbling all around her, but she didn't bother to distinguish the speakers. Someone said the word *shock*.

The doctor looked as if he'd dressed himself out of a yuppie handbook. Tortoiseshell glasses, a blue oxford shirt with contrasting white collar, and a red paisley tie. He even wore navy-blue suspenders. All he needed was an insincere grin and he'd look just like an ad for a J. C. Penney's Fourth of July sale.

"Now this is going to hurt, so just hold on." As the doctor pulled her jacket off, Annie took a sharp intake of air. The blood at the edge of the wound had started to dry and the fabric stuck to her skin. He cut away the thin material of her blouse and used a damp towel to daub at the gunshot wound. Each time he touched her she winced.

"I know, this feels pretty awful, but I want to make sure there aren't any bone fragments in here. Both an entrance and an exit wound—it looks pretty clean. The bullet must have missed the bone completely. It's still bleeding, though, so I'm going to apply some pressure." Someone handed the doctor a clean towel, which he wrapped tightly around Annie's upper arm. Through the babble of sounds she made out Barclay's voice.

"For God's sake, people, let me through. She's with me. Annie, Annie, are you okay? What happened, for chrissakes?"

The doctor glanced up briefly, then turning back to Annie, he spoke over his shoulder. "Please stand back a little, sir. Are you all right? Was anyone else injured?"

"No, everyone else is fine, as far as I can tell. Has someone called 911?"

"On their way, sir. Police and ambulance," a waiter replied, looking shaken.

As if on cue, an approaching siren was heard outside, shutting off abruptly at the restaurant's entrance. Instead of the ambulance it was a police car. Two uniformed officers, a man and a woman, rushed in, pushing the crowd aside. On their heels was a Channel 7 TV crew.

"Damn it all," Barclay muttered. "How did they know about this?"

Apologetically the waiter said, "I think they listen to the scanner, sir."

Barclay was still cursing when a microphone was shoved in his face. "Can you tell us what happened, sir? We understand you were with the woman who was shot."

Before Barclay could answer, he felt a hand on his arm. The

policewoman said, "You can speak to the press in a moment, sir, but first if you'd step over here?"

"Yes, of course. Thank you for getting me out of that."

The officer pulled out a notebook. After taking down Barclay's name, address, and occupation, she said, "Tell us everything you know about what happened."

He described the incident, explaining that he'd heard three shots. "Afterwards we could see that two hit the front fender of the car, near where I was standing with the valet. We were somewhat shielded, though, by the open door of the car." He gestured with his hands to demonstrate his position. "The third shot apparently struck Ms. MacPherson in the arm. She had been about to enter the car but suddenly remembered something that she had to go back for. I can't recall what it was. A coat, maybe? Anyway, she said something and started back for the restaurant door. That's when it all happened." The questioning officer nodded to her partner, who went out to examine the car. The officer led Barclay outside to look at the surrounding area.

"Any idea where the shots were coming from?"

Barclay surveyed the area. There were several eating establishments lining the waterfront, with large parking lots between them and the highway. No tall buildings or other structures stood near the restaurants. On the other side of the highway was a hillside dense with underbrush that rose sharply and was dotted with a few apartment buildings and homes.

"I would assume the shots came from that direction," Barclay said, pointing at the hillside, "from the way they struck the car."

The officer nodded and spoke into her radio. From the look on her face it was obvious she didn't expect to locate the shooter.

"And your relationship to the young woman?"

"A co-worker. We were discussing business. A, uh, legal case we were working on."

"I see. Any idea why someone might be shooting at you or at her?"

"Absolutely not, Officer. I can't think of a single thing. It would be absurd. Who could possibly want to shoot at either of us?" If the officer thought Barclay was protesting too much, she didn't say so.

"No angry spouses or ex-spouses running around?"

"Heavens, no. Annie is single, and my wife of thirty years is a thoroughly contented woman. Probably at home working in her garden right now."

The policewoman made jottings in her notebook, her face utterly devoid of expression. "We'd like to speak to her all the same, sir."

Barclay nodded. A faint film of perspiration formed on his upper lip.

"You're an attorney, you say? Do any criminal work?"

"None."

"How about the woman?"

"Annie? Yes, actually, I believe she used to do that sort of thing. She's only worked for us a short time. But you'd have to ask her. I wouldn't know anything about her past practice."

"What about business enemies? Clients who might be upset with you? Someone unhappy with a result?"

"No, that's absurd. Perhaps Ms. MacPherson, in her former practice. Domestic relations, minor criminal cases. Those would be the sort of people . . . My clients are insurance companies." He laughed nervously. "I can hardly imagine an insurance adjuster coming after me with a high-powered rifle."

"What makes you say it was a high-powered rifle?"

Barclay looked uncomfortable. "Why, I just assumed . . . a sniper attack. Isn't that what this was? From a rooftop somewhere?"

"That's yet to be determined, sir."

"I see."

The officer frowned. "It's not a lot to go on. You're sure

you can't think of anything else? Anything at all related to the business you were discussing?"

"Not a clue, Officer."

"Hmm. Is there a number where you can be reached?"

Barclay gave his office number. "May I speak to her now?"

"Certainly."

Barclay pushed through the crowd and crouched next to Annie. His expression was almost tender. "How are you feeling? Does it hurt?"

"Yes, but the doctor says it isn't serious. The muscle is torn. I'll have to go to the hospital for stitches. I guess an ambulance is on the way. I feel so silly to be the center of this much fuss."

"Not at all, my dear. I'll go back to the office, make sure your files are handled until you're feeling better. You will be taking some time off, won't you?"

"Yes," the doctor answered for her. "I've suggested complete rest for a few days, and then after that she can do what she feels like, provided she doesn't use the arm too much. She'll have to give that biceps muscle a good few weeks to heal properly."

"Weeks? That's ridiculous. Of course I'll be able to work, Gordon. I'll call in after I've been to the hospital and let you know when I'll be back."

The doctor just shook his head. "Stubborn one, isn't she?"

"So we've been led to believe," Barclay answered.

Halfway through her second glass of wine Annie's mood started to improve. The pain hadn't actually subsided, but its importance had begun to decrease.

"You could take the Darvon they gave you, you know. It won't kill you," Ellen O'Neill called from Annie's kitchen, where she was fixing a cashew chicken salad for dinner.

"Those things drive me crazy. One more glass of wine and I won't notice a thing."

"Suit yourself. Hey, it's five o'clock. I want to see you on the news. I bet you're the lead story." Ellen brought Annie's tiny portable TV out of the kitchen and plugged it in where they both could see it.

As the sound came on they heard the local news anchor saying, "And tonight's top story: a sniper attack on the waterfront. More after this."

"Hey, you're in the headlines, kid."

"I don't know which is worse. The pain in my arm or having to see myself bleed on TV. Aren't you supposed to look ten pounds heavier on television?"

"Shh. It's coming back on."

"Lunchtime patrons today at the fashionable Ray's Boathouse at Shilshole Bay Marina got more than the daily special when a sniper, estimated to be as much as half a mile away, opened fire on patrons leaving the restaurant. Local attorney Annie MacPherson was struck in the arm by a bullet and treated by a doctor at the scene."

The screen flashed to a picture of the red, white, and blue doctor.

"Hey, he's cute," said Ellen. "Sort of an academic Bruce Willis type."

"Isn't that a contradiction in terms?"

"No, really, did you get his number?"

"Come on, he looks all of twenty-four. Probably straight out of med school. If that. Who knows if he's really even a doctor? I never saw any ID. Maybe he just hangs out at restaurants posing as an M.D."

The doctor, obviously enjoying his moment in the limelight, was spouting off multisyllabic medical terms and fingering his beeper. "The way he describes it," Annie said, "it sounds like he wants a Nobel Prize for saving my life. He told me it was just a minor tear."

"Did you file a workers' compensation claim?" Ellen asked.

"What, are you crazy?"

"No, I'm serious. You were having lunch with your boss,

discussing matters of benefit to your employer. So you were injured in the course and scope of your employment. File a claim."

"Uh, slight problem with that scenario. We weren't discussing KLMD business."

"Oh, really?"

"Shh, there I am."

"Ms. MacPherson was rushed to Northwest Hospital for emergency care," the anchor said gravely. The picture showed Annie being strapped to a stretcher.

"God, I look horrible. Why couldn't they just show my high school graduation photo like they do for other crime victims? And can you believe they made me get on that gurney thing for a twenty-foot walk to the ambulance?"

"Sure, it's called fear of malpractice."

"They make it sound like such a big deal. I got four stitches, a sling, and a prescription for pain pills."

The news anchor continued, "Police have no leads on the identity of the sniper. This is what Gordon Barclay, the business colleague dining with MacPherson, had to say." The camera flashed to a close-up of Barclay's face.

"That's your boss?" Ellen asked, astounded. "He looks like a TV actor. No wonder you weren't discussing business."

"Shh," said Annie, as the camera focused on Barclay's face.

"I can't think what this would be about. Most likely an act of random violence. Ms. MacPherson has no enemies."

"He makes it sound like they were aiming at you!" Ellen said indignantly. "The sniper could have just as easily been aiming at him. Didn't you say the first two shots hit the car near where he was standing?"

"That's what he told me." The screen changed to an old photograph of Annie's father, the one he had used in the legal directory the year he was president of the bar association. "What the . . . Where did they get that?" Annie exclaimed.

The anchor continued, "The only possible lead police were able to obtain had to do with the fact that Ms. MacPherson is working on a biography of her father, George MacPherson, a noted trial attorney and past president of the Washington State Bar Association, who died in 1976. Action News learned this from a co-worker of Ms. MacPherson.''

"What are they getting at? I can't believe this.''

"Shh, look. Who is that?'' Ellen asked. The screen showed a close-up of Deborah Silver sitting behind her desk at KLMD. Either her face was flushed or she'd added extra makeup for the camera.

Deborah enunciated carefully, in the voice she usually reserved for the courtroom. "We all knew that Annie was working on her father's biography, especially the years he headed the state bar association. It's well known that during that time George MacPherson was *heavily* involved with the state's largest labor unions. I think it should be *obvious* that someone doesn't want that biography published.''

"Labor unions! What, as if unions are synonymous with organized crime or something.'' Livid, Annie struggled up from the couch. "Why, that little brown-nosing bitch . . .''

"You work with her?''

"I guess you could say that. But in her mind, no one works *with* Deborah, everyone is a rival.''

"I've known people like that. They think the only way they can succeed is by bringing other people down.''

"It's just a crock of lies.'' Annie turned off the TV when the news switched to a fire in Renton.

Ellen brought the salad, a warm loaf of garlic bread, and a bottle of wine to the table and dished up. Annie picked up her fork in her left hand and stared at the bowl of salad. "This is going to be very interesting.''

"Hmm, I guess I could have made something a little easier to maneuver.''

"No, no, this will be fine.'' Annie awkwardly impaled a piece of lettuce on her fork. It fell off before it reached her mouth. She tried again. Same result. She took a sip of wine and grabbed some bread. At least she wouldn't go completely hungry.

"What did you mean when you said you weren't talking business? Was this more of a romantic interlude than you've led me to believe?"

Annie almost choked on her wine. "Me and Barclay? That's absurd."

"Is it?"

"Yes," Annie replied, a little too emphatically. "I didn't say we weren't discussing *business*. It just didn't have anything to do with Kemble, Laughton, Mercer, and Duff. Barclay's leaving the firm and he offered me a spot in his new organization."

"Whoa, not exactly matters benefiting your employer, huh? What are you going to do?"

When she'd successfully maneuvered a piece of salad into her mouth and swallowed it, Annie said, "I'm not sure. It's a good offer. It would involve lots of trial work, big cases, less bureaucracy than a large firm. And besides, after Barclay leaves, I'm not sure there'd still be a place for me at KLMD, even if I did want to stay."

"Barclay's the one who had the affair with the secretary who killed herself? What kind of person would that be to work for?" Ellen had already finished one serving of salad and was helping herself to seconds. Annie had barely managed three bites.

Annie recalled her discomfort when she thought Barclay was getting a bit too friendly and expressed her hesitation to Ellen. "It's not that I don't think I could fend off any sexual harassment. I get the impression that Barclay just likes women. On a professional level, Barclay's a good attorney with a strong client base, and he gets a lot of respect in the community. And it would definitely be a step up from finding myself suddenly unemployed." Annie picked up an asparagus spear with her fingers.

Looking skeptical, Ellen helped herself to more garlic bread. "It's your decision, but I'm not sure I could work for someone like that."

They were interrupted by a knock on the door.

"Expecting someone?" asked Ellen.

"No, but it has to be someone from inside the building. The outside door should be locked."

"Want me to get it?"

"No, I can see if it's someone I recognize."

Annie gingerly opened the door a crack, feeling slightly embarrassed at her caution. It was her neighbor, Turek, from one floor below. As she let him in, Annie could see Ellen stifling a laugh at his white harem pants, Clark Gable T-shirt, and John Lennon glasses on a long, pointed nose. His myopic expression always reminded Annie of Mole from the *Wind in the Willows.*

"What's wrong with your arm?" he said, noticing her sling.

"You didn't see her on the news?" Ellen asked. Annie knew that he wouldn't have. Turek was a multimedia sculptor who didn't own a TV and was rarely aware of current events. Three weeks into the Persian Gulf war he had asked her what all the flags and yellow ribbons were about.

"I, uh, got shot at today."

"Really? Cool." He didn't inquire further. Such details weren't vital on Turek's plane of existence.

"Would you like some dinner? There's lots of salad."

"No, thanks. I'm cleansing today." Annie didn't ask for an explanation. "I just brought you this." He held out a letter in a KLMD envelope. "It got put in my box by mistake. I hadn't looked in there for a couple of days, so I'm not really sure when it came. Sorry."

"No, that's okay. Thanks for bringing it up."

Annie closed and locked the door behind Turek's departing ponytail.

"What is it?"

"It's a letter from the office."

"That's kind of weird. Don't you guys have in-boxes at work?"

"Uh-huh." Annie examined the outside. Under her name and address were the typed words EXTREMELY PERSONAL AND CONFIDENTIAL highlighted in blue.

Chapter 13

Annie struggled to open the letter, but it was difficult with her right arm in the sling. Ellen took it and tore open the envelope, then handed it back. Annie searched for a signature. There was none.

"What is it?" Ellen asked.

Annie shook her head. "It's bizarre. Here, take a look."

They took the letter into the living room where the light was better. It was a piece of office stationery, with only a few lines of type:

> You're sticking your nose where it
> doesn't belong. People get hurt that way,
> sometimes even innocent bystanders.
> STOP NOW BEFORE IT'S TOO LATE.

"Creepy. When was it sent?"

"Let me see," Annie said, examining the envelope. "It was postmarked on Saturday. Looks like five P.M. I probably should have gotten this Monday or Tuesday."

"Saturday. That's the day you and I had lunch at the Copa. Wasn't that also the day you went to the office and got caught in the crossfire between Barclay and Suzy Gulliver? Someone doesn't want you sticking your nose into Nancy's death."

Annie shook her head. "That doesn't make sense. Suzy and Barclay both knew I was involved that day almost by accident. I've been doing my level best to stay *uninvolved*."

"Then what about this business deal? Do you think someone knew Barclay was going to make you an offer and wanted to warn you off?"

Annie walked to the kitchen and grabbed the bottle of wine to refill their glasses. As careful as she tried to be, the bottle wobbled in her left hand, spilling a few drops onto the table. Frustrated, she wiped them up with her sling. Ellen was still talking. "Think. Is there anyone who would be upset if you joined Barclay's firm?"

"Upset?" Annie laughed. "That's hardly the word." Annie ran the list through her mind. Deborah Silver had hinted about Barclay running his own firm. She clearly would have wanted the offer herself. Fred Duff, of course, would be devastated. He was convinced that if Barclay pulled out, the firm he'd devoted his life to would collapse. Looking back on her conversations, it now seemed as if both knew more about the situation than they'd let on. Jed Delacourt? He hated Barclay. Maybe the letter could be interpreted as a warning not to get mixed up with Barclay rather than a threat. And then there was Alex Guiterrez, Barclay's right-hand man. Barclay had said he told Alex everything. And for whatever reason, Alex didn't like Annie. Just thinking about him gave her a chill.

"I think that's got to be it, Ellen. This letter was supposed to reach me *before* my lunch with Barclay today. It would seem that someone doesn't want me associating with him."

"What are you going to do about it?"

Annie sipped her wine and stared out the window. She suddenly felt overcome with weariness and pain from the day's events. "Who knows? But whatever I'm going to do, it's got to be tomorrow. Right now, I think I need some sleep."

Sirens blared all around her. Running down a dark alley littered with broken glass and debris, Annie realized she was hopelessly lost. On one of the rooftops lurked an assassin in a black ski mask. From another window the thin gray barrel of a rifle pointed at her. Suddenly she heard the sound of running footsteps, the squeal of a police whistle. The scream of the whistle got louder and louder, coming closer with every blast, until Annie realized it was the jangling of the telephone.

Her eyes jerked open. It was nine A.M.—she'd slept for over ten hours. Stretching to reach the telephone on the bedside table, she realized that her entire neck and right side were one giant mass of stiff muscles.

"Hello?"

"Annie? Annie, I just heard. Are you all right? How on earth could you let something like this happen?"

"Feinstein, you're the only person I know who would blame the victim for being careless enough to get shot by an unknown assailant half a mile away. But thanks for the sympathy."

"Hey, if we all just took certain precautions, a lot of these things could be avoided. Why do you think I left New York? But seriously, are you doing okay? Do you need anything?"

"Like chicken soup or something?"

"Don't knock it till you've tried it. Maria makes a chicken soup that almost rivals my grandmother's."

"No, that's okay. My cooking skills haven't been impaired in the slightest—I can still push all the buttons on my microwave."

"All right, if you say so. But you call us if there's anything we can do. Now here's somebody else who wants to talk to you." After a pause Annie heard another familiar voice.

"Annie, sweetie, how are you feeling? I saw you on the eleven o'clock news—I couldn't believe it."

"Val?" The last voice Annie was expecting was that of her former secretary. "Where are you calling from?"

"Why, the office, of course. Where did you think?"

"What are you doing there?"

"I'm working for you, hon. I knew you still had a temporary secretary after what happened to that poor, unfortunate girl, and then when I heard about your accident, I thought, My

God, Annie just won't be able to cope. So I said to myself, Val, honey, that girl *needs* you. You just have to call up her boss and tell him you'll be there to take over until Annie's feeling better, so that's what I did, and here I am."

Annie couldn't help smiling. Joel had once compared Val O'Hara to a mother hen, but a mother grizzly bear protecting her cubs would have been more accurate. When they'd agreed to the merger of MacPherson and Feinstein with KLMD, Val had said she wanted to retire, but Annie had wondered at the time if she was sincere. At sixty-three she was still sharp as a tack and had worked as a legal secretary since she was seventeen.

"But, Val, we gave you a retirement party. Remember, your grandkids made the cake? They were so happy because they were going to get to spend time with Grandma. Go to the zoo, make cookies, all those things grandmothers are supposed to do."

Val's raspy laugh was like a dull saw cutting hardwood. "Oh, honey. You should have seen me. Three days with those little darlings and I wanted to ship 'em off to Timbuktu. I'm not sure how I ever raised their mother 'cause I sure don't have the patience for it now. Working in a law office is so much more *relaxing* than grandchildren! But I hope you're not going to make me give back my retirement present, are you?"

"That suitcase was so you could take trips. Remember how you said you wanted to travel?"

"Oh, I will. One of these days I'll find the time. This is just temporary, till you get better and the firm hires somebody permanently. I didn't have a choice—there's no way your files would get looked after properly with one of those temps from an agency. Hell, some of those girls can't even spell subpoena duces tecum, much less know how to serve one. But don't you worry now. I've got everything under control. And that Mr. Barclay. Is he ever a charmer!"

Annie just shook her head. No need to worry about her files now. Sometimes Annie fantasized about a country run by legal secretaries, with the lawyers and politicians doing the grunt work. There'd be a balanced budget, everyone would have enough to eat and a place to sleep, and the trains would run on time.

"Well, don't let Barclay turn your head with compliments, Val."

"Oh, I've heard all about him. You wouldn't believe the reputation he's got in the staff lunchroom. But he's too old for me. You know it's those young fellas with the little behinds that I like." It had been a running joke ever since Val's granddaughter had given her a Chippendale's calendar for Mother's Day, which she had proudly displayed at her desk right next to the snapshot of herself holding up the winning daily double ticket at Longacres Race Track.

"Uh-huh, if I meet any of those, I'll send 'em your way," Annie said. Sitting up, she winced as the pain in her arm began to throb. "It looks like I'll be staying home for a day or two, so—"

"A day or two! Mr. Barclay said the doctor told you a few weeks, and he's *insisting* that you stay home and get well. And if you think I'm going to let you come back here before you're properly healed, young lady . . ."

Annie envisioned the mama bear rearing up on her hind legs, teeth bared. "Okay, I get the point."

Halfway through the midmorning talk shows Annie was bored out of her mind. Ordinarily she would have welcomed a few days off with no responsibilities. There was never enough time to sit and read a book or catch up on writing letters.

But how was she supposed to relax with everything that had happened recently? One woman dead under mysterious circumstances, a sniper attack, a threatening letter. And there wasn't a whole lot she could do about it while sitting at home in her bathrobe. Despite the pain in her arm, she had too much pent-up energy to sit still and do nothing.

Passing the answering machine on the way to the kitchen, Annie saw the red light blinking. In the confusion yesterday she hadn't noticed it. She pushed the button and heard the voice of the friend who was editing the book on Washington lawyers.

"Annie, this is Sylvie, it's about noon on Wednesday. I'm calling to see if you've fallen off the face of the earth or something. I know how busy you are with your new job and all, but I really *have* to have the outline of your chapter by the end of the week. Can you fax it to me on Friday? Thanks, I'm counting on you."

Annie groaned. She had totally forgotten about the deadline. Well, since Val wouldn't let her near the office to do her real work, there was no better time than the present. After starting a fresh pot of coffee, Annie threw on some jeans and dragged the box of her father's papers out to the dining-room table.

The box was a disorganized mess, papers jammed in every which way. It wasn't the way her father would have left it, so it had probably been thrown together by someone after his death. That became clear when Annie found several manila file folders, empty, stuck down the side of the box. She could only hope that what had once been *in* the folders was now in the box.

Laying the folders out in front of her, Annie decided that the first order of business was to try to re-create the various files. There were folders for bank statements, health records, divorce papers, correspondence, her school records, and a mysterious folder labeled "JW—$$."

The task turned out to be easier than she had expected it to be as she took one paper at a time from the tangled mess, discerned its category, and placed it in a pile. Everything that didn't have an obvious category Annie placed near the JW—$$ folder. She wondered if a pattern would emerge. The leftover documents seemed to be unrelated and gave no clear clue as to what JW—$$ might have meant. Payments to John Wayne? Jaywalking tickets? Knowing that her father had not been an indiscriminate saver, Annie figured that there must be a pattern that just wasn't apparent yet.

Finally, at the bottom of the box was an 8½ × 11–inch black-bound book that looked like a ledger of some type. Annie lifted it out and brushed off the dust. There, in her father's small, cramped handwriting was an entry: *"March 12, 1961—* Ginny left today, taking Annie. Moving down to live with her parents in Calif. Been coming for a long time, of course . . ."

Annie couldn't read any further. It was a diary, starting when her parents separated. She flipped to the back and saw that the last entries were sparse. One from 1964, two from 1965. Apparently by then the need, or desire, to keep a journal had passed. She set the book down on the table and took a deep breath. Reading such personal thoughts by one's father—it was almost like looking into his bedroom, invading his privacy. Annie wasn't sure she could do it. She set the journal aside. Right now, it was important to get on with the article about her father's professional life in order to meet Sylvie's deadline.

Remembering Deborah Silver's comments to the reporter, Annie thought about her father's labor union involvement. Nothing sinister there, of course. He'd represented a number of local unions over the years, working with them on collective-bargaining issues and contracts. Perhaps an article outlining his long involvement with the teachers' union . . .

As hard as Annie tried to concentrate, she kept coming back to the mystery pile. JW—$$ nagged her to look at it and discern its pattern. A quick look before moving on wouldn't hurt. She picked up the pile and shuffled the papers into chronological order.

The earliest document dated from July 1962, a bill from Tacoma General Hospital. It was obviously a second billing and didn't list the services provided, only the balance due. The latest was a bank statement with certain items circled. It was from 1976, the year Annie's father died of a heart attack at the age of forty-six.

Annie looked at each document briefly as she sorted through them. A receipt for a $500 gift certificate from a California menswear store in December of 1972. There were other gift-certificate receipts dating from various Decembers. Christmas gifts? A number of canceled checks and receipts for personal items: clothing, luggage, books. A delivery receipt showing a boy's bedroom set delivered to an address in Puyallup, Washington, in 1967. A catalog from a mail-order sporting-goods store—odd for someone whose idea of sports was a rousing game of chess—with a picture of a catcher's mitt circled.

But the most bizarre item was an envelope containing a brochure and two letters from the Hillswood Boys' Academy. The first letter thanked Annie's father for the generous $20,000 donation. Annie stared at the figure in disbelief.

To Annie's knowledge her father had had no connection to the Hillswood Boys' Academy or to any other private school. His father, Andrew MacPherson, had emigrated from Scotland in 1923 with nothing but two changes of clothes and a set of tools. He'd set up a jewelry and clock shop in Ventura, California, and although he had eventually made a decent living, private schooling for George or his sister would have been out of the question. George had gone to UCLA on a scholarship and to law school at the University of Washington on the G.I. bill.

The letter from the San Marino, California, boys' school was dated October 9, 1970, and stated in ebullient terms how much the boys of Hillswood appreciated the generosity of donors and that George could expect a personal reply shortly from the individual boy who received the MacPherson scholarship. At that time twenty thousand dollars surely would have paid for several years of schooling. Annie examined the brochure. From the style of the boys' uniforms and their well-trimmed hair, the school either hadn't updated its photos from the early sixties or held itself out as an enclave of conservatism in a changing world.

The second letter was a thank-you note on school letter-head. The language was so stilted and formal, Annie assumed it was a prescribed formula that all of the recipients had to copy. The letter was signed by an incoming third-grader named John W. Watney.

JW.

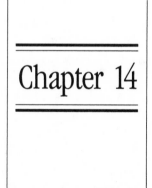

Chapter 14

Annie didn't want to face the facts, but they all added up to one thing. John Watney, a third-grader in 1970, would probably have been born some time in 1962, the year after Annie's parents had separated. Annie wanted there to be an innocent explanation for why her father would send gifts, furniture, and scholarship money to this young boy named John Watney, but she couldn't. The logical explanation was that John Watney was her father's illegitimate son.

Part of Annie wanted to stop there—not find out the truth. But part of her clung to the belief that it wasn't true. Perhaps the $20,000 had been a genuine scholarship donation after all. And she knew just whom to call to find out.

She'd recently gotten a call from an old school chum now living in San Marino, soliciting money for their college alumni fund. Even in college it had been clear that Madeleine Barnapple was destined for a Junior League life. Annie had muttered something about a fire in the kitchen and hung up before Madeleine had had a chance to really get into her spiel. Now she half regretted her rudeness. If anyone would have the scoop on the Hillswood Boys' Academy, it would be Madeleine.

As she struggled with left-handed awkwardness to dial the phone, Annie pondered ways to get through a conversation with Madeleine without actually donating any money. After rudely hanging up on the woman, no easy solutions came to mind. If she promised a donation, Annie suspected an Olympic-

class fundraiser like Madeleine would have the tenacity of a
bloodhound when trying to collect. But if Annie didn't at least
hint about money, the Queen of the Charity Ball might not
have the time to chat. As the call went through, Annie came
up with a plan.

"Maddy? Hi, this is Annie MacPherson. You remember, from
Binkley Hall?"

"Annie? Oh, yes. I called you last month. I just *knew* you'd
change your mind about giving to the alumni fund. Like I told
you, if our class can just increase our gift by *ten percent* over
last year we have a shot at taking the lead. And wouldn't that
be *stupendous*? We'd be listed *first* in the *Alumni News*! So,
tell me—"

It was like hitting the play button on a tape recorder. Madeleine hadn't even gasped for breath before launching into her
pitch. "Maddy—"

"What can I put you down for? For five hundred or more,
you get listed as a *benefactor*, but since you are an attorney,
you might possibly want to go higher into the *sustainer* cate-
tory—"

"No, Maddy, I—"

"As a *sustainer* you get free admission to all alumni lectures,
and of course there's breakfast at the president's house. His
wife, Tish, is *such* a lovely woman. Have you met her?"

As Madeleine gushed, Annie began to regret her strategy. She
tried to picture what her old acquaintance looked like now. In
the mid-seventies she'd been the only woman Annie knew who
wore curlers to bed. While everyone else dressed in torn Levi's
and Birkenstocks, Madeleine had worn lime-green wraparound
skirts with pink piping and espadrilles. She probably still did.

"No, Maddy. I'm not calling about the alumni fund."

"You're not?" Her voice was the little-girl whimper Annie
recognized from college. The same hurt tone had crept into
Madeleine's voice the day she found out she wasn't going to
be rushed by her mother's sorority.

"No, it's about my father's estate." Here's where the lying

began, she thought. For a basically honest person Annie took
an unnatural pride in her ability to fabricate. "I just got a call
from one of Dad's old law partners. He was the executor of
the estate. Well, it seems there was some money that my father
had earmarked for a donation that somehow got passed over
in probate. I was calling you to see if I could get some information on the institution he had planned to give it to. I thought
of you because it's there in San Marino." She tried to doodle
as she usually did while on the telephone, but her left-handed
curlicues were disappointing. She put down the pen.

"Oh, really?"

"Yes, the Hillswood Boys' Academy. I thought since you
live nearby . . ."

"Hillswood? Why, Annie, that's where our boys go! Andrew's in the third grade and Peter's in the sixth. James is on
the board of trustees and I'm PTA president. I just can't believe
this!"

Annie had hit it on the nose when she'd guessed the school
had catered to wealthy conservatives. From their college days
Annie recalled that James Barnapple had thought Richard Nixon
was a bit too liberal.

"Well, since you know the school so well, you might be able
to answer my next question. If my father's estate did make a
donation to the, uh, scholarship fund, is there any way that it
could be intentionally earmarked for a particular boy? In lieu
of paying tuition directly? My aunt's sons are just about the
right age . . ." More lies. Hopefully Madeleine wouldn't have
any way of knowing that she didn't have any cousins.

"Well, I can't say it's never been done," Madeleine said slyly.
"For the tax write-off, you know. If a relative just flat out pays
for a boy's tuition, that's not a charitable deduction, of course.
But if he gives a donation to the scholarship fund and it hap-
pens to get directed toward a particular boy's tuition . . . well,
you can figure it out."

Ah, these Republicans think of everything, Annie thought.
"So that's fairly common then?"

"Oh, common enough. Ordinarily, the student would have to meet the minimum qualifications for financial aid, of course, but if that's the way you'd like to go, I'm sure James can fix it up for you."

"Would there be any way, afterwards, to trace which boy the money had gone to?"

"Well, the school has to record which donation goes to which boy, but as far as I know no one's ever had a problem with it. You're a lawyer, you should know how to outsmart those nasty folks at the IRS."

"Yes, well . . ." Annie wanted to say that tricking the IRS had never been her area of specialty but held her tongue. Because there was one more favor she needed from Maddy Barnapple.

"There's just one thing I'm concerned about, Maddy. Maybe I'm being overly cautious, but you see, I believe my father made a similar type of donation in the past, with the same kind of setup, which went to a particular boy. If that scholarship went to someone in the family, I'm afraid it might look suspicious, don't you think? If I could just get the boy's name and address . . ."

"Hmm, I see what you're saying. You wouldn't want it to look like a pattern. Now, how large a donation did you say you were planning this time?"

"I'll have to check with the executor of Dad's estate, but my guess is that it would be in excess of fifteen."

"Thousand?" Annie could hear the lilt in Madeleine's voice as she struck pay dirt. "Hmm. Why don't I have James look into it! Today's his golf afternoon, but I'm *sure* he wouldn't mind dashing down to the school office for a moment or two. Seeing as how it's for an old *friend* and all."

"Oh, could he, Maddy? You are such dears." Annie wondered if she was pouring it on too thick. Poor Maddy. When she found out the "executor" had been mistaken after all and the extra fifteen thousand had gone to those "nasty folks" at the IRS . . .

"Don't think a thing about it, darling. Can I call you back in an hour or two? Where can I reach you?"

"I'm working at home today." Annie gave her the number.

"All right, then. I'll get right on it. Ta."

Ta? Did people really say that? Annie hoped all of her prevarication had not been in vain.

Forty-five minutes later the phone rang. The taste of a fifteen-thousand-dollar donation must have really built a fire in Madeleine's engine. Annie picked it up on the second ring.

"Annie, darling? I've great news!"

"Oh, do you? Tell!" Annie was aware she had an unfortunate habit of mimicry. Whenever she spoke to anyone with an accent or a particular speech pattern, it only took moments for her to take on his or her speech. She cringed as she heard her own voice whimpering in perfect harmony with Madeleine's.

"Well, you were right about your father making a donation to the scholarship fund. Quite a hefty one, too. Twenty!"

"Really?" Annie faked amazement.

"Yes. And the paperwork was quite specific that it go to a particular boy who'd started third grade in 1970. The money was placed in a special account for his scholarship."

"I see."

"But the good news is, it went to a poor boy from Washington state. The family was on *public assistance*, so I'm *sure* there could be no relation." Madeleine held herself at arm's length from the words "public assistance," as if she could get a social disease just by mentioning it. Annie withheld comment.

"You'd better tell me the name and address, for my files."

"Right, let's see. James wrote all the information down for me. . . . Watney. His name was John Woodrow Watney, Jr. Lived in Washington state with an aunt and uncle in a place called—oh, my—Poo-yaw-loop, uh, Pwee-a-lope?"

"You mean Puyallup." Annie pronounced it easily. The town was the site of the Western Washington Fair each year, and its mangled pronunciation was a sure way to tell the tourists from the Northwest natives.

"The boy's guardian is listed as Mrs. Alexandra Osterhaus." She read off the address, which matched the one Annie had seen in her father's papers. "Does your family know them?"

"I haven't heard the name before today."

"Well, then. The scholarship office must have selected the boy at random. So if your father's estate wanted to have some scholarship money go to your nephews, I can't see any problem—"

"Yes, that might just work out," Annie cut in. "Well, it's been terribly nice talking to you, Maddy. Thanks for all the help."

"But don't you think I should get some more information? The name of the executor, perhaps. I could have James give him a call to explain the procedure."

"No, I'll explain it to him. We'll call if we have any questions. Thanks again. Ta."

As she hung up, Annie thought briefly about changing her phone number so that Maddy couldn't track her down to get that scholarship money. It hardly mattered, though, since her father had no nephews, there was no estate and no executor, and there certainly was no fifteen thousand dollars to give to a scholarship fund.

John Woodrow Watney, *Junior*. Who was this boy—and who was the "senior" he was named after—from a family on public assistance? He was probably born in 1962, the year Annie's parents were divorced. Also the year George MacPherson had a falling out with Gordon Barclay and left Kemble, Laughton, Mercer, and Duff to start his own firm. But before Annie could speculate on any possible connection, there was a pounding at her door as if someone were trying to break it down.

Annie instinctively tensed. Nothing like being shot at to make a person paranoid, she thought. She had to keep reminding herself that this was a security building. It was probably her neighbor, Turek, again.

Nevertheless, she moved to the door cautiously, regretting that she'd never had a peephole installed. She stood to one side of the door. "Who is it?"

"It's Jed, Annie. Damn it all, hurry up. I'm dripping all over the carpet out here." She opened the door. "Whoa, what happened to you?" Jed said, walking into the apartment. His Burberry was drenched with rain and his blond hair was plastered to his forehead. Annie carried his dripping coat into the kitchen and draped it over the back of a chair.

"How'd you get in?" A note of anger crept into her voice.

"Huh? Oh, some weird guy with glasses and a ponytail. He let me in as he was going out."

She should have known. Turek had commented once about not believing in doors. That probably meant he didn't believe in locks, either.

"So, come on, what's with the arm? D'you fall down roller-skating at Green Lake?"

"You mean you didn't see me on the news last night? I was shot at. A sniper from a rooftop."

"Jesus, why?"

Annie debated whether it was safe to tell Jed the details about her lunch with Barclay. She decided it would be prudent to wait until after Barclay made the news public on Monday. After all, Jed was not exactly a charter member of the Gordon Barclay Fan Club. She shook her head. "I've no idea."

After getting the blow-by-blow account of the shooting and her trip to the hospital, Jed said, "What a godawful mess. Kind of puts a damper on my news."

"What news?"

"Just that getting canned by Barclay may have been the best thing that's ever happened to me. I've got three job interviews lined up for Monday and all of them sound promising."

"Jed, that's fabulous."

"I came over to see if I could take you to dinner, sort of to pay you back for hospitality beyond the call of duty the other night. But if you don't want to go out I'd understand . . ."

"No way. I'm going stir-crazy here. I can at least *pretend* my life is normal."

With potential job offers close at hand, Jed was feeling generous. He took Annie to the Palomino Bistro in the Pacific First Centre, one of the current "places to be seen" downtown. Annie blanched slightly when she saw the prices but reminded herself that job or no job, John Edward Delacourt III could no doubt afford it. He always had the trust fund to fall back on.

The specialties of the house were from the open-fire wood oven. Annie ordered the garlic chicken with rosemary and Jed went for roast pork loin with currant sauce. When the waiter asked about drinks, Jed opted for mineral water. Annie looked at him inquiringly.

"What? So I don't feel like having a drink tonight, okay?"

"Fine with me."

"Look," he said, suddenly defensive, "it's not like I'm some kind of alcoholic or anything."

"I didn't say anything."

He brushed it away. "Nah, I'm sorry. I know you didn't. It's just there's so much attention paid to drinking these days. Like the only legitimate reason *not* to drink is if you come out and make these grandiose statements admitting you're an alcoholic and saying what a wonderful time you had at the Betty Ford Clinic. I mean, I think a person can want to cut down a bit without having *that* kind of problem."

The waiter brought a basket of bread. It had been brushed with olive oil, sprinkled with garlic and rosemary, and toasted in the wood oven. Absolute heaven. Jed laughed bitterly as he tore off a piece. "They said it was one of the reasons I was being fired. What a bunch of hypocrites."

"What do you mean?"

"As if I'm the only one who ever drank too much. You went to one of their parties. Did you see all those old guys? They toss the stuff back like it was water. At every goddamn firm social event half the attorneys end up drunk. And if you try to hold back a little, they think you're not 'tough.' And if you don't match all the other guys drink for drink you're not a 'team player.' Barclay was one of the worst—he'd buy rounds of tequila shooters for the table, then see who was 'man' enough to keep up with him." He shook his head. "Barclay didn't fire me because I drank. He fired me because I couldn't hold it."

Annie didn't say anything. Was Barclay really the villain here, or was Jed just trying to shift the blame for his own failure? "Whatever the reason," she said, "I think you're doing the right thing now."

"Yeah, that scene the other night, that was some sort of breaking point." He picked up his fork and concentrated on polishing a spot off it to avoid eye contact. "I just wanted to say that I'm glad you came to the rescue."

For the first time Annie began to see Jed in a more favorable light. He was still the arrogant rich kid she'd known in law school, but he wasn't without feelings.

As they chatted through dinner, Annie suddenly felt the need to talk to someone about her day's research. Her discovery of "JW" was still distracting her. She still didn't want to believe that the child was really her father's son. Jed listened, without a single wisecrack or crude comment, to the whole story. At the end she said, "But I'm sure there's a good explanation."

"Whoa, there, Cleopatra, Queen of Denial. I think you're sugar-coating this a little. I mean, he's going to shell out twenty thousand dollars for some poor kid he's not related to? I'm sure he was a generous guy and all that . . ."

Annie clenched her fist under the table. "That's just it. He wasn't." She spoke so quietly her voice was barely audible over the noise in the restaurant.

"What?"

"Look, you're thinking that I don't believe he fathered an illegitimate son because he was so 'good.' That's not it at all.

I'm not saying he wasn't a good father. He always provided very well for us, he never mistreated me in any way. And I loved him, I really did. But, Jed, he was one of the *coldest* men I have ever known. Maybe it was shyness or a reserve, I don't know. But he never showed any emotion. To him, giving me my weekly allowance was a massive display of affection. I simply can't believe he'd give of himself like that, not unless he had to. It would just have been totally out of character. He never even dated after the divorce. When I lived with him during high school, the only thing he was interested in was his job. He didn't have any friends outside of work, never took a vacation. I couldn't even get him to go to the movies. It just wouldn't have been possible. Not the man I knew."

"So why don't you go find out?"

"What do you mean?"

"You have the name and address, don't you? Of the boy's aunt? Go talk to her."

"Oh, I couldn't."

"Sure you could. I'll drive you out there, go along for moral support."

"Why?"

Jed shrugged. "You've got me curious now. And I've got nothing to do until my job interviews on Monday. Besides, you need to chaperon me so I don't go off on a bender, right?" He picked up the plastic table tent and started reading. "Let's see, should I have a fuzzy navel, a blueberry tea, or maybe a kioki coffee? I've got it, I'll get a gallon of Thunderbird and go lie on a bench in Occidental Square. . . ."

"You can be so obnoxious, you know that?"

"That's what makes me so adorable."

Chapter 15

"I don't know why I let you talk me into this," Annie said when Jed showed up at her place early on Friday morning. "As if I didn't have better things to be doing." Annie struggled with her shoulder bag, which held, among other things, the manila folder on JW.

"Like what? You're not going to get much work done without the use of your right arm. What better way to take it easy than to take a nice ride out to the country—"

"Puyallup is hardly the country."

"It is to someone who grew up in Boston."

"Let's just get this silly trip over with, all right?"

"You're the boss," said Jed. Leaving her apartment, Annie was careful to check the dead bolt on the door and to make sure that the exterior door closed tightly. Something about the fact that her attacker had been anonymous made what had happened all the more frightening.

The morning was threatening rain, so it made sense not to take Annie's convertible. Settled into the driver's seat of his reasonably new BMW, Jed popped a cassette of *La Bohème* into the tape deck. He grinned mischievously. "So I have good taste in music, what can I say?"

They rode silently down Highway 167, past car dealerships and gravel pits. The town of Puyallup was located about thirty miles south of Seattle in the fertile lowlands in the shadow of Mount Rainier. The area had been used for farmlands since the

1890s and was still mostly agricultural. But as land values increased, housing developments and minimalls were starting to encroach on the strawberry fields and Christmas-tree farms. As Annie looked at the lush fields, blanketed by a low bank of clouds, she hoped that suburbia could be held at bay for a few years longer.

Entering downtown Puyallup on Meridian, they followed the yellow flowers painted down the middle of the street, reminders of April's Daffodil Parade.

"Where is this place again?" Jed asked.

"The address is on Mill Creek Road. Pull into that gas station. We can ask directions."

"I can find it."

Annie sighed. Were all men genetically unable to ask for directions? she thought. This could take all day. "I could use a rest stop," she lied.

"Oh, okay, then. I guess we could use some more gas, too."

On the way back from the rest room, Annie walked over to the service bay, where an older man in greasy coveralls was peering into an engine. While Jed was paying for the gas, she asked for directions to Mill Creek Road.

His friendly expression told her he didn't mind being interrupted. "Mill Creek? You folks looking for the egg barn?"

Annie shrugged. "I'm not sure. We're looking for Mrs. Alexandra Osterhaus."

"Yeah, that's it. I never will figure out why all you yuppies drive way out here to get your eggs, when Zan sells them to the Safeway in Seattle. But that's your business, I guess. It's real easy to find. You just go down to the second light, take a right on Pioneer, and go about four miles out of town. You'll see a sign for Mill Creek to your left. Can't miss it. And tell Zan that Jack at the Arco station wants a kickback for all the business I send her way."

After giving Jed the directions, Annie debated about asking him to turn around and take her back to Seattle. Now that they

were so close, the idea of finding out the truth about JW made
her fidgety. She stifled her urge to run.

"There it is, turn left."

Jed screeched into the driveway, barely missing a slow-
moving German shepherd. "Sorry." He laughed at himself. "If
I drive like this sober, isn't it a good thing I gave up drinking?"

The driveway led to a gravel parking area, big enough for
about six cars, next to a two-story white-frame house and a
freshly painted red barn. A sign reading ZAN'S WELL-FEATHERED
NEST was decorated with geese wearing gingham kerchiefs and
little yellow rainboots and carrying baskets of eggs. To make
the point doubly clear, the flagstones leading to the barn were
decorated with dancing eggs, their little egg arms pointing the
way.

"I can wait here if you like," said Jed, grimacing at the de-
cor.

Annie shook her head. "No, I think I need moral support
against a barrage of country cuteness, or should I say 'kountry'
with a 'k'?"

As it turned out, their fears were well founded. The cuteness
only intensified as they neared the barn. Following the dancing
eggs, they encountered a wind sock in the shape of a pig, a
revolving cat weather vane whose legs rotated convulsively as
if dislocated at the shoulders, and a sign on the barn door of a
pudgy child with tears in his eyes that said CLOSED—SORRY WE
MISSED YA!

Annie looked at her watch. It was ten to ten, almost opening
time. "Want to try the house?"

"Why not?"

They retraced the dancing eggs to the farmhouse. Lace curtains woven into a cow pattern framed the windows of a darkened living room, but it looked like a light was on farther back
in the house. The door knocker was a witch made out of dried
apples, which Annie bypassed in favor of the doorbell.

The plump woman who came to the door looked to be in

her late fifties, with Clairol-russet hair showing a touch of gray
at the roots. She wore a ruffled apron over a denim skirt and
fluffy slippers. Her eyes darted briefly to Annie's sling before
she brightened and asked, "Don't tell me you've come about
the bears already? I thought the ad wouldn't run till this afternoon."

"Bears?"

"My teddy bears, of course. If it's eggs you want, they're in
the barn. We open at ten."

"No, actually . . ." They were interrupted by a timer going
off in the kitchen.

"Well, come on in and make yourselves comfortable, I need
to take care of something in the oven." Before they could answer, the woman had dashed off to the back of the house,
leaving the front door standing wide open. Annie wasn't sure
what to do.

"Let's humor her a little," Jed whispered, leading the way
into the living room and flipping on a light. The room exceeded all of Annie's expectations of cuteness. Every flat surface was covered with doilies and crowded with clutter, with
most of the objects representing some form of anthropomor-
phized animal. An entire zoo's worth.

The plump woman returned. "The cookies will be out in
just a minute. I'm Zan Osterhaus, by the way. I see you've
already made the acquaintance of Edgar Bear and his sister,
Eloise." Seated on the sofa was a pair of antique bears. Edgar,
wearing a coat and tie, was missing some of the stitching around
his mouth and had one loose eye, making him look slightly
senile. Eloise, wearing a baby's pinafore and black patent-
leather Mary Janes, stared vacantly into space and smelled of
mothballs.

"They're both quite old," said Zan, beaming like a proud
grandmother. "You can have them with or without their out-
fits. Or I have other clothes for them—there's a lovely sailor
suit that fits Edgar, though I have to say I'd hate to part with
it. Anything you like. As long as they're not split up." When

Annie looked confused, the woman said, "They're quite attached to each other, of course."

"They're, uh, lovely," said Annie. "Why are you selling them?"

Zan sighed heavily. "Space problems, I'm afraid. I can't put old bears like this up into the attic—much too damp, you know—and now that my collection's up over a hundred, well, there's just no more room. I simply hate to part with these two. They really are like family. But if I can't give them a good home, it's my *obligation* to find someone who can."

"I see." Annie wondered if there was a Society for the Prevention of Cruelty to Teddy Bears that enforced such matters. "Actually, we didn't come about the bears."

Zan looked befuddled. "Let's see, we're all out of daffodils and it's too early for strawberries. We always have eggs, of course, and our jam selection." Cottage industry seemed to be Zan's middle name. "Oh, and the Easter decorations are marked down." She pointed to a table filled with hand-painted wooden ornaments, pink and blue bunnies, colored eggs, and ducks with parasols, all on little ribbons. Annie wasn't quite sure what one was supposed to do with them, hang them on the Easter tree?

"How do you ever find the time?" Annie asked, struggling to come up with something polite to say. All of Zan's "creations" were just too adorable for words.

"Oh, it doesn't seem to be a problem. I just love working with my hands—I lose all track of time. I don't know what I'd do if I couldn't keep busy!"

"We'll take some eggs," said Jed, pulling out his wallet. "And this." He picked up a small wreath made of dried flowers and lace. Because it was missing a couple of roses, it was half price.

Sending a glare in Jed's direction, Annie said, "Actually, we didn't come to buy anything. There was something else. I need to ask you some questions about John Watney, Jr. I understand you're his aunt?"

The woman's face closed up, taking on a martyred expression. "I'm afraid I can't tell you anything. It's been years since he's called or written. . . ."

"It's actually the past I'm concerned about. If you don't mind. I need to find out his relationship, if any, to a man named George MacPherson." She paused, watching Zan's face for a reaction.

"MacPherson?" Zan looked blank for a moment, then her eyes grew wide. "Oh, my." She picked up an Easter ornament and nervously polished it with the corner of her apron.

"Did you know him?" Annie asked, even though that was obvious from the woman's discomfort.

Zan nodded, chin quivering.

"May we sit down?"

"Yes, yes, of course. Here, let me move Edgar and Eloise. I . . . I need to go to the kitchen for a moment, excuse me." She padded out, leaving Annie and Jed alone. Jed reached over and gave Annie's hand a squeeze. They could hear Zan puttering in the kitchen, taking longer than seemed necessary. When she returned carrying a plate of warm cookies and a pot of coffee, her face was flushed. She placed them on the coffee table and sat down opposite the sofa, her hands fluttering in her lap like a wounded bird.

Annie realized Zan hadn't even asked who they were, she'd been so flustered by the question. Quietly she said, "George MacPherson was my father."

Zan's eyes met Annie's. "Oh. Yes, of course."

"You said you knew him," Annie prompted.

"Yes."

Annie wasn't quite sure how to proceed, but Zan finally spoke up. "You'll be wanting to know about the boy then."

Annie could sense Jed looking at her and refused to meet his eyes. "Yes. Is this a good time?"

Zan nodded. "Yes, it's just been so long, I . . ." She glanced at the table. "Dear me, I forgot the coffee cups." Before Annie could stop her, Zan had dashed back to the kitchen.

Annie stifled the urge to run. She tried to think of some way, any way, she wouldn't have to hear the words that her father had a son. But even if he did, certainly this woman, the boy's "aunt," couldn't be the mother. Picturing her father in this room . . . it defied belief.

Zan returned and fussed over pouring the coffee, while Jed ate three cookies.

"There." Zan sighed, returning to her seat. She was more composed now, as if she knew she couldn't put off the conversation any longer. "I should have recognized you, I guess, from the red hair. George used to talk about you all the time, you know."

Annie swallowed and must have looked confused.

"He didn't tell you about the boy, then? Probably just as well. Although I'm surprised Johnny never tried to find you. Always a curious lad, so precocious. It could be he was jealous, of course."

"Mrs. Osterhaus," Jed interjected. "I think you'd better start at the beginning."

Annie nodded. "All I know, and I just learned this recently, is that back in the seventies my father paid for the education of a boy named John Watney. I take it that's the boy you're talking about?"

"Yes, my little Johnny. Such a sad story. And your father was so kind. So very kind. He didn't have to do it; he wasn't obligated, of course."

Annie held her tongue. If Johnny was her father's illegitimate son, he probably should have done a lot more. She let Zan go on with her story. Now that the initial shock had passed, the woman had regained her composure and her eyes took on the hazy glow of remembrance.

"Well, I guess the beginning would be when Lucy met George."

"Lucy?"

"My sister. Stepsister, to be exact. The boy's mother. Oh,

dear Lord, you didn't think that I . . . that the boy . . . ?'' A
hand fluttered up and touched her hair, as if deep down she
was flattered.

Annie didn't want to drag it out any further. ''So Lucy was
the boy's mother? How did she know my father?''

''Why, she worked for him.''

Suddenly Annie remembered. ''Did she have long dark hair,
very pretty?''

''Oh, yes, that was Lucy.'' Zan smiled. ''Two years younger
than me. I always think of her as my sister because she came
to live with us when I was only four and she was two. I always
wished I could look like her. I was always trying to lose weight,
while she could eat anything she wanted and stay slim. My hair
was totally unmanageable—it used to be dark auburn, you
know—but always limp and frizzy. Hers was so long and thick;
she always wore it straight, to her waist. About the only thing
I was good at that she wasn't was cooking—Lucy could barely
boil water. Here, I'll show you a picture of her.''

Zan left the room and came back a few minutes later carrying
a photograph in a silver frame. Annie was surprised to see that
it was a wedding picture of sorts. A young woman, no more
than a girl really, with long dark hair posed holding a bouquet
of flowers next to a stocky, bearded man. Annie thought she
recognized the marble hallway from the King County courthouse. The woman was wearing a summery white dress and
the man wore a suit that didn't fit well, as if he'd borrowed it.

''See how pretty she was? She was only eighteen when she
married Woody, but to me it seemed like she never aged a day.
She looked just like that the last time I saw her. But I'm getting
way ahead of myself.''

Annie's head was spinning. This was too much information
too fast.

''How did she come to work for my father?''

''Well, it started when she ran off and got married. I'm not
quite sure how she met Woody. I'd graduated from high school
by then and was going to the junior college to learn account-

ing. She was still in high school and met this fellow who worked on the railroad, the Northern Pacific. His full name was John Woodrow Watney, but we never called him anything but Woody." Zan's tone turned bitter when she said his name. "Lucy was an A student, popular. In all the right clubs. We all thought she was going to go to college, really make something of herself. But she dropped out two months before she would have gotten her diploma and married that man. Oh, he was a rough character—and a foul mouth you wouldn't believe. Our family never approved of him. But she was headstrong. Once she had her mind made up, there was no persuading her otherwise."

Annie was starting to regret asking Zan to begin at the beginning. The way she reminisced, it might be a while before she got to the relevant parts. "So she married Watney," Annie said, trying to nudge Zan on.

Zan nodded. "They got a little apartment in Seattle—a horrible little place down in the central district. I never knew how Lucy could stand it after being accustomed to the farm. But she seemed happy. At first, anyway." She bit her lip.

"Then something happened?"

"Lucy got pregnant. They'd been married about five months or so. I remember when she told me, she was so happy about it. But she wasn't sure how Woody would take it. As it turned out, she probably never should have told him."

"What did he do?"

"He got angry. At least he didn't hit her, we can be thankful for that. All the time she knew him, bless her soul, he never laid a hand on her. But he didn't take the news well, said he never intended to have kids. He left that very night."

Annie became hopeful. Surely this was the little boy that her father helped send to school, for whatever reason. But her hopes for a neat solution were soon crushed. "What happened to the baby?"

Zan pulled a Kleenex out of her apron pocket and wiped her eyes. "A miscarriage. I'm sure it was the stress of being left on

her own, no job or anything. She stayed in that dingy little
apartment for a while, taking in typing projects to make a go
of it, but eventually she came home to the farm. Dad was upset,
of course, but he took her back without a word. She finished
school and then got a job as a secretary for a lawyer here in
town, a friend of Dad's." Zan fussed about, pouring more coffee, rearranging the cookies on the plate.

"What about Watney? Did she ever hear from him again?"

Zan flushed, her voice quivering with anger. "I wish to God
that man had just stayed away, but he didn't. His work for the
railroad took him all over the country, but then when he was
in town he'd call her. She knew Dad hated him, so she'd sneak
off, meet him in Seattle. Sometimes . . . sometimes I'd lie to
help her see him. I wish now that I hadn't, but we were both
young and didn't know any better. Dad wanted her to divorce
him, but she refused."

"When did she go to work for Kemble, Laughton, Mercer,
and Duff?"

"Let's see now, that was the same year I married Otto—
1961, around the first of the year, I think. I was twenty-seven,
so she would have been twenty-five. That's where she met
George. They started dating."

Annie flinched. The idea of her father "dating" . . .

"I knew about it, of course," Zan continued. "We were very
close, being only a couple years apart and all. But Dad never
knew. He was so incredibly strict. He was horrified enough
when Lucy got married before she'd even finished school, but
if he'd known she was dating a married man, and her still a
married woman, why, I'm not quite sure what would have happened, but it might have involved a shotgun."

"So you met my father when he was seeing Lucy?"

"Oh, Lord, lots of times. We'd do all sorts of things together,
George and Lucy with me and Otto. Go to the movies and
such. They were so sweet together, so much in love. That's
when I heard all about you. You were just a little tyke then; he
showed us pictures. Your father talked about the divorce he

was going through, how you and your mom had gone down to California to live. Gosh, he missed you something awful.''

Annie realized her teeth were clenched. She couldn't figure out if she was angry or heartbroken. If only her father had *shown* some of that caring, told her that he missed her. He'd rarely even telephoned. She looked up and met Zan's eyes and must have conveyed some of that anger, because the older woman said, ''This must be awful hard for you to hear.'' Jed was sitting quietly, paying close attention.

''No, really. I want to know. How often did they see each other?''

''Oh, several times a week, I guess. They went to movies and the park. I remember one time she told me about, they went for a walk in the arboretum when the rhododendrons were blooming. George brought along a book of poetry and read to her under the trees. Now if that isn't the most romantic thing you've ever heard. But she still had to keep it a secret from Dad, always came home to the farm at night. Drove herself so Dad wouldn't catch on.''

''And . . . did she love him?''

''Oh, my, yes. Just like she was eighteen again. If it hadn't've been for that damned—I'm sorry . . .''

''What?''

''That damned husband of hers. Coming back just at the wrong time. It was right before Christmas 1961. Lucy told me she was going to stay in Seattle with friends, so she could go to the office Christmas party and not have to drive back late. I was all for it, because I thought she was going to be with your father and all, even though she never did tell me any specifics. Six weeks later, she came crying into my room. She'd just found out she was pregnant.''

Annie felt a wrenching in her gut. Hadn't the woman just said Lucy had stayed overnight in Seattle, to be with George MacPherson? ''Did she tell you who the father was?'' Annie asked, leaning forward on the couch.

''Well, hard as it was to believe, that's when she told me

she'd seen that damned—excuse my French—husband of hers over Christmas. That weekend she stayed in Seattle. He was in town so she decided not to go to the office party but to go out with him. And she said one thing led to another . . ."

Annie caught Jed's glance. His expression seemed to ask if the woman could really be that naïve.

"So Lucy said it was her husband's child?" As Annie said it, she couldn't keep the note of skepticism out of her voice.

"That's what she swore up and down to me. He denied it later, of course, but that's just the kind of man he was. Not honest like your dad."

"What do you mean, later? Was there a paternity suit?" Jed interjected.

"A what?"

"Did Lucy take him to court, to prove he was the father?"

Zan, looking petulant, smoothed her apron and nodded. "Later, when Johnny was about to enter school, we tried to find Woody and make him take some responsibility. We never did talk to Woody—I guess he didn't want us knowing where he was—but we dealt with some lawyer fellow out in Eatonville, said he represented Woody. His name was Eaton, just like the town, which made us all think he was some kind of big shot. I remember something about blood tests that this lawyer said *proved* beyond a shadow of a doubt that Woody wasn't the daddy. Otto and I, we wanted to take it further 'cause I just don't put much stock in those tests, you know. But we asked our lawyer and he said it would be no use."

"So what happened?"

"Well, Lucy had to quit her job in April when she started to show at about four months, of course. Back in those days even married ladies didn't work when they were pregnant. You can imagine how Dad took it. She lived here at the farm till the little guy was born. I can't believe she actually named him after that . . . that man. John Woodrow Watney, Jr., she called him.

Poor little guy, having to grow up without either a mommy or a daddy like that."

"Why? What happened to Lucy?" Jed asked, leaning forward.

"Well, she always was crazy when it came to that man Woody. I never did understand it, to tell you the truth, because from what you could see, she loved that baby more than life itself. Come October of that year she'd barely got her strength back—and the little guy, he was sickly at first, needed lots of special attention—she tells me she has to go to Seattle for the weekend and would I take care of him? I say I will, but I think, darn it, that man must be back in town again, and sure enough, she shows me the divorce papers that she had all drawn up for his signature. She admitted that she had to see him one last time, to make it final. She never said so, but I think your dad asked her to marry him."

Annie wished she'd been taking notes. The way Zan rambled, it was hard to keep all the characters in her story straight. "So Lucy said she was going to meet her husband?"

"And she did, too. We never saw her again after that—the last we heard of her was that she was in Alaska of all places, with Woody, and she weren't coming back."

"You mean she never came back for her baby?" Annie asked, shocked.

"She never did. I raised that boy like he was my own son." Zan sniffed, but Annie suspected they were tears of self-pity. "I never will know how she could abandon him like that."

"But when you heard from her," asked Annie, "didn't she say why she left?"

Zan's eyes brimmed with tears. "I wished she'd had the common decency to call us. Worried sick, we were, three whole days, till we got the news. But all she did was telephone that boss of hers at the law firm."

"You mean Annie's father?" Jed asked.

"George? Heavens, no. I'm talking about that Barclay character. The tall, good-looking fellow. Gordon Barclay, I believe his name was. That's who called us with the news."

Chapter 16

"Where to now, kemo sabe?" Jed asked. They were driving back toward Seattle, having finally gotten away from the Well-Feathered Nest with three dozen eggs, two jars of raspberry preserves, and the half-price dried flower wreath that was destined for some future garage sale.

Jed kept talking. "Why don't we drop this stuff off at your place, then we can figure out who to interview next. You know, this research is kind of fun."

"Stop it, Jed. The game's over. There aren't going to be any more interviews." Annie's voice was brittle with irritation.

"What?"

"This was all a setup, right? You knew all along about Lucy and her son and you just used me to get out and talk to Zan. That's why you were so anxious to go out there with me, isn't it? You're still out to crucify Barclay."

"I can explain—"

"Yeah, well, start talking."

Jed squared his shoulders. "Okay. After Suzy got me thinking about Barclay and his involvement with Nancy, we did some more checking. I went and talked to Fred Duff. I thought he would know if Barclay had had problems in the past with any of the women he'd been involved with."

"You're not saying he and Lucy—"

"No, no. Everyone knew that Lucy and your father were romantically involved, even planning to be married. But Fred mentioned a conflict between Barclay and Lucy that sounded very strange. He told me that a couple of months after her baby was born, Lucy came to Fred and requested her job back. Fred didn't believe the story Lucy concocted about seeing her husband, by the way. He said it was pretty well assumed that it was your father's child, but no one would have dared mention that around George. Well, anyway, Lucy came and talked to Fred. She said she'd written to the hiring committee about coming back to work but hadn't heard anything. Fred gave her the bad news. They'd filled her position and didn't have any other openings. Fred said the hiring committee had turned down her application to come back because they didn't feel a new mother, especially one without a husband to support her, could do the job."

Annie shuddered. "I'd forgotten that they used to be able to get away with things like that. But what does that have to do with Barclay?"

"Well, I did a little more checking. Turns out Barclay was the head of the hiring committee back then. All the other members voted to bring Lucy back, but Barclay vetoed them."

"He's conservative. Maybe he was just expressing the morals of the time . . ."

"No, Annie. You can't stick up for Barclay this time. I talked to one of the other partners—someone who was at the committee meeting that day. He said Barclay was livid at the mere mention of Lucy's name, called her a little Jezebel and swore he would leave the firm if she ever set foot in the office again. The partner said he'd never seen an explosion quite like it before."

Annie was quiet. She had wanted to believe in Barclay, the same way she had wanted to believe in the memories of her father. But she was starting to understand that she couldn't hide from the truth any longer.

"And you knew that Mrs. Osterhaus was the child's guardian?"

Jed nodded. "I bribed one of the secretaries to pull Lucy's

old personnel file out of the archives. Mrs. Osterhaus was listed as next of kin in case of emergency. I was trying to think of a pretext to go out and see her when I talked to you. I'm sorry, Annie. I did use you to get to her. But it's for your own good, too. Barclay is dangerous. I had to make you see that."

"Just because he got angry at a committee meeting?"

"There's more. That meeting was the week before Lucy disappeared. Forever."

They drove for a while in silence, with Annie trying to process what she'd learned. It was almost one, and Annie realized she hadn't eaten all day. Even so, the gnawing pain in her stomach was probably more from tension than hunger. After dropping the bombshell about Barclay, Zan had gone on to talk about the nephew that she had raised from infancy. Somehow Annie doubted that he was the paragon of perfection his aunt described, but she let it pass as "motherly" pride. As Zan talked about George MacPherson's involvement in the boy's care, it became harder to deny that the paragon was the half brother Annie had never known.

"We were so poor back then," Zan had said, "we never would've made it without your father's help. When my Otto died in sixty-nine, that's when it really got hard. I had the farm, but things were real tight, with a little boy to take care of. We had to get food stamps even. That's when your father made arrangements for Johnny to go to that boarding school down in California. I guess he knew someone on the board of trustees, got him admitted even though other kids had been on the waiting list for years. It was a real fine thing George did."

"Did he look like . . . Woody?" Jed had asked cautiously.

"No, not one whit. Took after his mother, small and dark; he had those big brown eyes like she had, like to melt your heart, they would."

"Where is he now?"

Zan sniffed. "I guess he doesn't care much for his old auntie.

I saw him a couple of times when he was home from college. Got a full scholarship to one of them fancy-schmancy private schools they have back East. Top of his class, too. Going to be an engineer—Johnny was so good with mechanical things and math. But he's drifted away. Got all smart and sophisticated from all that schooling, I guess. He was living in San Francisco, or thereabouts, last I heard. I used to call him now and then, even though it was so expensive. But one day I called him and his number had been disconnected. And I couldn't even find him with directory assistance."

"And he never came back to visit you?" Annie had asked, feeling sympathy for Zan.

The older woman had looked around the living room at the teddy bears and jams and Easter ornaments. "I got the idea, last time he was here, that he was sort of, well, embarrassed by all this." She'd looked back at Annie and shrugged. "He wouldn't understand. Without him, and without my Otto, this is all I've got left."

Annie jumped at the sound of Jed's voice. "I said, am I forgiven? You're really giving me the silent treatment."

"Oh, no. It's not you," she said, gazing vacantly out the car window. "I was just thinking."

"Kind of a rough day, finding out all this stuff about your dad, huh?"

Annie turned in the seat so she was facing Jed. "Were you close to your father?"

He shook his head. "No. He was a very successful orthopedic surgeon. Partner in a prestigious Boston medical group, lecturer at the Harvard School of Medicine. He usually got home from work about nine o'clock at night. Mom would parade the three of us kids out in front of him for about five minutes to tell him about our day before we went to bed. He never looked tremendously interested. Over the years our relationship has been distilled down to the obligatory Christmas telephone call. In five minutes we can exchange enough pleasantries to last a year."

Annie turned down the car's air conditioner. The subject was cold enough without help. "When I lived with my dad during high school, we were close, all right. There wasn't anything I could do that escaped notice. He monitored my grades—always excellent. My boyfriends—never good enough. My social activities—'That'll look good on the résumé,' he'd say. The goal was clear. I was supposed to think like him, act like him, grow up to be just like Dad."

"And you rebelled?"

"I had no choice. For the most part, though, I did it subtly. Rather than directly disobeying him I just figured out ways to do what I wanted to do, then make him think it was his idea. But that didn't work when it came time for me to tell him that I didn't plan to go to law school."

"Uh-oh. Direct defiance."

"Like a declaration of war. He'd assumed from the day I got my first A in elementary school that by the time I was twenty-five we'd be MacPherson and MacPherson, Attorneys at Law. He practically had the stationery ordered. God, he was *stubborn*."

Jed glanced sideways. "Not like anyone else we know."

"I know. A chip off the old block. I realize that now. But at the time I thought we were so *different*. He was constantly harping at me to be more organized, get serious about my life. I did the same to him, telling him to relax, make more friends, get in touch with his feelings—this was the seventies, you know. I told him to go barefoot, read Jane Austen. I couldn't understand why he was so rigid."

Jed smiled. "Yeah, I knew everything when I was in college, too. Funny how that doesn't last. When did your dad pass away?"

"February of 1976. I was twenty, in my junior year in college down in California. I'd seen him at Christmas and we'd spent practically the entire time fighting about my career plans—as usual. I'd finally decided what I wanted to do, which was to go to graduate school in English literature. I wanted to

teach, travel, maybe write. He was livid. Told me how rotten
the job market was for English professors—that I'd probably
have to go live in Kansas or Arkansas or someplace if I wanted
a university job. That I'd never make any money and he was
damned if he was going to support me for the rest of my life."

"It sounds ugly."

"It was. It was the worst fight we'd ever had. I mean, we
had discussed all these things before, but this was the real thing.
Remember, this was a man who kept all his emotions bottled
up inside—when he did finally explode it was bigger than
Mount St. Helens. I think windows were rattling as far away as
Idaho."

"And what happened?"

"Nothing. We argued. I left in a huff, went back to school.
Didn't write or call for a month and a half."

"Who finally blinked?"

When Annie looked down at her hands, she realized she'd
been pulling on a cuticle and it was bleeding. She stuck the
finger in her mouth. "I got the call at school that he was dead.
He'd had a massive heart attack on the golf course and died in
the ambulance on the way to the hospital."

They had reached Annie's freeway exit. Jed pulled off on
Roanoke and turned onto Tenth to head toward Annie's place.
At a stoplight he looked over and gave her a wan smile, like
that of a faithful dog who knows its master is hurt.

Annie laughed sadly. "It doesn't take much of a psychiatrist
to figure out why, after one year of grad school, I switched to
the same law school Dad had graduated from. Or why I continue to sit at his desk, read his law books. Damn it all, here I
am working at the same firm he worked at."

Jed braked suddenly for a kid on a bicycle who'd darted out
into traffic. "Well, at least now I understand why it's so hard
for you to accept the idea that he had a lover, even a child."

"You see? It doesn't fit at all, does it? Not the man I knew
as my father."

Shaking his head, Jed said, "No, that's not it."

"What, then?"

"All this stuff we heard today, that he fell in love with a beautiful woman and took walks in the park and read poetry to her . . ." When they reached Annie's building, Jed pulled the BMW into the parking lot and slid into the guest slot. "He was a lot more like you than you want to admit. I think you're afraid that you might have to stop hating him."

Annie looked over at Jed but couldn't acknowledge the truth in what he said.

Balancing three dozen eggs in her good arm, Annie slammed her door as she got out.

"Wait," said Jed. "You forgot something." He picked up the preserves and the dried flower wreath. "Frankly, I think this will look just *dahling* over your mantelpiece."

"Oh, gee. Pity I don't have a mantelpiece. I guess *you'll* have to keep it, Jed. Especially since *you* liked it so much to buy it."

He placed the wreath on his head and sashayed across the parking lot. "I could be the queen of the May for Halloween. What d'ya think?"

Annie rolled her eyes. And only a few minutes ago she was starting to think Jed Delacourt might actually have some substance. Right now, she'd had entirely too much of him for one day. She wished he'd just leave, but he reminded her that he'd left his coat in her apartment.

When she reached the side door of the apartment building and saw it propped open with a magazine, it was almost more than she could bear.

"Damn it all, this is not funny." Picking up the magazine, she saw that the address label said Turek Zinzer. She let Jed in, then threw the magazine on the floor and started to pull the door shut, making sure it locked behind them.

Jed was still clowning in the hallway, tossing the wreath in the air and catching it behind his back, when Annie reached the door of her flat. She knew immediately that something was wrong. The door wasn't shut tightly. In fact, up close she could see that the jamb was broken. She pushed with her foot and the door swung open. With a whimper she let three dozen eggs slide out of her hands and onto the hardwood floor.

"What is it?" Jed ran into the room behind Annie, stepping over the eggs.

"Look." The middle of the living-room floor was covered with papers. All of her neatly separated piles were in a jumble on the floor. It looked as if someone had gone through them on hands and knees.

"A burglar?"

"I don't know." Annie went quickly from room to room. There wasn't much to check. The ten-year-old portable TV was still on the end table in the living room, and her jewelry box in the top drawer of her dresser was untouched. The stereo she'd bought in college was still in its cabinet. As far as she could tell, nothing else had been disturbed.

She returned to the mess in the living room. "I don't think so. Nothing seems to be gone. This looks like all they were interested in." Annie sank down and started looking through the mess. "Oh, no . . ."

Jed got down on the floor next to her. "What?"

"A black book, it looked like a ledger. Do you see it?"

He shuffled some papers. "No."

Annie sat back with a sigh. The lines in her face revealed the weariness of the long day, and it was almost more than she could do to keep from crying. "My entire life, he shut me out. Now here I have a shot at learning something personal about him, an emotional side to him, and it's gone. You'd almost think he came back from the grave and took it himself."

Chapter 17

Jed brought Annie a glass of water and a couple of Advils. "How's the arm?"

"Not as bad as it was, but that's not saying much." She slipped off the sling and stretched her arm out, wiggling her fingers. "But I'll never play the piano again."

They looked down at the mess of papers. "I think we can assume that whoever broke in here got what they wanted," said Jed.

Annie nodded. "My father's journal."

"Had you read what was in it?"

"No, I . . . I was going to, but it seemed so personal. I needed to get my courage up. But from glancing at it, I remember that it started at the time of my parents' breakup, in 1961. It ended in 1965."

"So it would have covered the time period when Lucy disappeared. This has to be Barclay's doing."

Annie knew what she had to do. She walked to the phone and dialed KLMD. "Gordon Barclay, please."

"What are you doing?" Jed asked. "Are you crazy?"

Waving her hand at him to be quiet, Annie listened to the receptionist. "Working at home? Was he in the office this morning? No? All right, thanks." After looking up the number in the firm directory, she dialed again, then slammed down the receiver when she got a busy signal. If Barclay was finalizing the details for his secret split from KLMD, the phone could be tied up all afternoon.

"I'm going to go over there."

"Annie, I don't think that's a good idea. The man is dangerous."

"We have no proof of that. All we have are some suspicious circumstances involving his relationship with Nancy and with a woman named Lucy Watney over twenty-five years ago. I just want to ask him some questions, that's all. Besides, it's not like he's going to attack me in broad daylight."

"At least let me go with you."

Annie shook her head as she gathered up her things. "No, he wouldn't talk to me with you there. You know he doesn't like you. I'll say I've come to talk to him about . . ." She remembered she hadn't told Jed about the new firm Barclay was planning. Now wasn't the time. "Anyway, he'll talk to me. I'll call you in an hour or two and let you know I'm okay."

"Are you okay to drive?"

Annie flexed her arm. It hurt to move it, but she had good grip strength. "Yeah, I'll manage. Barclay just lives over by Volunteer Park and it's only a couple of miles from here." She grabbed her keys, then looked at the broken door with dismay. There was no way she could lock it until the damage was repaired. Jed saw her dilemma.

"Tell you what. I'll stay here and clean up this mess and call a repairman to fix that busted doorjamb. You can call me here if you need me."

Annie agreed, then left.

Barclay's neighborhood was only a few minutes away. Capitol Hill has two distinct personalities. The intense trendiness of Broadway lived in friendly coexistence with the stately old wealth of Volunteer Park, where Seattle's founding fathers had built their elegant homes. Slowly guiding the Fiat through the narrow, tree-lined avenues, Annie searched for a parking place near the Barclay home, a three-story brick Tudor a stone's throw from the Seattle Art Museum's grounds in Volunteer Park. The house seemed almost small in comparison to the pseudo-antebellum mansion next door.

Annie found a parking spot about a block from the house and walked back. The front yard was small, with the house and curved driveway taking up most of the lot. Flagstone steps led up to the front door, which was flanked by two rhododendrons the size of small trees. She rang the bell.

On the drive over Annie had been rehearsing what she'd say to Barclay, that she was sorry to disturb him at home, but she needed more information about his new firm before she could give him an answer. Once she was inside and talking with him she'd figure out a way of asking her questions about Lucy Watney, though she wasn't quite sure how she'd broach the subject. Perhaps a direct confrontation would be best. As she was turning her speech over in her mind, the door opened. But it was Adele Barclay who stood in the doorway wearing a wrinkled apron over loose-fitting slacks and a man's white shirt rolled up at the sleeves.

The woman smiled vacantly. "I know you. We met at the funeral. You're . . . Sandy, aren't you?"

"Annie."

"Yes, I knew it was a name that sounded like Nancy." Adele just stood there without inviting Annie in.

"Is Gordon home? There are some things I need to speak to him about."

"Gordon?" For a moment Annie got the oddest sensation that Adele didn't know who she was talking about. "He would still be at the golf course, wouldn't he?" She looked at her watch. "Four o'clock. He should be home soon, though. He always golfs on Fridays unless the weather's too awful. Why don't you come in and wait for him?"

Annie wasn't sure she could make small talk with Adele very comfortably, but waiting seemed like the logical thing to do.

"If it wouldn't be too much trouble."

"Oh, no. You can help me in the kitchen." Without waiting for an answer, Adele turned and started back through the house.

Annie would have preferred to sit in the living room with a magazine, but that hadn't been offered as an option. She followed Barclay's wife, trying to gather as much information as she could on the way.

Her first impression was that she'd walked into a photo layout for *House Beautiful*. The decorating was not just expensive, it was exquisitely done. Unlike Gordon's office at KLMD, which had "interior designer" written all over it, Annie sensed that the Barclay home was Adele's personal creation. It had the same sense of artistic flair that she had seen in the wreath Adele had designed.

The entry hall was richly paneled in a dark wood, mahogany perhaps, with a staircase leading up to a banistered landing. On the hall table was a bouquet of red tulips in a silver pitcher, opened so wide they almost looked like oriental poppies. Old photographs in silver frames lined the stairwell. Annie followed Adele down a hallway to the back of the house. Covering the hardwood floor was a deep blue Chinese rug with a pattern of dancing dragons.

Past a closed door to the left was a room that looked like Adele's private space, with white wicker furniture and rose-patterned chintz cushions. An antique writing desk at one end held stacks of papers, a basket of correspondence, and a telephone. And at the far end of the room, surrounded by a large bay window looking out on the garden, was an upholstered chaise longue, the kind Ginger Rogers might have had in her bedroom in the movies, with a stack of books on the floor next to it. It looked like Adele was in the middle of D. H. Lawrence's *Women in Love*.

Even though she only got a glimpse, it was a room Annie would have liked to spend more time in. It made her reevaluate Adele's statement that she only wanted to be left alone to her own interests. At the time, the comment had implied low self-esteem. Now, seeing the woman in her own environment, Annie had to wonder if Adele simply had better things to do than spend time worrying about Gordon Barclay.

The kitchen confirmed this opinion. Where the sitting room revealed part of Adele's personality, the kitchen held the real key. It was a huge room, obviously expanded after the house was built, and designed for function more than beauty. The center was a cooking island, with an industrial-size gas range beneath a ceiling rack holding a complete set of Calphalon cookware. In the area that at one time might have been a breakfast nook stood a huge butcher-block work table. At one end sat a delicately crafted birdhouse, still smelling of glue and sawdust.

Adele went to the other end of the table, where she was working on an elaborate dessert with sponge cake, strawberries, and white chocolate in a springform pan.

"Here," she said, directing Annie to a chair at the kitchen table. In front of her were a bowl of melted dark chocolate, a paintbrush, and a pile of fresh mint leaves. "You can help me."

"But I really don't think—"

"Oh, it's so simple. I've just washed these mint leaves. All you have to do is paint the chocolate onto the leaves, about this thick"—Adele took one and demonstrated—"then put it on the cookie sheet. There you go."

Annie tried one and realized it wasn't as hard as it looked. Maybe she'd have to make a stab at cooking one of these days. After taking time out to baste a chicken roasting in the oven, Adele started slicing the sponge cake into ultrathin layers.

"Are you having company?"

"Hmm? Oh, no, I just had some extra time, so I thought I'd try some new recipes. Gordon probably won't even stay for dinner. He's been so busy with work lately."

"Won't this go to waste?"

"Oh, no. We have a housekeeper who comes every other day. Juanita always takes the leftovers home to her family."

"Doesn't Gordon enjoy your cooking?"

"If he's home. The man's hopeless in the kitchen himself, can barely even make a ham sandwich. But most of the time he prefers eating at his club."

Annie continued to paint leaves as she pondered the Barclays' unusual marriage. She could understand now why Adele would stay with Barclay—it would be hard to live the Martha Stewart life-style without a substantial income. And Gordon's motivation? A lovely home and a contented wife who didn't intrude on his business, or other, affairs. Was that the nature of their relationship?

"How are you and Gordon getting along these days?" Adele suddenly asked Annie. "It's so hard to get him to stop working. Does he have much time for you?"

Annie was taken aback at what the question implied. "Excuse me?"

"You mean you're not . . . Oh, how embarrassing. I'd just assumed . . . ?"

"No," Annie replied adamantly, dropping a paintbrush full of chocolate into her lap. She looked around for a towel.

"Oh, good heavens," said Adele, her pale eyes widening. "Here, this will fix it right up." She reached into a cupboard and handed Annie a bottle of clear liquid. The label had been covered up with a large 3. "Oh, it's stain remover. I have to do that for Juanita—she doesn't read English. I was so afraid she'd mix the wrong things together by accident."

Annie took the fluid and swabbed at the chocolate. Miraculously it looked like the stain was going to come out.

"I just thought . . ." said Adele. "It's just that Gordon's showing all the classic signs again."

"He's what?"

"Of starting a new romance. He starts spending more evenings away, not coming in till late." She laughed her little-girl giggle. "It's so cute. He gets kind of high-spirited, I guess 'manic' is a term I've heard. You know, revved up. I'd just assumed it was you."

"Mrs. Barclay, just to set the record straight, if your husband is having an affair with someone, I don't know about it. And it certainly isn't with me."

Adele shrugged. "It's not that I mind, of course. I just thought . . . you were having a private lunch together, the day that . . . you know." She nodded at Annie's arm. She wasn't quite as oblivious as she seemed. "Must be someone else, then." She went back to work, lining the edges of the mold pan with strawberry halves, facing outward. Annie felt as if she'd stumbled into a Fellini movie and no one had handed her a script.

"Of course, it could just be excitement over this new business venture," Adele continued. "Gordon and Daddy have been having so many chats lately. You've met Daddy, haven't you? Did Gordon introduce you at the dinner-dance?"

"Your father? No, I don't think so. What is his name?"

Adele laughed, although it sounded more like a high-pitched birdcall. "Why, John Quinn, of course. I thought everybody knew that."

Senator Quinn. It made sense. In addition to a nice home and a wife who left him alone, Barclay got to be the son-in-law of Washington's senior senator, the head of the Senate Judiciary Committee, and a personal friend of the president.

Annie had a thought. "Has Gordon ever talked about a career on the bench?"

"You mean being a judge? Why, of course. For thirty years that's been his goal. Even before we were married. He'd be wonderful, I think."

For many attorneys the most fitting culmination of a brilliant legal career was an appointment to the federal bench. The power and status were unparalleled. And the only way to get there was by political appointment. It made Barclay's bizarre marriage come into sharper focus. Annie wasn't quite sure how Barclay's new law firm fit into the scheme, but she wasn't sure that Adele would be able to enlighten her.

Adele had finished lining the pan with strawberries and was now folding white chocolate into whipped cream. For the second time that day Annie realized that she hadn't taken the time to eat and it was practically killing her. She watched as Adele poured the chocolate mixture into the pan, using a spatula to smooth it evenly. On the one hand it seemed like Adele operated on a different plane, not quite hitting on all cylinders, as her mechanic might have said about Annie's Fiat. But in other ways she seemed highly focused, able to follow complex recipes and perform miracles of craftsmanship.

Annie glanced at her watch. She'd been there for over an hour and still no sign of Barclay. Watching Adele making dessert on an empty stomach was almost more than she could bear. If she didn't get some food pretty soon, who knows what dastardly deeds she might be capable of. Yet if she mentioned her hunger she was afraid she'd get stuck eating roast chicken with Adele. She decided to call Jed, tell him she was all right, then come up with an excuse to leave. She asked to use a phone.

"Oh, certainly, dear. Let's see. The morning room is so cluttered. Why don't you go on into Gordon's office and use that extension. It's the closed door off the stairway."

Annie couldn't believe her luck. A chance to snoop in Barclay's office when he wasn't home. She tried not to show her anticipation.

It felt a lot like breaking and entering as Annie turned the doorknob and pushed open the door of Barclay's office. She didn't want to take more than a few minutes in case Adele came looking for her. And since she had no idea what she was looking for, Annie had no idea where to start.

She closed the door and glanced around. The office had been converted from a small bedroom and was no more than ten by twelve feet. A large desk and an overstuffed chair made the room seem even smaller.

Annie could guess why the door was kept shut. This room hadn't been "done," like the rest of Adele's beautiful house.

The secondhand furniture was mismatched and the faded wallpaper looked as if it had been in place since the depression. Besides a telephone and a fax machine, there was little to indicate that Barclay did any work here. No supplies except a near-empty pencil holder; no filing cabinets. The room's true purpose was revealed by the floor-to-ceiling bookshelves lining one wall, filled with paperback novels. Barclay's secret passion appeared to be spy novels by the likes of Robert Ludlum and John le Carré.

Annie opened the closet door and peeked in. Nothing sinister there—only winter coats smelling of mothballs and a dusty stack of board games. Somehow Annie couldn't picture Barclay and Adele playing Trivial Pursuit on a winter's night.

A quick search of the desk drawers proved equally fruitless. Rubber bands, a few staples, a sticky deck of cards. The center drawer held half a yellow legal pad and a stack of office time sheets—probably for those times when Gordon took a phone call at home regarding a file.

Annie was about to give up when she spotted the wastepaper can. It was a small metal cylinder tucked far under the corner of the desk. She pulled it out from under the desk. Feeling a little like those poor souls who rummage through garbage cans for their next meal, Annie started sifting. Gas station receipts, several candy wrappers, outer envelopes for bills. Annie was starting to think the only secret she would discover was Gordon's covert love of Snickers bars when some color caught her eye. At the very bottom of the can were several scraps of stiff paper that had been torn into pieces the size of quarters. Laying them out faceup on the desk, Annie could see that together they would form a picture, about four by five inches, of Monet's water lilies.

Chapter 18

At least this time the outside entrance was closed and locked. The last thing Annie needed was another surprise waiting for her in her apartment. The only way to end such a mentally draining day was with a glass of wine and a long, quiet soak in a hot bathtub.

She could hear the raucous laughter and loud music before she got to the top of the stairs. No, she thought. Not tonight. Tell me the next-door neighbors aren't having a party. The way I feel, I don't think I can handle it.

But when she passed her neighbor's door, there wasn't a sound. The noise was coming from somewhere else.

It was coming from her own apartment.

They didn't notice her at first as she pushed open the door with its newly replaced jamb. And Annie barely recognized her apartment. It was clean. Jed was standing on a chair changing a light bulb, and Turek Zinzer was vacuuming. A woman who looked like a friend of Turek's, dressed entirely in black from her pierced nose to her hobnailed boots, was cleaning the glass French doors with Windex.

"Could someone please tell me what's going on?" Annie yelled over the blaring stereo.

"Hey, Annie's here." Ellen O'Neill came out of the kitchen wearing rubber dishwashing gloves. Someone turned off the music.

"It was sort of a situation of great minds having a single thought," she said, wiping some soap bubbles off her nose. "We all knew you'd be tired from doing too much when you were *supposed* to be recuperating from your wound, so I stopped by with a pizza for dinner—"

Joel Feinstein appeared from the bathroom, where he'd been mopping the floor. "And after you gave me such a hard time, I had to come by with some chicken soup."

Jed spoke up. "I had plans to meet Suzy later this evening, but the carpenter wasn't through with the door, so I called and told her to come on over here. She brought a big green salad." They heard Suzy yell from the kitchen, "Dinner's almost ready, Annie."

"And we just wandered by," said Turek, looking a little befuddled. "It seemed like the place to be. Zola"—the woman in black smiled at the mention of her name—"made a carrot cake with stuff from my place."

"Everybody sort of showed up at once," said Jed. "We started just picking up the mess of papers but kind of got carried away. I think everybody's just about done."

"Yeah," said Ellen. "Time to eat."

"Food," Annie muttered. "I think that's a very good idea."

After a dinner of pepperoni pizza, chicken soup, a huge salad, and Zola's homemade carrot cake, Jed cornered Annie in the kitchen. "How'd it go with Barclay?"

"I didn't see Barclay. But I found something that's convinced me that you may be right."

Jed's eyes widened. "So you think Barclay's guilty?"

"We can talk about it in a bit, after everyone's left."

Pleading exhaustion, Annie herded everyone toward the door, but only after promising Joel she'd rest and finish the chicken soup the next day. Jed spoke to Suzy, and they hung back. Ellen, the true-crime fanatic, was like a bloodhound when it came to sensing an investigation in progress and stayed as well. When they sat down in the living room, Suzy eyed Ellen warily.

"It's okay," said Annie. "Ellen knows about most of what's happened so far. She can help us be objective." She didn't mention that the last time she'd been mixed up in a murder investigation she had made a mistake that almost got Ellen O'Neill killed. Annie owed her one.

She started by filling Ellen and Suzy in on the visit to Puyallup and the ransacking of her apartment. After the disappearance of her father's journal, she was starting to believe that the events were connected somehow. Then she described her bizarre visit with Adele Barclay.

"And the strangest part is she knows about all the affairs and it doesn't seem to faze her. She actually thought he and I were sleeping together."

"And are you?" Suzy Gulliver asked sharply.

"Of course not! Why does everybody keep thinking that?"

Suzy shrugged. "Jed said Gordon talked about you incessantly. And you defended the old man pretty strongly the other evening."

Annie reached for her purse. "That was then. I'll admit I thought you and Jed were charging off half-cocked. I wasn't sure about your motives—I thought maybe you were just out for revenge. But after what I found at his home, I think you may be right about Barclay." She pulled out a sheet of yellow paper folded into a square. Inside she had placed one of the scraps from the wastebasket that clearly showed the picture of the water lilies.

Suzy gasped when she saw it. "That's Nancy's stationery. It was at Barclay's house?"

Annie nodded. "There was a pile of them. Torn into little scraps like this. I left all but this one. You can have it analyzed to see if it matches Nancy's note."

"You left them there?" Suzy yelled. "How could you? Now

he can destroy them, get rid of them. Then no one will be able to prove—"

Quieting her by placing a hand on her arm, Jed explained, "Annie was right. If she'd brought them all, it wouldn't have proven a thing. She could testify as to where she found them, but it would be pretty shaky evidence. A jury could easily dismiss the evidence as fabricated. Much better that the police should find the scraps and be able to prove a chain of custody."

"So have you called the police?" Ellen asked.

"No, and I'm not sure we should just yet. This still isn't much to go on. You could never get a conviction on this kind of evidence. And the police closed this file as a probable suicide. From what I know from years of working with the police on criminal matters, a detective's percentage of closed cases is a lot more important than whether a guilty person has been apprehended. They won't be anxious to reopen without something solid."

"So how do we get something solid? Trick him into making a confession?" asked Suzy.

"That's not as easy as it looks in the movies," said Annie. "Like him or not, Barclay's smart. I don't think we could outwit him. I think we just need to keep digging until we find something that will force the police to reopen the investigation."

"So," said Jed. "Where does that leave us?"

"I've heard from the document specialist," said Suzy. "The note was definitely in Nancy's handwriting, and it matched the rest of the box of stationery. I can give him this fragment and see if it matches as well."

Ellen had grabbed a legal pad and was jotting down notes. "We have Nancy's death, Annie's attack by an unknown sniper, the anonymous letter on firm stationery, the missing journal of George MacPherson, and questions about the disappearance of George's secretary thirty years ago. All of these things concern

Annie, or her father, except for Nancy's death. I don't see how that fits in. You didn't even know Nancy before you started working at the firm."

Suzy sat forward on the edge of the couch. "What did you say about an anonymous letter?"

"Here, I'll show you." Annie pulled the letter out of her purse and handed it to Suzy, who stared intently at the envelope with its blue highlighting, then looked at the letter inside.

"What is it, Suzy?"

"Nancy told me about some letters like this. Barclay had gotten several of them. It was one of the things they fought about right before she died. Every single letter had some reference to the word *Paradise*. Nancy was sure they were from some old girlfriend. She was jealous and wanted to know who was sending them."

"Did she ever find out?"

Suzy stood up and paced, trying to remember. "It just didn't seem important to me. She babbled about lots of things that night. We talked for hours, and most of it was about Gordon. I admit, I didn't listen as carefully to all of it as I could have. The Paradise Letters, she called them. They said things like 'Paradise lost,' 'a fool's paradise,' 'paradise on earth' . . . Wait. Yes, she did say something about the letters. She was complaining about the way he always ignored her and said, 'He wasn't even grateful when I told him where paradise was. I thought he'd be happy that I figured it out for him.' "

"*Where* paradise was?"

"That's what she said. It didn't make any sense to me, so I guess I kind of ignored it."

"That's got to be it," said Ellen, still scribbling on her pad. "That's got to be the missing link. Nancy knew something about those anonymous letters, which are somehow linked to the attacks on you, Annie. It's the only way it all fits together."

Annie rolled her eyes. "Come on, Ellen. Maybe it won't all fit together. Life isn't always that convenient, especially where a crime is involved."

"No, I think Ellen's right," said Jed. "I think we should concentrate on what those letters mean and how they might be connected to your father's journal."

Annie was glad she wasn't the prosecutor on this one. She'd made lots of tenuous arguments to juries in weak cases, but this one would have left the defense attorney snickering.

"We need a plan of attack," she heard Ellen say.

Annie tried hard to force her exhausted brain into action. "Okay, tracing the letters will probably have to wait until Monday, when the office is open. I'll have Val get into the computer log, see if she can find if they were typed on in-house equipment. Jed, you said you've got Lucy Watney's personnel file from the archives?"

"It's here. I had Suzy bring it over so you could take a look at it."

"Good, I'll go over it again and see if there's anything that would give us a lead on where she might have disappeared to. Why don't you and Suzy work on tracking down John Woodrow Watney—either junior or senior. Lucy's husband might have come back and settled in this area. Look through phone books, check with the Northern Pacific Railroad to see if they have any personnel records. The last-known location of the son was the Bay Area. You can check San Francisco and vicinity to see if anything turns up on him."

"I'll call one of my insurance-adjuster clients," said Jed. "Get him to run a DMV check on senior and junior."

"Good."

Ellen asked, "Didn't you say there was a lawyer involved when they were trying to prove Watney's paternity? Wouldn't that be a lead to check out?"

"That's just what I was thinking. An attorney named Eaton in Eatonville. Ellen, why don't you and I take a drive tomorrow?"

The next morning Ellen showed up with croissants, fresh orange juice, and the Saturday morning *Times* to read in the car.

Annie resented her being a morning person, especially after she revealed that she'd been up for hours but had cut her run short at only twelve miles.

All night Annie's dreams had swirled and spun in the past. She'd seen her father dancing with a beautiful long-haired beauty, gliding across a dance floor like Rogers and Astaire, passion radiant in their faces. She'd awakened with a crick in her neck. Somehow she'd fallen asleep on the couch and slept like concrete till morning.

They took Ellen's Toyota Camry for comfort, and the ample leg room, air-conditioning, and good shocks made Annie wonder if it might be time to trade in her little convertible. No, too much sentimental value was attached to the old Fiat.

They took the same route Jed and Annie had taken to get to Puyallup but continued south another twenty-five miles on Highway 167, pulling into Eatonville around ten. In some ways it was a typical western Washington small town, with a commercial district about six blocks long and a couple of Victorian houses mixed in with 1950s architecture. The main street, with its Big Foot Tavern, Sears Catalog store, and American flags, was like a Norman Rockwell scene revisited forty years later, when everything was badly in need of a coat of paint. But there were also signs that Eatonville was struggling to enter the modern age. A sign in the Tall Timbers restaurant proudly proclaimed that espresso was available—Annie made Ellen stop and wait while she got a latte to go—the Roxy theater was showing the latest Schwarzenegger adventure flick, and the gas station–mini mart at the end of town was so new that the cedar siding practically glistened.

"Where to first?" Ellen asked as they cruised down the main street. It didn't take long, so she pulled a U-turn and cruised the six blocks again.

"The library, and let's hope it's open on Saturday morning." They pulled into the lot of the small, one-story brick building bordered with giant irises. Annie's plan wasn't complicated: Call everyone named Eaton in a twenty-mile radius and start asking if they knew a lawyer who'd been practicing in town in the sixties.

Annie pulled out the local phone books, searching both the yellow and white pages for anyone named Eaton. There were several, but none were lawyers. She copied down the numbers. As she did so, Ellen passed the time looking at the bulletin board. A purple flyer caught her eye. She took it down and brought it over to Annie. It advertised HOBO DAYS—JULY 3 THRU 7 in historic Elbe and showed a picture of a steam engine, reading VISIT THE COAST STARLIGHT DINING CAR—CHILDREN WELCOME! At the bottom it said, "And don't miss the 14th annual chili cook-off. See if you can top Chef Woody's secret recipe!"

Ellen and Annie exchanged glances. "This would be too easy, right?" Ellen asked.

"It's sure worth checking out." Annie turned to the section in the telephone book for Elbe. There was no listing for John Woodrow Watney, but she copied down the number for the Coast Starlight Dining Car restaurant. "Let's find a phone."

The voice that answered sounded like a teenager's. "Yeah?"

"Is this the Coast Starlight?" ·

"Yeah, we ain't open yet. Open for lunch at eleven. Bye."

"Wait a second—" But it was too late. The boy had hung up.

"I think we should go up there," Annie said. "Elbe's only about ten miles up the road. We can phone these names on our way back if we have to."

They began to gain elevation after leaving Eatonville, the curving road cutting a tunnel through tall hemlock, cedar, and fir trees. Looking into the woods, Annie wondered how the original settlers had ever managed to force their way through the tangled undergrowth with shrouds of moss and lichens dripping from tree branches and thick ferns growing out of fallen timber. It was impossible to walk through woods like these; one had to scramble over giant tree trunks and fight through barriers of low branches.

Occasionally the road would open onto a cleared pasture,

where cows grazed and the purple ridge of the Cascades could be seen in the background, patches of late-spring snow still visible on the cone-shaped peaks. Shortly after they reached the shore of Alder Lake, appropriately named for the deciduous trees that shared the lakefront with evergreens, they pulled into Elbe.

The town of Elbe was a fraction of the size of Eatonville, barely filling a crook in the highway. To the left, snuggled up against the mountainside on the north side of the highway, was the residential part of town, mostly clapboard houses in need of repair. Rusted machinery and the ruins of old cars were a testament to the harsh mountain weather. What should have been the town square was a dumping ground for crumbled bricks, scrap lumber, and general debris.

But to the right were the trains.

Ellen parked the car and they got out to take a look. Permanently parked on the railroad siding was the Hobo Inn, a line of eight vintage cabooses all brightly painted in primary colors with wooden steps leading up to the cars that had been turned into a motel. Annie picked up a brochure that someone had dropped on the ground. It said that three of the cars were the last bay-window Milwaukee Railroad cabooses, built in 1944, on the West Coast. The "honeymoon suite" included a hot tub in an old logging caboose, which was attached to another caboose for sleeping.

Next to the motel was the Coast Starlight Dining Car. Two coach cars—a Southern Pacific and a Great Northern—formed the dining areas, with a bright red caboose for the entryway. A Chicago-Burlington coach car named the Sidetrack Room served as the bar.

At the other end of the siding was the Mount Rainier Scenic Railroad, an authentic steam train made up of three cars and an engine, which several times a day carried passengers along a fourteen-mile trip to Mineral Lake and back. The train was loading for the 11:00 trip, with "conductors" in blue-striped overalls and red bandannas herding passengers aboard. The sign advertised live music and scenic views.

"This place is a real hoot," Ellen said. "All the times I've been to Mount Rainier I've never really noticed it."

"You'd miss it if you blinked twice. But I haven't been this way in years. The times I've been to the mountain it's generally the northern side, along Carbon River or the Sunrise area. It's so much more accessible when you're coming from Seattle. Well, it's just about eleven. Let's go see if this Woody is our Woody."

They walked into the restaurant. The linen-covered tables were all empty and a waitress was still putting out the flower vases.

"Two for lunch?" the hostess asked. She wore a Gibson Girl blouse and a ruffled apron.

"No, we're actually looking for a man named Woody Watney, and we were wondering if—"

"Woody? He's in the back. I'll go get him. Just a sec."

Annie barely had time to compose her thoughts when the hostess returned with a ruddy-faced man in his midsixties. He was only about five eight, stocky, but fairly muscular. He wore a well-splattered apron over his T-shirt and blue jeans.

"How can I help you ladies?"

"My name's Annie MacPherson. Is there somewhere private we could talk?"

His expression darkened. "What's this about? You gals don't look like bill collectors or cops."

"I need to ask you some questions about Lucy."

He looked from Annie to Ellen as the hostess shifted uncomfortably, trying not to listen. Ellen, sensing Watney's ambivalence, excused herself and said she'd wait for Annie outside. Watney didn't look happy as he said, "All right. I can give you a few minutes before the lunch crowd gets here. Come on back to the manager's office."

They passed through the kitchen, a converted rail car, to

another caboose. Inside was a cubicle barely large enough to hold a desk stacked a foot high with invoices and order sheets and a couple of chairs. They crammed into the small space and Watney pulled the door shut. "This is likely to be pretty quick," he said, "as I haven't heard that lady's name in over twenty years. But first off I'd like to know just exactly who you are and why you're here."

Annie pulled a business card out of her purse. "I'm a lawyer in Seattle, but this is really a family matter. My father, George MacPherson, was Lucy's boss—and friend—about thirty years ago."

"George MacPherson, huh? He was her boss at that big downtown place, wasn't he? And you're his daughter." He took in the information but didn't offer any of his own.

"Yes. I . . . I feel somewhat awkward talking about this, but I've just recently learned that my father and your wife had a relationship—after you were separated—and that she disappeared shortly after giving birth to a son."

Laughing good-naturedly, Watney said, "Yeah, I know all about the little bastard. Pardon my language, but if he wasn't mine, then that's exactly what he'd be, wouldn't he?"

After Zan Osterhaus's comments Annie had expected the worst. But she found herself liking this rough-hewn character. "Right now I'm mostly concerned with finding out what happened to Lucy. Her sister, Mrs. Osterhaus, thought she ran off with you."

Watney guffawed and shook his head. "She really believed that, did she? Well, ain't that sumthin'. I should try to sell that woman the Tacoma Narrows Bridge. So let me get this straight. You don't have anything to do with Zan Osterhaus or her family?"

"No, I talked to Zan, but that's all."

"Well, that's okay, then. I don't mind talking to you. See, that Zan, she was forever trying to get me to take responsibility for Lucy's kid, to the point where I finally had to get me a lawyer to get her to stop. Now don't get me wrong, I sure did love Lucy, and I'm sorry as heck that that little boy had to grow up without no daddy, but he weren't mine and I wasn't about to pay for his upkeep. Hell, she's the one ran off and left the little guy. That weren't any of my business."

"So, you mean Lucy didn't run off with you when she left her baby?"

"Only in my dreams, sweetheart. In my fondest dreams. Look, I don't know who's been telling you tall tales, but it do sound like someone's been feeding you a line. That Zan never could keep her facts straight." They were interrupted by the phone. "Just a sec." Watney leaned out the office door and bellowed into the kitchen, "Sally, hon, can you cover the phone? I'm gonna be tied up here for a bit. Thanks, sweetheart. Now, where were we?" He rummaged around the desk. "You probably don't have a cigarette on ya?"

Annie shook her head.

"I quit a week ago, but it's not taking too well. If I were a bettin' man, which I am, I'd put short odds on my not making it through Hobo Days."

"How did you meet Lucy?"

"Well, I was just a kid, barely twenty-one, and she was seventeen. It was in the fall of 1953, and I thought I was so growed-up. A real tough operator. Left home and got a job with the railroad when I was sixteen, so I'd been on my own for a while. I started out working a run based out of Seattle and we had a few days off, so me and some of the guys decided to go to the state fair for something to do, the one over to Puyallup. Lucy was working one of the food booths, can't remember which one, selling bratwurst or some such thing. I swear, she was the prettiest girl I think I'd ever set eyes on. She had this hair like you wouldn't believe, dark brown and silky, fell almost to her waist. I swear even lookin' at a picture of that hair was about enough to give me a . . . 'Scuse me, I don't mean to be crude. I never was sure what she saw in me, 'cept maybe that I was older and I'd been a few places. She wanted to travel, see things. We'd go on these dates and I'd tell her about places.

Hell, half the time I made it up, but she didn't know that. I think maybe she saw things in me that I didn't see myself.'' Watney had a look of fond remembrance in his eyes, and Annie could almost picture the rugged charm he must have exuded more than thirty years back.

"When did you get married?''

"It was the next spring. We'd only known each other about three months, but she wanted to get away from home real bad. I didn't mean for her to quit school or nuthin', it's just that once we started living together, it took more money than I'd planned for and my salary didn't quite cut it, so she had to quit and find a job. And I think she thought if we got married, I'd take her to some of the places I'd been.'' He shook his head and his voice sounded wistful. "I knew in my heart that getting married wasn't a good idea.'' He looked around the office, finally locating a pack of cigarettes under a stack of papers. He pulled one out, lit it, and took a long drag. "Why is it that I love everthin's that bad for me?'' He coughed spasmodically. "All this could give you the wrong idea 'bout who I was. I mean, I look pretty settled down now. Got this job cooking, damn, it's gotta be almost fifteen years now, but back then I just couldn't stay out of trouble. I had a 'problem with authority' was how they put it in school. Fights mostly. Had a couple of assaults on my record 'fore I was nineteen. I knew damn well I wasn't a stable sort of character. Not worthy of somebody like her. But she was so hot on the idea I just couldn't say no.''

"Zan said the family never approved.''

"Her family? Hell, no. They thought I was the devil incarnate taking their baby doll away from them. And I have to tell you, the dislike was mutual. Stuck-up bunch of Norwegian farmers they were. I was glad to get Lucy out of there, but there wasn't a whole lot I had to offer. We had this tiny little dump of an apartment down on Twenty-third in Seattle. Lousy heat, cockroaches. I was damned ashamed she had to live in a place like that.''

Watney was leaning back in his chair and addressed his comments to the ceiling. It was clear his memories were as crisp as if the events had happened days before.

"Lucy's sister said you left after about six months."

Watney nodded and looked at Annie. "And she probably told you I was a heel and a scoundrel, too. If that woman had had a brain in her head, she woulda seen I did it for Lucy."

"What do you mean?"

"Those days it was damned hard for a woman to find a decent job, especially without a high-school degree. Smart as Lucy was, all she could find was working in some old garment factory sitting at a sewing machine. They paid you by how many shirts you could sew in a day, and sewing, that wasn't Lucy's strong point. She was as good a seamstress as she was a cook, which was plumb lousy. She made a lot of mistakes, so they was always docking her pay for this or that. She wanted to go back to school so she could get a better job—smart as a whip, that girl. But we just couldn't afford it. I knew if I left she'd have to go back to her family, and without me in the picture they'd take care of her. I loved that woman like my own right arm, and I hope to God I never again have to do anything as hard as leaving her. But I knew it was the right thing. The railroad was looking for guys to work out of Anchorage, and I took the transfer. I left her a note saying I weren't coming back and she'd better call her family to come and get her. I told her she could get in touch with me through the company and that I'd give her a divorce anytime she asked."

"And did you ever hear from her?"

"Not a word till 1962. She wrote me a letter, care of the railroad, saying she finally wanted to meet with me." With a homesick look in his eye Watney said, "At first I had this silly notion she wanted to get back together. But no, she told me she'd met somebody new and she finally wanted her divorce. I guess that must of been your daddy."

"And how'd you feel about that?" Annie felt she had to pursue the possibility that Watney could have been jealous enough to do something violent, but it wouldn't have seemed in character for this gentle bear of a man.

He shrugged. "I still loved her, but I knew I didn't deserve her love in return. I was the one that'd left her. I couldn't ask anything more of her. Besides, by that time she'd already gone and had that baby. I always figured it was his."

"You mean you never even saw her until after the baby was born?"

"What you're asking is, am I absolutely sure it weren't mine? Hell, yeah, I'm sure. I hadn't laid eyes on her since the day I left. I take it her sister still thinks I diddled her?"

"Yes."

"Well, it figures that she'd hang on to that fool notion. Lucy told me back in '62 that she'd lied to her sister about it, listed me as the daddy on the birth certificate, for appearance's sake, since we was still married, but that she'd never ask me for money or anything. But it was years later, after Lucy was gone, and Zan was raising the little guy, that they threatened to bring that lawsuit."

"A paternity action?"

"Is that what you call it? Where they would try to prove I was the daddy so I'd have to pay to bring the kid up? Well, now, if Lucy herself had asked me for anything, I would have given her my life itself and then some. But that sister, no siree. Not one penny was going to go to her. So we had to go through all this folderol with blood tests and everything. Took my blood and compared it to the kid's. I don't quite know how it worked, but the lawyer I talked to down in Eatonville said that the blood tests proved hands down I couldn't of been the daddy and they didn't have a case. But that doesn't surprise me that her sis wouldn't believe it. She probably thinks I rigged the results somehow."

"Do you still have any of those documents? The blood-test results or the lawyer's letter?"

"Nah, those'd be long gone by now. I chucked 'em once the lawyer told me their case had been throwed out."

"When was the last time you heard from Lucy?"

"Well, now, the last time I was *supposed* to hear from her she stood me up. It was a Tuesday night, October 8, 1962. Reason I remember so exactly, the Yankees were in the World Series and it was the night of the last game, and I was missing it just to see her. That's how crazy the lady made me! So I was plenty mad when she didn't show up."

"What happened?"

"I got this call from her. She had divorce papers drawn up and she wanted me to sign 'em. As I told you, I didn't have no problem with that, 'cept I was sorry that's the way it had to turn out. I even volunteered to come out to the house, but she didn't want me to. Asked if we could meet at the Sorrento Hotel, in the bar." He laughed. "Leave it to her to pick one of the few bars in town that didn't have the game on TV."

"And she never came?"

"Never did. I waited there for about three hours, though I knew if she wasn't there right at seven that she wasn't coming. Lucy was never one to be late."

"Could you have been confused about the place?"

"Not a chance. The Sorrento, that's where we spent our wedding night. Damn, it took every cent I had in the world for a night at that place, but it was worth it to see the look on her face when I told her that's where we was going. We couldn't really afford a wedding or nothing, just went down to the courthouse and had a judge marry us. But that night, champagne in the bar, a big fancy room, I swear that made it all worth it. I'll never forget that night."

"And you haven't heard from her since?"

"Nope."

"Didn't you ever want to follow through with the divorce?"

"Didn't have to. See, a couple years later I hooked up with my current lady, her name's Helga. She'd been married twice before, and both her husbands went and died on her. She thought it was her fault, her being a bad-luck charm or something. Hell, after what she'd been through, I couldn't drag her to the altar if I'd wanted to. We're happy as clams. I call her the missus and ain't nobody the wiser. Frankly, I think not getting married is good for my health, knowing what happened to her first two, if you know what I mean.''

Chapter 19

When Annie came out of the Coast Starlight Dining Car, the early low clouds had given way to brilliant sunshine. Ellen had just picked up her order and was seated at a picnic table on the other side of the highway in front of a fast-food stand named the Scaleburger.

"Here, you want half of this?" she said as Annie arrived. "Sorry I didn't get you anything, but I wasn't sure how long you'd be, and I was starving."

"Gee, what a surprise. How are you going to eat that thing?" The burger in Ellen's hand had to be at least five inches high.

"Doesn't it look great? It's called the Overlimit—bacon, cheese, the works. Sure you don't want some?"

"No, I'll just scarf some of your fries."

"This town is great, Annie. I took five minutes and saw the whole thing. This food stand was where the old logging scale was, and over there is this adorable little church—*Ripley's Believe It or Not* calls it the smallest church in the world. It's just a tiny little room with a few pews and a big steeple. And this is the best part. See that over there?" Ellen pointed to a modest one-room structure that looked like the town's hardware and general-supply store. "That's the Elbe Mall. Don't you just love it? So, what did the dastardly ex-husband have to say for himself?"

"He's far from villainous." Annie recounted what Watney had told her, then took a long sip of Ellen's Pepsi.

"So you really like the guy, huh? You know, you've been fooled before. Lots of seemingly nice guys murder their wives."

"Do you have these evil thoughts about everyone? I swear you've got to stop reading those true-crime books."

"No way, I just bought Ann Rule's latest and I can't wait to sink my teeth into it. You'd be surprised what horrid things ordinary people can do to their loved ones." Struggling, Ellen tried to sink her teeth into the humongous burger. Although it was a noble effort, she only managed to make a small dent. Undaunted, she dove in again.

"To answer your question, no, I don't think Woody did away with his wife. After all these conniving lawyers I've been hanging around with lately, it's really refreshing to meet someone who's happy with a decent job and a simple family life. I got the impression that he really loved Lucy, but that the timing for them was just wrong."

Annie looked up at the mountains rising behind the small town. It was a different world up here, away from the mad pace of the city. This was the kind of peace David Courtney found on his sailboat. She wondered for the thousandth time why she was unable to find that kind of peace in her own life. Lost in thought, she suddenly realized that Ellen was saying something.

"What did you say?"

"I said, I was curious about what Watney said about the blood test, about the fact that it conclusively proved he wasn't the father."

Annie shrugged. "I just took that as more proof that the baby was my father's son."

Ellen was frowning, trying to swallow a large bite of burger. "Not necessarily. Did you bring Lucy's personnel file along?"

"Yeah, I've got it right here." Annie pulled the file out of her shoulder bag and handed it to Ellen.

After glancing through the pages, Ellen found what she was looking for, a preemployment physical. "Great, it lists blood type. Do you know what your father's was?"

"AB negative, same as mine."

"I can't believe it. Annie, this is incredible."

"What?"

"Both Watney and Mrs. Osterhaus said the blood test was absolutely conclusive, right? No room for doubt?"

"Right, words to that effect."

"If that's true, then it not only proves that Watney wasn't the father, but it also shows that the baby was *not* your father's."

Annie reached over and took the medical report. It showed Lucy's date of birth, making her twenty-five when she started work at KLMD. Husband's name: John Woodrow Watney, address unknown. No prior health problems.

"Look at the second page," said Ellen, "where it lists blood type."

"Okay. It says AB negative."

Ellen looked expectant. "See, that proves it. Don't you get it?"

"Get what?"

"What this means. The blood type's the same as your father's."

"But we don't have enough information. We don't know what the baby's blood type was, or what Watney's was, for that matter."

"No, but we don't have to know. I'll spell it out. Genetics 101." Ellen turned to a fresh page on the legal pad she'd been jotting notes on and drew three circles. One said "Lucy—AB negative," the next had a question mark, and the third said "George—AB negative." Below, she drew a circle labeled "baby" with a question mark.

"Okay, we know that a baby has to have the same blood type as one or both of its parents, right? That's elementary."

"Right." Annie was glad Ellen hadn't added, "my dear Watson."

"If both parents have the same blood type, such as AB negative, what blood type is the baby going to have?" She drew lines from Lucy's circle and George's circle.

"AB negative. Nothing else it could be."

"Right. So if George was the father, the baby would have had AB negative blood. But if he did, how much would that prove about the father?"

Annie suddenly saw what Ellen was getting at. "Nothing, because the baby could have inherited that blood type from Lucy. If the baby had the mother's blood type, the father could have been anyone. The blood tests would have been inconclusive."

"Precisely. But if the tests *conclusively proved* that Watney wasn't the father, then that means the baby must have had a blood type that not only didn't match Watney's but also didn't match the mother's. That would be the only way paternity could be absolutely ruled out."

Annie nodded, feeling foolish for being so dense. "And if the baby wasn't AB negative, then it couldn't be my father's child."

"Not bad, for an English major."

It took a moment for it all to sink in. After trying to get used to the idea that she had a half brother, Annie felt a sense of mixed relief and disappointment that it wasn't true. She was still feeling dazed a moment later when, seeing a loaded Grayline bus roll by, Ellen asked, "How far from here are we from Mount Rainier National Park?"

"I don't know. I'll look at the map." Annie pulled it out of her purse and opened it on the table, where it soaked up a grease stain from a previous patron's Scaleburger. "It looks like it's about fifteen more miles to the entrance of the national park and about the same distance on to . . . Oh, my God. Why didn't we think of this?"

"What?" Ellen stopped eating.

"We're about thirty miles from Paradise."

———

As they neared the park entrance the road grew steeper. The terrain was subalpine now, the trees weren't as tall, and the lush undergrowth was gone. Later in the summer, when all remnants of the winter snowfall had melted, the meadows would be white again with fields of avalanche lilies, then on fire in the fall with mountain ash and huckleberry. Neither woman spoke as they made their ascent up the mountain. They weren't sure what they were looking for but felt compelled to go forward to see Paradise.

After paying the five-dollar entrance fee, they were given a brochure with a map of Mount Rainier National Park showing the points of interest and the dozens of ridges and glaciers on the peak that rose more than 14,000 feet above sea level. Annie stared at names like Point Success, Disappointment Cleaver, and Cathedral Rocks and could almost feel the emotion of the thousands of adventurers who had been attempting the trip to the summit since the late 1800s. Given Gordon Barclay's passion for the mountains, Paradise had to have some significance.

As they passed the viewpoint at Narada Falls, the road began turning sharply. Typically for May the sides of the road were still banked with four or five feet of snow. At 5,400 feet they reached the Henry M. Jackson Memorial Visitors' Center, a spool-shaped building with viewing windows high enough off the ground to provide viewing even under fifty feet of snow in winter.

They parked the car and went inside, where they found a variety of displays telling the history and geography of the mountain. While interesting, neither could believe that the mountain's past was relevant to their present quandary.

Annie and Ellen skipped the displays and climbed the spiral corridor up to the observation area. There the view of the snow-covered south slope of Mount Rainier rose so sharply, it filled the entire viewing window. Annie overheard the exclamations of surprise as groups of tourists entered the room. To someone from the eastern or plains states who'd never seen a real mountain before, the sight was almost unbelievable.

Telescopes were positioned so that visitors could see groups of climbers heading for the top, on what was the most popular route of ascent. Although it was a bit early in the season for favorable weather, they could see a group of about fifteen climbers working their way up the icy slope.

"Barclay has climbed the mountain," Annie said, letting Ellen look through the telescope. "He had a picture in his office of him standing at the summit. But I know my father was never interested in mountain climbing. I could never even get him interested in day hikes."

"Didn't the brochure say there's a lodge here at Paradise?"

"A famous one. Just up the road a little. It's been a popular tourist spot since the twenties. Let's go on up there. I don't think we're going to learn anything here."

The Paradise Lodge was a large, A-framed wooden structure with several outbuildings. According to the brochure, it was built in 1917 and was unique in that it was made completely from cedar taken from the surrounding forest. Inside, the lobby was spacious and inviting, with rough-hewn timbers and rustic-styled furniture. There was a stone fireplace at each end, and around the perimeter at the second-story level was a balcony made up of a series of alcoves for quiet reading or conversation. High above them, hanging from the rafters, were huge cylindrical lampshades painted with botanical designs, reproductions of the originals from the twenties.

"Wouldn't it be great staying in a place like this?" Ellen asked, peering into the large dining room, already laid with linen tablecloths and silver for luncheon. "It's like going back in a time machine."

"Can't you just imagine it in the twenties?" said Annie. "Plucky travelers coming up here in their Model-Ts, getting ready to put on their knickers and lace up their leather boots to explore the mountain."

After they'd had a good look around, Annie walked over to the reception desk and asked for the manager.

"Speaking."

"This is an odd request, but is there any way I could find out the names of guests who might have stayed here in the sixties?"

The manager thought for a moment, then shook his head. "No, those records would have been destroyed a long time ago."

"How about a history of the lodge? Would anything cover that era?"

"Well, there is the scrapbook, but most of the clippings in there are older. You're welcome to take a look, though. It's there at the end of the counter."

"Thanks."

Annie flipped through the pages, which, as the manager had said, contained mostly items from the twenties and thirties. The later clippings mostly had to do with climbs, both successful and tragic, up the mountain. The only reference to the sixties was a newspaper write-up from 1960 announcing the remodeling of the new wing, which added several luxury suites with full kitchenettes.

"Anything there?" Ellen asked, joining Annie at the book.

"Lots of interesting history, but nothing that seems very relevant. The answer may have something to do with this place, but I don't think we're going to find it here."

"Are you going to talk to Barclay?"

"Not yet. First there's someone else who I think hasn't been telling me the entire truth."

After dropping Ellen at her place, Annie headed for the southwest shore of Lake Washington. Since she had been there once before, Fred Duff's house was easy to find. But before she could ring the bell, the gate swung open.

"Heavens, dear, you scared me half to death," said Vivian Duff, looking fluffy in a white cotton cardigan. She was holding a canvas shopping bag stamped with the logo for Puget Consumers' Coop. "I was just heading out to the store."

"Is Fred here? I really need to talk to him."

"Yes, surely. He's in the garden. You go right on down."

On his hands and knees at the far side of the yard, Fred Duff was carefully placing dark purple petunias and yellow marigolds in a bed.

"Annie, what a nice surprise. You were in the neighborhood, I suppose?" Using his cane, he pushed himself slowly to a standing position. "I always like to get my annuals in early. That way they're blazing away by the Fourth of July. Summer's short enough around here—can't waste a minute of it."

"I'm terribly sorry to bother you like this, but I need to talk to you."

Picking up on Annie's serious tone, he asked, "Is this about Gordon Barclay, by any chance?"

"In part."

"I see. Come on in the house."

The house felt cool after the bright sun outdoors. But Annie also knew she was flushed with anticipation. She was surprised to see a rifle on the kitchen table, with materials for cleaning it.

"Oh, don't worry. It's not loaded. Just getting her all cleaned and polished so she'll be ready for deer season."

Annie was the world's worst authority on guns, and she knew even less about hunting, but she'd always thought deer season was in the fall. Fred saw her look of concern and chuckled. "Were you picturing me sniping from a rooftop somewhere?" As he said it, Annie realized she was being foolish to even suspect the old man. After declining his offer of food and drink, they sat in the living room.

"Before you say anything," the old man began, "I want to assure you that I know all about Gordon's secession this coming Monday. I don't know if that's what you were coming to talk to me about, but I wanted to set you at ease that you weren't betraying any secrets."

In all the chaos since the sniper attack on Wednesday, Annie had almost forgotten about Gordon's plan to leave KLMD. "How did you find out?" she asked.

"Oh, that doesn't matter. What matters is how I'm going to stop him."

As Annie looked back toward the kitchen table, Fred read her thoughts and laughed.

"Good God, Annie, you don't think I meant . . . No, I can assure you, my dear, I was thinking more along the lines of *legal* remedies to stop Gordon."

"You'll file a lawsuit?"

"Most likely. Annie, like I was telling you before, as much as Gordon and I have disagreed over the years, his significance to KLMD can't be ignored. If he goes, it could spell the end for us. I can tell you honestly that I'd do anything—*within the law*—to stop Gordon Barclay from leaving KLMD. Now I also know that Gordon's approached you with an offer. If he promised you more money, a partnership, I'll match it, if I can. But I can't promise anything now since there will undoubtedly be layoffs if he succeeds."

"I didn't come here looking for any special favors. But I've decided I won't be accepting Gordon's offer."

Fred stood up and walked over to the liquor cart, where he poured himself a bourbon. He held up the bottle to Annie, but she shook her head. "I get the impression that's not the reason you're here."

"No." She wasn't sure how to start. It was clear from her last conversation with Jed that Fred knew far more about past events involving Lucy Watney than he'd revealed to Annie. She decided to be blunt. "Fred, I need to know the *whole* truth about my father and Lucy Watney. And where Gordon Barclay fits into the equation. I know it may be painful for me to hear, but I'm entitled to know."

Taking a deep breath, Fred Duff thought for a moment. "Never having had children myself, I guess I do tend to be a little bit fatherly toward the young folks who work for me. I was trying to shield you, Annie. And you're right. I shouldn't have. Let's go outside. It's getting a little stuffy in here.''

The lawn chairs were already set up in a patch of sunlight down by the edge of the lake. When they reached them, Fred sank into one with a sigh that brought back to Annie the fact that Fred was in his eighties.

As he stared at the tranquil lake, he began to talk. ''Four of us started this firm back in 1946, after Kemble, Laughton, Mercer, and I came home from the war. Built it from the ground up, using every cent of cash we could lay our hands on, working long hours. But it paid off. By the late fifties we were one of the top firms on the West Coast, and we've stayed at the top ever since.

''One of the reasons we did so well, and I take most of the credit for this, was our ability to spot talent. George, your father, had it. I knew from the beginning that he'd do well for himself. As a young lawyer he was a little bit shy socially, but when he got in front of a judge or jury, you should have seen how he came alive. Did you ever get to see him in action, Annie?''

She nodded. ''One time when I was in high school he wrote me an excuse to miss class so I could come to court and watch a trial.''

''So you know what a powerhouse he was. But Gordon Barclay, there's another story altogether. I knew from the start that his was more than an ordinary legal mind. He had the charisma to go with it, the innate knack of getting people to eat out of the palm of his hand. You've felt his charm, we all have. He seems to be especially appealing to women, which he's used to full advantage over the years. But I knew right then when we hired him that Gordon would make this firm invincible.''

Annie noticed for the first time how old Fred's hands looked as they gripped the arms of the lawn chair. The mottled skin looked almost transparent and was as brittle as parchment. He went on.

''My own pride in the firm, my desire, like that of a father, to see my 'family' do well, was probably what kept me from doing anything about Gordon over the years. I knew, rationally, that his personal morals were practically nonexistent, but I chose to turn a blind eye in order to keep him here at KLMD. Undoubtedly the worst instance of my own selective blindness had to do with dear Lucy."

"Something happened at the firm Christmas party, didn't it?" Annie asked tentatively.

"Yes, you've figured out that much, haven't you? The poor thing, I should have known she was no match for Gordon's powers of 'persuasion.' Such a tiny little thing she was. This was the Christmas before she took her maternity leave, I believe she'd been with us about a year."

"Nineteen sixty-one?"

"That sounds about right, yes. We held our Christmas party where we always did, at the Cascade Club. We'd take over the whole place for the evening. I remember that party being especially festive that year because Gordon stood up and announced his engagement to Adele Quinn, and everyone was toasting the couple and having a grand old time. Your father and Lucy had both come alone, but that was just a facade. Everyone in the firm knew George was sweet on Lucy, but they were always discreet, since both of them were still married at the time. These days it wouldn't have mattered, of course, but you have to remember what the times were like then. Divorce was a social stigma, and the marriage vows were taken quite seriously.

"It was very late in the evening. The band was playing, quite a few folks had had more than a little to drink. I was wandering down one of the corridors in search of the men's room when I heard a sound. It was like a muffled cry, then voices arguing." As if to illustrate the point, they heard a screech and looked up to see the bald eagle circling overhead.

"The sound seemed to be coming from one of the service stairways at the back of the building. Understand, this was a large space and there were only fifty or sixty people at the party. Whoever had gone back there obviously thought they wouldn't be disturbed."

"But you went to see?"

"I had to. It sounded like a woman in trouble. I opened the stairwell door and there, one flight up, were Lucy and Gordon. She had tears streaming down her face, her dress was all disarrayed, her nylons down around her ankles. And Gordon"— Fred's voice quavered slightly—"Gordon was zipping up his pants."

Annie shifted in her chair, not wanting to hear more but knowing she had to.

"The girl was obviously upset, but seeing me at that moment, the look on her face was sheer terror. After everything else she'd been through, being seen by the managing partner— she probably thought I was going to fire her on the spot. I asked her if she was all right. I should have known she wasn't, but she just turned her face to the wall and nodded."

Fred paused, as if gathering strength for the rest of the story. Annie noticed the firm set of his jaw, the resolute stare. He didn't want to relive that night any more than she wanted to hear about it.

"What did you do?" she asked softly.

"Of all the things I have to feel guilty for in my life, Annie, the worst is the fact that I did nothing about that evening. The next Monday, when I ran into Gordon at the office, neither of us said a word about it. I think it was at that moment that Gordon knew he could get away with . . ." Fred stopped himself before he could say "murder."

"And my father. Did he ever know?"

Fred nodded slowly. "I got the impression that he did, but he didn't learn it from me. In my heart I always wanted to tell him. For God's sake, he and Gordon were best friends. But I never knew what to say. It only got worse when we learned that the girl was pregnant. She made up that cock-and-bull story about seeing her husband, but I always knew that was a lie.

And I was so selfish, so damned concerned for the welfare of my firm, that I never confronted Barclay about it."

The story answered Annie's question about the father of the baby boy, but it didn't explain why George MacPherson had helped to pay for his upbringing. It also didn't explain Lucy's disappearance in October.

"I understand that my father helped care for the child. Could he have believed it was his?"

"I don't think that was the reason. As I say, I always got the impression from George that he knew the truth. But the general gossip around the office . . . of course everyone assumed it was his child. Perhaps he was just keeping up appearances."

Annie didn't buy that explanation. Her father had never been one to care much about what other people thought and certainly wouldn't have spent twenty thousand dollars just for appearances' sake. There had to have been something more.

"I never heard any more about the little tyke after he was born that July," Fred continued.

Annie quickly counted months. "July? But if she got pregnant at the Christmas party . . . ?"

"From what I understand, she didn't make it past seven months. Complications of some kind, gave birth prematurely sometime around the fourth. But as far as I know, both she and the baby did fine. Leastwise she was well enough to go off with George on that trip in October."

"What trip?"

"Oh, you didn't know about that? To tell you the truth, I'm real unclear on the details. But I know it was after Lucy's request to come back to work was turned down."

"Jed told me about that—how Barclay blocked her from coming back."

Fred looked glum. "I wished I'd had the chance to talk to her about it. She called me after she got Barclay's letter, horribly upset, going on and on about having to go back to some garment factory to work and how was she going to support her baby. I told her to come on in the following Monday and we'd talk about it. But maybe she sensed that I really couldn't override Gordon. She never came in to see me.

"I've never stopped feeling guilty about how we treated the poor girl. These days we never would've gotten away with behavior like that, especially her being Mexican and all, or I guess I should say Hispanic."

Annie must have looked surprised. "I knew she was adopted, but I didn't know . . ."

"Well, she didn't make much of it. In fact, I think she was a little ashamed that her parents had been farm workers. She always tried real hard to fit in, be just like all the other girls we had working for us back then."

"But do you know what happened to her?" Annie asked anxiously.

"The story I heard was that she stood your daddy up. George had told me about some special trip he had planned to the mountains someplace. I remember even then, after the baby, George did everything properly. He made sure to tell me that it was all on the up-and-up, another couple was going along to share rooms. The ladies in one, the men in the other. I asked him the next week how it had been, and he was so upset he could barely speak. Seems she'd run off with her ex-husband and left him in the lurch."

The same lies. Even so, Annie had learned more than she'd expected, more than Fred Duff knew he had revealed. One phone call would be able to tell her if her suspicions were correct.

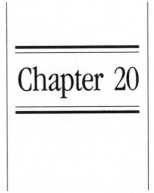

Chapter 20

Driving across the Evergreen Point Bridge to the east side of Lake Washington, Annie tried to formulate what she'd say to him. Before her telephone call to Zan Osterhaus it had been just a hunch, based on nothing more than a few coincidental dates and places. After making the call and checking his biography in the firm marketing brochure, she was now certain her theory was correct. She just didn't know what she was going to do about it.

The Pebble Shore Condominiums were easy to find. Taking the Kirkland exit off Highway 520, Annie looped around to the north onto Lake Washington Boulevard, where there was a string of condominiums and apartments right on the water. Literally.

They had all been built before the restrictive Shoreline Protection Act. All jutted out into Lake Washington on stilts, which gave each owner a one-hundred-and-eighty-degree waterfront view and no need to worry about landscaping. It was about a quarter to six when Annie rang the bell at number 401.

"Just a second." Annie jumped when she heard the female voice and carefully checked the address she'd copied from the firm directory to make sure she hadn't made a mistake. Then the door opened abruptly.

It was hard to say who looked more embarrassed, Annie or Deborah Silver, keys in hand and purse on shoulder, ready to walk out the door.

"Uh, Annie? Well, isn't this a surprise."

"Deborah. I was looking for Alex. I didn't mean . . ."

"Uh, yeah, he went for a bike ride about an hour ago. But he'll probably be back anytime." Deborah jingled her keys, obviously anxious to get away. "Look, I'm supposed to meet someone downtown at six and I'm running late. But why don't you come in, if you want to wait." She looked at her watch. "I've really got to go. Make yourself comfortable."

With that, Deborah practically ran for the elevator, leaving Annie alone in Alex's condominium. She felt slightly uncomfortable about it, but she had, after all, been invited in.

She scrutinized the very masculine room. From the looks of it Annie doubted that Alex and Deborah cohabited. Except for a pair of Papagallo pumps under a chair, there wasn't a feminine trace in the room.

The living room was sparsely furnished in Danish teak and dark leather. It was clear that Alex spent his hefty associate's salary on "toys." A massive entertainment center filled one wall: television, VCR, laser disk player, and an ultramodern stereo system.

The bookshelves, as always, drew Annie's attention. Wedged between African artifacts used as bookends were volumes on everything from quantum mechanics to classical architecture. But before Annie had time to browse through the books, she was distracted by an all-too-familiar item. Sitting on one end of the shelf, partially hidden under a stack of magazines, was a hardbound black book. Her father's journal.

It wasn't a complete surprise, given what she now knew about Alex, but she'd hardly expected to find it under such circumstances. Now she was torn between desire to confront Alex with her newly acquired knowledge and to get the journal away to a safe place, where she could read it and find out what was so important in it that had made it worth stealing.

She opted for the latter, quietly letting herself out of the condo and locking the door behind her. She glanced at the elevator, but she didn't want to take the chance on running into Alex on his way back and so took the stairs.

She threw the journal onto the seat of her car, got in, and turned the key. The only sound was Annie's own frantic breathing. Not even a click to indicate a dead battery. More likely it was the defective starter switch that Jurgen had replaced last month. At least he was supposed to have done so.

She quickly ran through her options. Alex (or possibly Deborah?) had been willing to break into her apartment to get the journal. There was little chance that he would let her have it back without a fight. Alex's building was on a bus line. If she rode into downtown Kirkland, she could find a place to stash the journal—possibly mail it to herself—then come back and confront Alex.

She buried the journal in her shoulder bag and jogged down Lake Washington Boulevard to a bus stop several blocks away. Partially concealed by trees, and not too close to the front of Alex's building, it seemed like a reasonably safe place to wait. She collapsed on the bench and prayed the bus would come quickly, before Alex returned home.

In the meantime she pulled out the black book. When she opened it, a white square tumbled to the ground. It was a black-and-white photo that Annie was sure hadn't been in the journal originally. It looked like the kind of photos she'd seen as a child in the fifties and sixties, where three sides of the paper were smooth and the fourth was ragged, like a book page. It was a group photo taken from a distance of about twenty feet. Four adults, all wearing sunglasses and heavy jackets, were standing in front of the Paradise Lodge at Mount Rainier. It was easy to make out her father—Annie had seen photographs of him as a young man before. Next to him, his arm around her shoulders, was a diminutive long-haired brunette—obviously Lucy Watney. A tall man stood next to Lucy and a blond woman with frowsy hair was on the end. Even though they were thirty years younger, Annie quickly recognized Gordon and Adele Barclay.

On the back was a date stamp showing when the photo had been developed: October 1962.

Annie heard the backward spinning of gears behind her but didn't attach a meaning to the sound until it was too late. From behind her she felt one gloved hand on her shoulder, while another hand reached around and grabbed the journal. She looked up into the angry face of Alex Guiterrez.

"Sorry, Annie," he said, stuffing the journal into his bicycle pannier and buckling the strap. "But I took this for a reason."

She turned around on the bench to face him. His wiry body was tense, and sweaty from the ride. In his black bicycle pants and domed helmet he was practically indistinguishable from all of the other cyclists swarming the Kirkland waterfront on a sunny Saturday. Except for the gleam of pure hatred in his eyes.

"We need to talk, Alex."

His eyes narrowed. "All right." He hoisted his bicycle on one shoulder and grabbed her left arm. She winced in pain from his powerful grip but was glad that he hadn't grabbed her wounded arm. There was no point in trying to get away. Alex was both stronger and faster than she, and they both knew it.

He marched her back to his condominium, maintaining his hold until they were inside. Once there he pushed her in the direction of the couch and directed her to sit. Not saying a word, he hung his bicycle on two hooks in the entryway, unstrapped his helmet and set it on top of the bookshelf, pulled off his gloves and set them down next to the helmet. Then he walked into the kitchen and grabbed a can of Diet Pepsi, tipped his head back, and drank half of it without stopping. He glanced once in her direction and walked into the bedroom. When he came back he was carrying a gun.

He sat in the leather recliner across from the couch and set the gun on the end table next to him. It was a large handgun, like something Annie assumed the police might use. Certainly the type that could kill a person with one bullet.

Alex smiled when he looked at her, seemingly enjoying her uneasiness.

"What, not comfortable around guns?"

"As a matter of fact, no. I've never owned one, never fired one, and don't have any plans to change that."

"Don't worry, I don't want to shoot you. A bullet from this, see, would go right through you, hit the furniture or something. This is all leather, be a bitch to repair. No, I just want to leave it there to remind you not to leave before we've finished our discussion."

From the way he was treating her, she could only assume that he was the one responsible for breaking into her apartment. She tried not to dwell on the possibility that he might also be a killer.

"Maybe you should have said you don't want to shoot me *again.*"

He raised one eyebrow. "You thought I did that?" He shook his head, taking another sip of his soft drink. "Kinda too bad I can't take credit. But I was at a Rotary Club meeting. My presence from twelve to two can be verified by about forty of this city's most respected citizens." He chuckled. "Too bad, huh?"

For the first time all day the wound on her right arm began to throb. Trying to suppress her fear and sound in control, Annie said, "So, are you going to tell me why you broke into my apartment to steal that journal? Or should I just leave that up to the police? I've called them, you know."

Steely-eyed, Alex didn't acknowledge her question and obviously didn't believe her claim about the police. Annie had never been much of a poker player—bluffing didn't come naturally.

"Why did you come here?" he asked. "How did you know I had the journal?"

"I didn't. I came because I wanted to ask you some questions. About your parents." She paused. "Gordon Barclay and Lucy Watney."

If Alex was surprised, he didn't show it. He finished his Diet
Pepsi, then crushed the can in his hand. "So you figured that
out, have you? It's kind of funny. Barclay almost treats me like
a son, but he's never even suspected that I really am. But then,
I don't look much like dear old Dad."

"No, you take after Lucy."

The hatred in his eyes was now tempered with wariness.
"You said you didn't read the journal. So how did you put it
together?"

She told him that she had learned about Lucy and the baby
from her visits to Zan Osterhaus and Woody Watney. "But I
didn't suspect you were Lucy's son until I talked to Fred Duff
and he told me—" she paused, not knowing how much of the
story Alex knew "—enough to implicate Gordon Barclay as the
father of Lucy's child. He also said that the baby had been born
prematurely. In July 1962. The month and year you were
born."

"Along with about a million other people."

"Zan Osterhaus told me that Lucy's son went to college at a
fancy private school back East, where he was at the top of his
class, then moved to the Bay Area. The firm brochure says that
you graduated summa cum laude from Harvard, took a year
off, then went to Stanford Law School."

Alex listened with an expression of amusement on his face.
"Coincidence?"

"That's what I thought. But I confirmed my hunch by calling
Zan and asking what the name of your mother's family was,
before her parents were killed and she was adopted by Zan's
family."

Alex smiled. "Good investigative work, Counselor. You
learned that my mother came into this world as Lucinda Maria
Guiterrez."

"Why did you change your name?"

"My mother was taught to be ashamed of her heritage, subtly, by Aunt Zan and her family. Sure, they loved Lucy, but
they did everything they could to get her to assimilate into her

adoptive family. Aunt Zan wanted me to do the same, to simply ignore who I am. The year I took off between college and law school I did a lot of thinking, reevaluated who I wanted to be. I decided I could never be content unless I acknowledged my heritage."

"You didn't tell your aunt?"

"The crazy old thing, I didn't want to hurt her. She wouldn't have understood. It seemed easier to simply break away."

"But you didn't break away completely. You took her name as well. Alexandra."

"You're very good at this. Have you ever thought of being a reporter for a sleazy tabloid? Then you could pry into other people's lives and get paid for it," he said venomously.

His spite made Annie furious. "What is it, Alex? Why are you so angry at me? What have I ever done to you?"

His black eyes bored into her. "What have you done to me, Annie MacPherson? You deprived me of the only father I ever knew."

Chapter 21

"What are you talking about?" Annie shouted, jumping up off the sofa. "I don't have anything to do with Gordon Barclay despite what everyone in the world seems to think. I don't want to work in his damned firm. I never wanted any of the attention he seems to want to give me. And you"—she leapt up, ignoring Alex's gun on the table—"if you've got problems with your father, it is not my fault."

"Sit down, Annie," Alex said calmly, not threatening her. "I'm not talking about Barclay. You're right, he is my biological father. I'm talking about the man who was a father to me when I was growing up. George MacPherson."

In a symbolic gesture Alex opened the drawer of the end table and placed the gun inside. "I'm sorry," he said. "I'm acting like a spoiled three-year-old. Deep down, I know you're not to blame. It's just that I've hated you for as long as I can remember."

As if expressing an opinion, Annie's stomach rumbled so loudly that they both heard it. They laughed. "You hungry or something?" Alex asked.

Annie realized she was. "I guess I keep forgetting to eat."

"Come on, I'm sure I've got something in the fridge."

They went exploring and found some slightly wilted green salad and some leftover barbecued chicken. Alex set out the plates and twisted open a couple of beers. The flip-flops in Annie's stomach immediately quieted, though she didn't know if it was from the food or from no longer having a gun pointed at her.

"It wasn't loaded, you know."

She shot him a nasty glance. "You shouldn't do that to a person."

"I never have before. I got it for protection, but I've never pointed it at anything but a target." He paused to wipe some barbecue sauce from his mouth. "There was a time I thought of you as my sister. I hated you, but I hated you as a sister. Did you even know I existed?"

Annie shook her head.

"Uncle George. From the time I was old enough to remember, he was around. Took me places, to ball games, things like that. Aunt Zan always described him as a 'friend of the family.' When I was old enough to ask questions about my parents, she gave me a sugar-coated history about my mother being an angel who loved me very much but who had to go away one day. She never mentioned Woody except to say they'd been married for a while, long before I was born. But whenever Zan talked about George, she'd get almost reverential, telling me how I always had to be polite and well-behaved so that Uncle George would be sure to come back and visit. I think I was about six when I decided that he was my real dad. I had it all planned out how I was going to go live with him so we could be together all the time. Then you came along and ruined everything." The laugh that followed was bitter.

"How?"

"I was about eight. Zan's husband, my uncle Otto, had died the year before, and money was real tight. About every two weeks your dad would come to visit and bring a carload of groceries. I think he tried to give Zan money one time and she wouldn't take it. But if he showed up with food, she couldn't refuse. Well, I was all set to tell Zan that I wanted to go live with George when the bombshell hit. Out of the blue Zan tells me I'm being sent away to school, to some fancy boarding school down in California. They said it was because of money, but I figured it was because you were coming up here to live with your father. That was the summer of 1970.''

Alex was right. That was the year Annie had started high school in Seattle.

"The way I saw it," Alex continued, "you were his number-one kid. I was just a substitute. Now that he had you to take care of, he didn't need me anymore."

It made more sense now. Alex's anger was rooted in childhood jealousy. But what still didn't make sense was why her father had felt such an obligation toward Alex.

"When did you find out that he wasn't your father?" she asked softly.

"It was the summer I turned thirteen and was right about to start high school. You were away somewhere, rafting on the Colorado River, I think. I came to your house, saw your room, all the evidence of you. George and I sat down and had a 'man-to-man' chat. It was the last time I saw him before he died." Alex went to the living room and retrieved the journal. He took out the photograph.

"Your dad gave me this that day. It's probably the only picture in existence showing *both* my parents," he said, acid in his voice. "The great Gordon Barclay."

The photograph confirmed that Gordon and Adele were the other couple at the lodge that weekend. Annie hesitated. "How much did he tell you?"

"Almost everything. He told me about the . . . the rape, how Barclay got her pregnant the same night he announced his engagement to Senator Quinn's daughter. And how he refused to acknowledge the child, even blocked my mother from getting her job back because he was afraid she'd try to extort money from him or something."

"You said 'almost everything.' "

"There was one thing he wouldn't talk about and that was what had happened to my mother. All he'd say was that I had to believe him, that she hadn't abandoned me. He told me she was dead."

Annie closed her eyes. She'd felt, ever since she'd talked to Woody Watney, that Lucy hadn't run away. But to hear it said washed her in a wave of sadness. "Was it that weekend at the Paradise Lodge?"

"He wouldn't say any more," said Alex, shaking his head wearily. "No matter how much I pushed. But it has to be. That's the last time she was seen alive."

"So that's why you stole the journal."

He nodded. "When I saw that article about you in the *Bar News* and it mentioned that you had his papers, I just had to check for myself. I didn't know what I was looking for. Letters, more photographs. Anything that would explain what had happened to her."

"And?"

"Something terrible happened that weekend, Annie. I'm not entirely sure what. A few days before they were about to leave he described in the journal how the four of them were going away to the mountains. Neither couple was married, so George and Gordon were going to share a room, as were Lucy and Adele. They'd reserved the largest suite in the new wing at the Paradise Lodge. They'd divided up the duties. Gordon was going to drive and George was responsible for buying all of the groceries and supplies for the three-day weekend and so on. The next entry is pretty incomprehensible, but it sounds like Lucy got violently ill—vomiting—and had to be taken to the hospital. There's nothing more until the day after they got back. It doesn't say anything explicit, just ranting and raving about feeling so awful, how he doubts he'll be able to live with the knowledge of what's happened. And he mentioned feeling responsible for her baby—me."

So that explained his commitment to the child, thought Annie. There was something her father had felt terribly guilty about, something so awful he couldn't even write it down. And she'd never known a thing about it.

She looked up. "You're sure he said 'the *knowledge* of what's happened'?"

He nodded. "I can show you the page. The way I read it, he didn't say that he'd *done* something but that he *knew* what had happened. Witnessed it perhaps. Or helped cover something up."

Independently, both Annie and Alex had the same thought.

"You think it was Barclay, don't you? He was afraid that she'd want money from him or cause a scandal."

"Don't you think it's incredibly odd that he would single-handedly keep her from getting her job back at KLMD, then the very next week go off on a happy holiday foursome with her? I'm sure he killed her, and for whatever reason your father knew it, too, and covered it up."

Annie tried to make sense of the muddle of information. "But what about Nancy Gulliver? Where does she fit into all of this?"

"I think she learned something she shouldn't have. Innocent people get hurt when they stick their noses where they don't belong."

A chill ran up Annie's spine. "What did you say?"

"Innocent people get hurt," he repeated, his gaze intense.

"It was you. You sent the anonymous 'Paradise' letters. Why, Alex?"

"Your letter was a warning. After what happened to Nancy, I was worried that he'd go after you if you started digging into the past. Granted, you're not my favorite person in the world, but I still didn't want you to come to any harm. The letters to Barclay—I don't know. It was a plan to flush him out, I guess. That was my single goal in coming back here, getting a job with him. I wanted to get close to him so I could watch him, wait for him to make a mistake. Do something revealing. It was easy enough getting close to him. He's a vain man, and he never had a son with Adele. I think subliminally he saw parts of himself in me. I guess I thought that when he saw all the references to Paradise, he'd get frightened and make a mistake. Lead me to some evidence of what he'd done to my mother."

Annie understood immediately. " 'The play's the thing wherein I'll catch the conscience of the King.' "

"What?" Alex asked, looking confused.

"*Hamlet*, act two, scene two, where he plans the play about his father's murder to gauge his mother's and stepfather's reactions. It worked for him."

A smile played on Alex's lips. "That's right, your dad said you were majoring in English at college. I was an engineering major—I haven't read *Hamlet* since high school."

"But did it work? Did he show any reaction?"

"In a way, yes. It visibly upset him. But as angry as he was, he wasn't revealing any information."

"He didn't suspect you?"

"No, and I have you to thank for that. The timing was perfect. I sent the first one right after that article about you came out—the one that mentioned you had your father's papers. I left a copy of it, open to the article, lying on his desk. Of course he made the connection immediately."

"What? He thought *I* sent the letters?"

"He told me as much. I hate to break it to you, Annie, but that's why he hired you, then made all those efforts to get close to you. He wanted to find out how much you knew. I'm sure he would have seduced you if it came down to that."

It was like getting a bucket of ice water in her face. The worst part was, she thought, she'd almost fallen for Barclay's act. Not wanting to show her embarrassment, Annie got up and cleared the table. They'd eaten all of the leftovers in Alex's refrigerator, and she could have eaten more. "So do you think Barclay killed Nancy Gulliver?" She thought about the incriminating scrap from the "suicide" note that she'd found at Barclay's home.

Alex's face darkened. "That's the problem. I don't know who killed Nancy, but I know it wasn't Barclay."

"You mean, you have no *proof* that he did it?"

He leveled his gaze at her. "Worse than that, Annie. I have ironclad evidence that Barclay *didn't* kill Nancy Gulliver."

"What do you mean?"

"I mean that he had an alibi."

"Alibis can be manufactured. Maybe he bribed someone on—"

"No, Annie. Barclay was with me. We were both at the office that Friday night working on the plans for the new firm. We didn't finish until six A.M. From what the autopsy said, Nancy Gulliver was dead long before that."

"You were with Gordon the entire time? No breaks at all?"

"The only time he was out of my sight was for about an hour, maybe an hour and a half, when I was working in the law library on the eighty-seventh floor. When I came back to our offices on the eighty-eighth floor, he was at his desk working. I'm sure he couldn't have gone and been back by then."

"But it had to have been Barclay. Nancy had no enemies. No one else benefited from her death."

"A hired killer?" Annie asked.

"I thought of that, too. But the method—entering her apartment and faking a suicide? That's not one a professional would use. Too risky—the killer easily could have been caught, especially when he started the car. Trace evidence could have been left in the apartment. And it wasn't foolproof. Nancy could have awakened, a neighbor could have called the police. Any number of things could have gone wrong. It just doesn't have the look of a hit."

Annie had to agree. Ellen had lent her enough true-crime books for her to recognize the classic patterns. Perhaps if Nancy had died from an attack in a dark alley, an execution-style killing, even arson, a hired killer would have been believable. But carbon monoxide suffocation? It didn't seem likely.

"Wait, Alex. I know how we can find out if Barclay left the building that night. The security guard keeps records of who's in the building after hours. And there are videotapes of the lobby and the garage. If he left the office at any time, those tapes will show it."

"You're right." He jumped up. "Just let me change out of these bicycle clothes—we'll go now. The more I think about it, the more convinced I am that Gordon's tricking us somehow."

They took Alex's 280Z. At 8 P.M. on a Saturday night there was little traffic in the financial district, and they pulled into the underground parking lot twenty minutes after they left Kirkland. The elevator from the parking lot brought them up to the lobby. But they knew as soon as the doors opened that something was terribly wrong.

In addition to the building's security officers, the lobby was overflowing with police. They were stopped as soon as they exited the elevator.

"Names?"

They answered, then hesitated when asked what their business in the building was. "It's all right, Sergeant. I know them two. They work at KLMD." It was Bob, the security guard Annie had encountered during her first week of work. When she started to tell him what they'd come to find out, Alex stopped her. "We were just here to pick up a file for a trial that starts on Monday. Is something wrong?"

Annie was disturbed that Alex felt it necessary to lie, but the expression on the guard's face worried her even more. "Well, now, I'm not really at liberty—"

"Sergeant Cooley," a voice called. "Medical examiner's here. You want him to go on up?"

"Medical examiner?" asked Alex. "What the—"

There was a sudden outburst of confusion, as all three local news stations' crews arrived simultaneously, the reporters trying to find someone, anyone, who could tell them what was happening. Annie and Alex were pushed back in the confusion.

Suddenly recognizing Annie from the sniper attack, one of the crews came rushing over. With the camera whirring and the spotlight on her face, the reporter asked her what she knew about the incident and whether she thought it was related to her own attack on the previous Wednesday.

"I don't know what's happened here, so how can I know if it's related?" she stammered as Alex pulled her away from the camera.

"Turn that thing off, man. We don't have anything to do with this. We're just here to pick up some files. Come on, Annie, let's get out of here."

Annie winced as Alex accidentally pulled on her wounded arm. "Sorry," he said.

"Wait a second." With the camera off, Annie asked the reporter what was happening.

He shrugged. "We don't know much yet. Just that there was a probable homicide on the eighty-eighth floor." Annie and Alex froze.

"The victim?" Alex asked, practically grabbing the reporter's lapels. "Who is it? Who is it, damn you?" He looked ready to throw the guy to the floor to get an answer when another reporter ran up. "I've got the information, hurry, let's go live."

The camera whirred into action again, and the second reporter gave the facts gleaned from the police. "The victim appears to be a Caucasian woman in her early thirties, black hair, blue eyes, who police say was an associate of the prestigious law firm Kemble, Laughton, Mercer, and Duff. Her name will not be released until the family has been notified. She was found by a security guard approximately twenty minutes ago, apparently dead from inhalation of chemicals taken from a janitorial cart. Police say a strong mixture of chlorine and ammonia was poured into a bucket and left just inside the office door where the woman was found. The case is being treated as a probable homicide, and possible rape, as the woman was found in a partially clad, disheveled condition. The medical examiner has not yet determined if there is evidence of sexual violation. . . ."

Annie looked up at Alex, whose face had taken on a ghostly

pallor. "No, no," he murmured. She could barely hear his strained whisper as they listened to the reporter.

The reporter concluded by saying, "The woman was found lying on a sofa in the corner office of her immediate supervisor, the prominent trial attorney Gordon Barclay. Barclay's car was observed leaving the building shortly before the body was discovered, and a warrant has been issued for his arrest. We'll break in with an update on the situation as soon as we know more."

Annie grabbed Alex's arm to steady him. They both knew the victim was Deborah Silver.

Chapter 22

"Come on." Alex pulled Annie's arm, this time ignoring her cry of pain. She followed him down the stairwell into the parking garage. "We've got to find Barclay." They raced to the car, and Annie barely had time to fasten her seat belt before Alex was gunning the car up the ramp. He inserted his magnetic parking card into the slot, then roared out of the building as the gate opened.

"Where are we going?" Annie didn't ask why. She could see the hatred blazing in Alex's eyes.

"If Barclay did this, then he's gone to hide out. He's got a place in the mountains, hardly anyone knows about it. He goes there to get away—from the firm, from his wife. He took me there after we climbed Rainier." Alex laughed dryly. "It was almost like a father-son chat—the day he told me about the new law firm he was planning. He told me then—and I didn't really understand it at the time—that it's the only place he really feels safe."

"How far is it?"

"It's near the Crystal Mountain Ski Resort on the northwest side of Rainier. It'll take us about two hours, or less if I push it. We might even be able to overtake him, depending on how fast Gordon's driving. Keep a lookout for his black Mercedes."

They drove in silence. It was dark by the time they passed Enumclaw and turned onto Highway 410 toward the mountains. Even if they had overtaken Barclay, it was impossible now to tell anything about the other cars on the highway. Occasionally Alex pulled ahead to pass someone, but they saw no large black sedans.

Knowing how much Alex hated Barclay, it was hard for Annie to believe what a good actor he'd been to become Barclay's trusted assistant. "What were you planning to do once Gordon started the new firm, Alex? Were you really going to go with him?"

"Only as long as necessary to make the case against him. I worked my way close to him to try to learn what had happened to my mother. I admit, I wasn't succeeding very well on that front, but I had picked up some other bits of useful information. I'd decided that if I couldn't get Barclay for my mother's murder, I could at least send him to jail for his other crimes."

"Like what?"

"Your basic white-collar variety: fraud, embezzlement, conspiracy to bribe a public official."

Annie looked at Alex, startled. "He confided all this to you?"

Keeping his eyes firmly fixed on the road, Alex said, "Hell, no. He trusted me, but not that much. But I was around him enough to know where he kept his personal documents. There was a locked filing cabinet—he thought he had the only key. I managed to steal it and make a duplicate one time when we were working out at the club. It's all in there—how the firm was going to be financed. I found out that Barclay wasn't putting up any of his own money. He had a silent partner secretly putting up the funds. Now that in itself violates the code of professional responsibility, the rule that says a nonlawyer can't be a partner or own any interest in a law firm. But it gets worse than that."

Annie suddenly recalled her conversation with Adele Quinn as the pieces fell into place. "Senator Quinn was the silent partner?"

Alex nodded. "Barclay had no idea that I was on to him. He was going to pay Quinn off out of the firm's profits for the first couple of years, as well as provide cut-rate legal services to

Spectrum Defense International, another venture Quinn had a substantial interest in. When the time was right, Quinn would see that Barclay was appointed to the federal bench, his life-long dream. There were hints about other long-term deals as well, like Barclay promising to be 'friendly,' as a judge, to the special-interest groups that supported Quinn, such as the timber lobby and the NRA.''

As much as she wanted not to believe Alex, his story just rang too much of the truth. "You got all this from his papers?"

"Not all. I also figured out a way to bypass the computerized phone system. Sometimes when we worked late at night Barclay would get a private call from Quinn. He'd ask me to leave the room, of course, so I'd go down the hall to my office, shut the door, and tap right into the call. I've got tapes that will send both of them to prison for many, many years.''

"I can't believe it,'' said Annie.

"Can't you? The FBI had no difficulty with it—they've been trying to hook Quinn for years but have never been able to get anything on him. Last week, after the sniper attack, I decided it was too dangerous to continue on my own. I turned over everything I'd gotten so far. They were planning to wait until the new firm was up and running next week, when there'd be a solid paper trail of money changing hands, then move in. I was still hoping I'd learn what had happened to my mother before Barclay's whole world crumbled. The ten or twenty years he'd get for conspiracy to bribe a public official wouldn't be a fraction of what he deserves.''

Annie recalled another conversation, the one where Deborah hinted at the persuasive power of the right kind of information. "Alex, I know you probably don't want to talk about this." He kept his eyes straight ahead. "Did Deborah know about Senator Quinn's involvement?"

Showing no emotion, he nodded. "I feel so responsible. We've been lovers for the past year. I thought I could trust her. But if I hadn't told her . . .''

"No, Alex, it's not your fault. She must have tried to use that information to coerce Barclay into giving her a job or to blackmail him."

As the road narrowed and they began to gain elevation, Annie gripped the door handle as Alex took the tighter and tighter switchback turns. He was an excellent driver, but that didn't make the ride any less terrifying. What was most frightening was Annie's speculation of what Alex planned to do once they found Gordon Barclay.

Finally they turned onto an unmarked, unpaved road off the main highway. Alex doused the headlights. There were only a couple of other houses on the road and no sign that any were occupied. A single light shone in the upstairs window of the cabin at the end of the cul-de-sac, about a quarter-mile away.

Alex hid the car in a thick stand of evergreens. Annie finally got up the courage to ask Alex what he planned to do.

"I'm not sure," he said, reaching into the backseat to get his coat, which was folded into a bundle. "But I intend to be prepared."

Seeing him unwrap the coat to reveal his handgun, Annie protested, "Alex, violence isn't going to help. We have no reason to think that Barclay is armed."

"We have no reason to think he isn't. I'm taking this in there."

She looked at him. "It's still unloaded, isn't it? You said before—"

"I lied."

Annie tried to get past her near-irrational fear of guns. To her, they were like time bombs, capable of exploding spontaneously at any moment. She tried once more to persuade him to leave it behind. "Alex, Barclay may be guilty of bribery, but the more I think about it, the surer I am that he didn't kill Nancy, your mother, or Deborah." Seeing his skepticism, she explained who she thought the murderer was and why. Alex was stubborn, but he couldn't fail to see the logic in her theory. "Barclay probably ran away because it would look like he was the killer, don't you see?"

"All right, we'll do it this way. We'll take the gun in your purse. That way Barclay won't see it. We'll tell him we've just come to talk. That all we want is the truth about Lucy. But you'll keep the purse with you and stand next to me the whole time. I want it within easy reach."

Annie had to acquiesce. She knew her theory was correct, but she also knew there was a risk involved in confronting Barclay. They placed the gun in her shoulder bag, then walked quietly toward the cabin, staying out of sight under the cover of the trees.

They didn't hear him approach. He jumped them from behind, swinging an iron rod of some kind. Alex put his hand up but failed to completely deflect the swing so that he took it on the side of his head. Stunned, he stumbled to the ground. In the faint moonlight Annie saw that the tool was a heavy, wrought-iron fire poker. She barely had time to dodge and roll away as the second blow fell. The third swing caught her on the side of the kneecap, sending a stab of excruciating pain up her leg.

Standing over them, Gordon Barclay wielded the poker like a warrior's club. When Alex regained his equilibrium, Barclay ordered them into the cabin, then grabbed Annie's purse off the ground. In agony with every step, Annie limped after Alex toward the lighted doorway.

Chapter 23

Where Barclay's Volunteer Park home was a display of his wife's tastes and his office the product of a decorator, the small mountain cabin reflected the man himself. The furniture was solid and well worn: an overstuffed leather armchair and ottoman discolored from sunlight; a faded tweed sofa, long enough for a tall man to stretch out on; a bookshelf crammed with *National Geographic*s that must have gone back at least twenty years. From the light of two oil lamps Annie could see that the walls were covered with framed photographs of Barclay's beloved mountains.

Annie and Alex sat on the sofa where Barclay had directed them. Annie tried not to show the pain she was feeling, but she could see that her knee was already beginning to swell. At least Barclay hadn't discovered the gun. As they had entered the cabin, he had tossed Annie's purse, gun and all, down by the door without searching it. Annie had to fight to keep her eyes away from it, not wanting to clue Barclay in to the gun's presence.

"What now, Gordon?" Alex sneered, his words full of hatred. "Are you going to kill us like you killed the others? Like you killed Nancy and Deborah? *Like you murdered my mother, Lucy Guiterrez Watney?*"

For a moment Annie thought she saw a look of shock on Barclay's face. Annie had been so sure that Barclay wasn't the killer that it was hard to believe she'd been fooled by him again. Barclay didn't reply. Still holding the poker and staying within striking range, Barclay took a coil of rope off a hook on the wall. It was the type of rope that rock climbers used for rappelling, strong as steel and braided in a manner so as to resist fraying. Practically unbreakable. It looked brand-new.

"Put your hands on your heads." As they did so, Barclay moved around behind the couch and in one swift movement looped their wrists together in that awkward position, securing the rope tautly with a knot.

"How did you know we were coming?" Alex asked.

"I recognized your car behind me at one point. Luckily there's another route to this cabin. It's shorter, but over rougher road. I knew if I took it, I could get here at least twenty minutes before you." Barclay looked around the room, concentrating, as if formulating a plan. "Now let's see. Two bodies found upstairs in the bedroom, a fire started down below when an oil lamp tipped over. Yes, I think it will work. But it's too early. There's still traffic on the road. Someone might see the smoke. We'll have to wait till after midnight." Barclay seated himself on a wooden chair directly opposite them, as if preparing for a long wait.

"Gordon, please." Annie spoke up for the first time. "This isn't necessary. You're just doing this to protect the *real* killer."

Alex eyed her warily, apparently unsure about whether she meant what she was saying or was trying a ploy to get him to release their hands. But she did mean it.

"Oh, really?" Barclay asked, seemingly amused.

"She's wrong, Barclay," Alex cut in. "She told me her theory, but it doesn't play out. You're the killer. You're the only one who wanted all three women dead. You might as well admit it."

"Well, Annie. Your cohort here seems to disagree with you. We've got plenty of time. Why don't you enlighten us. You apparently don't think I'm a killer."

Annie weighed her options. Barclay clearly intended to wait

until the middle of the night before killing them. Engaging him in conversation couldn't hurt.

"Alex is right as far as Lucy and Deborah are concerned. You did have the motive to kill them."

"And why is that?" Barclay asked.

"Lucy, Alex's mother, was planning to go public with what you had done, how you had raped her, unless you agreed to give her her job back. She was planning to talk to Fred Duff about it the following Monday." The bit about going public with the story was speculation and Annie knew it, but it was the only thing that made sense based on what Fred had told her about the appointment Lucy had failed to keep. "Why else would Lucy agree to go on that trip to the mountains? She was desperate; she needed to talk to you. This was her last chance to try to work things out."

Annie kept her eyes on Barclay's face. "You were in a bind. You didn't want her back in the firm, where she could continue to threaten you, yet what were your alternatives? A man in your position, a rising young trial attorney, couldn't have survived even the allegation of a rape. The publicity would have destroyed your career."

Barclay sat opposite them with his legs crossed, examining his nails as if uninterested in what Annie had to say. But she could see from the tension in his shoulders that his casual attitude was an act. He was extremely interested.

Barclay looked up and gave Alex a look that was smug beyond belief. "And Deborah? You think I wanted *her* dead, too? When our little fling had just gotten off to such a lovely start?" Annie could sense Alex's bottled-up fury. "Don't worry, Alex. I didn't *rape* Deborah. She was a very willing participant." Alex strained at the ropes holding his wrists.

Annie wasn't put off by Barclay's act. "Oh, you might have enjoyed her company, Barclay," she said. "But Deborah was far too dangerous. She had a six o'clock appointment with you this evening at the office. Was that when she presented you with her offer? She'd keep secret your deal with Senator Quinn in exchange for what? A partnership at the new firm?'' Barclay listened impassively, the iron poker flat across his lap. "She believed information was power and that she could use what she knew to get a partnership in your new firm.''

Barclay stood and began pacing slowly, almost ambling around the cabin, tapping the poker against his hand like a riding crop. "An interesting scenario. But why would I kill poor, sweet Nancy? Nancy who would never hurt a fly?''

"My point exactly. Nancy's death was the one that confused everyone. She learned something, didn't she? What was it, that the letters about 'Paradise' referred to the lodge? Was she getting dangerously close to an unpleasant truth? Probably. But even before Alex told me about your alibi that Friday night, I couldn't believe you would kill Nancy. You didn't perceive her as a threat. She adored you. Surely you could have found some less violent way of silencing her, if you had wanted to.''

Barclay stopped pacing and turned to face her. "This is all very interesting, Annie. But you said you thought I *wasn't* the killer. If I'm not, then who is?''

"Your wife, Barclay. You're protecting Adele, aren't you? Adele's motives are linked to yours. She'd do anything to preserve your career, so that you can support her.

"Both Lucy and Deborah were threats to your career—she couldn't let anything happen to cause you to lose your livelihood. And Nancy—you may not have viewed her as a threat, but Adele did. To your marriage. She saw what we all did, that you truly cared for Nancy, more than any of the others. Adele saw how much you adored Nancy and felt that she would eventually destroy your marriage.''

A faint smile played on Barclay's lips. "But you were a criminal defense attorney, Annie. You know that motive can't prove murder.''

Annie shifted, trying to ease the growing pain in her knee. "You're right. What really convinced me that you didn't commit the murders is the manner in which the deaths were brought about. As you've demonstrated here tonight, Gordon, you're a man of action. A decorated war hero, a Silver Star for bravery in action, proud that you have the physical stamina of a man half your age. A man like you isn't going to use such indirect methods as carbon monoxide suffocation, chemical inhalation . . . or food poisoning." Barclay flinched when she mentioned the last.

"Go on" was all he said.

Annie continued. "Deborah's death. That's the obvious one. If you're like most men, you wouldn't even know that mixing chlorine and ammonia releases deadly fumes that can cause a person to pass out within seconds. But anyone with experience with household-cleaning materials knows that. Adele told me how she has to explain such matters to her housekeeper, who doesn't read English.

"Lucy's food poisoning . . . Who else could have pulled that off that weekend at the Paradise Lodge? You were staying in a kitchenette suite in the new wing. My father brought along all the groceries so you could have home-cooked meals. But of the four of you only Adele knew anything about cooking. The rest of you were as hopeless in the kitchen as I am myself. No doubt everything you ate that weekend was personally prepared by Adele. That's how Lucy came to be violently ill."

Barclay rose slowly and again walked around behind the couch. Despite her impassioned speech, Annie was shocked that he was actually letting them loose. But, of course, she was wrong. He exchanged the poker for a hunting knife that was hanging on the wall behind the couch, slowly untied their hands, and ordered them up the steep stairs. He held on to Annie and laid the blade of the knife against her throat. He didn't need to tell either of them what he planned to do if they made any sudden moves.

"An intriguing theory, Annie," he said as they entered the small loft bedroom. "But I'm afraid it's only partially correct." He gestured to Alex to move to the far side of the room. He loosened his grip on Annie but still kept the knife close to her skin. "You're right that Adele committed the actual deeds. But only because I needed her to. That weekend at the Paradise Lodge—which you seem to know so much about—that's when I learned how much Adele truly cared for me.

"You're right, Lucy had come to me and told me that she would go public if she had to. She needed that job to support herself and her son. Our son. I didn't know what to do, so I talked to Adele about it. I just needed a sounding board, someone to hear my thoughts. Adele was the one who suggested we all go away for the weekend, that it would give us time to talk and reach a solution. But that conversation never took place because Lucy became ill after our first dinner. Violently ill in the middle of the night. George and Lucy suspected nothing, but of course I knew what was happening. You're right, Adele prepared the meal. The way she looked at me as we were taking Lucy to the hospital, I knew."

"You took my mother to the hospital?" Alex asked. "Couldn't they save her?"

"No, it was too late for that. She was delirious by the time we made it to Eatonville—the nearest town with a hospital. Adele is nothing if not a perfectionist. She knew how to get the dosage right."

"But why didn't anyone know? Why did my father go along with the lie that she'd run off with her ex-husband?"

"I was able to convince him that we had to avoid any hint of scandal. George was still in the midst of his divorce at that time. I convinced him what the media would do with such a story. A prominent attorney has an affair with a married woman, who gives birth to an illegitimate child—assumed by all who knew them to be the attorney's. A few months later, the woman mysteriously dies while away for the weekend with her lover. Not only would George's career have been ruined, but there was a good likelihood that such a scandal would deprive him of ever visiting his only daughter. He had too much to lose."

So that was it. The source of her father's lifelong guilt. He'd known that Lucy had died but never suspected she'd been murdered. He had felt guilty about the fact that they'd covered it up.

"When we got to the hospital," Barclay continued, "Adele took Lucy in to register her. By this time, Lucy was practically comatose. But instead of identifying her, Adele said the woman was a hitchhiker we'd picked up, that we had no idea who she was. And, of course, she had no ID on her. Adele left her in the emergency room and refused to leave her name."

"Adele did it for you then?" Annie said.

He nodded. "And Nancy? I did love the girl. I never could have brought myself to kill her. But she was a terrible risk. I knew that. So I let Adele believe I was ready to end our marriage in order to marry Nancy. I left hints around the house, how to get into her apartment. Nancy's little love notes. I knew sooner or later the deed would be done. The same with Deborah. Adele didn't know anything about the blackmail, only that I was going to meet Deborah at the office. I knew she'd followed me there, so I made certain that Adele saw us making love, heard me tell Deborah how she was the only one I cared about, how we'd always be together."

"You bastard," Alex spat out. "You were just using Deborah."

Barclay chuckled. "You were wrong to love her, Alex. Oh, I knew about you two. She told me, in fact. We had a good laugh about it. We'd been seeing each other for weeks. Deborah was the one who used people. She was using you to get close to me, and all she wanted from me was a boost to her career. I knew that from the start."

Barclay pulled Annie closer and laid the cool blade of the knife against her cheek. "And you, Annie. You with your research into your father's past. How did you think that made me feel, knowing that someone was going to be rooting around in all those dark secrets? I knew you'd find out about Lucy sooner or later. Did you think I could let that happen?" He stared her directly in the eyes. "You knew, of course, that Adele thought we were having an affair?'' The implications of his statement made Annie go rigid with fear. The new job, the cozy lunches—it had all been a setup from the beginning. It was Barclay's oblique way of setting Annie up as Adele's next victim.

Suddenly there was a noise on the stairs below. In the pale glow of the oil lamp they could see Adele Barclay at the foot of the stairs, grasping Alex's gun in both hands. "I think you're the one who doesn't have the story quite right, Gordon," she said. Her hands quivered slightly, but her voice was steady. "You think I did it all for you?" She laughed, her high-pitched, squeaky laugh sounding inappropriate in the masculine cabin. "Everything I've done I've done for myself. I thought you knew that. I don't even like you, Gordon." Another laugh. "But you've provided me with a wonderful life all these years. Money, a beautiful home, all the time I want to work on my projects, my cooking. I knew that Daddy wasn't going to support me forever. I needed to take care of myself." She backed down the stairs. "Toss down the knife, Gordon, then come down here where I can see you better."

"Adele, put the gun down. Someone's going to get hurt." Barclay tried to sound authoritative, but it was obvious he was frightened. Another shrill laugh from Adele. He threw down the knife, and in single file they slowly descended the stairs into the living room. Adele kept the gun pointed at Barclay's stomach.

"What are you going to do with that thing, Adele? You don't know how to handle a gun."

Adele giggled. "Isn't it funny, Annie, how long you can be with a man and they still don't know everything about you? Gordon knows Daddy's a hunter, always has been. Who do you think he took elk hunting all those years, when he never had a son? Oh, I'll admit, I'm not real sure of handguns like this, but it can't be that different from shooting a rifle."

Barclay looked dumbfounded. "It was you shooting at us— that day at Ray's? Adele, you could've killed me."

"That was the general idea." Looking at Annie, she said, "Sorry about grazing you like that, dear. I really need to get in for new glasses. I don't see well out of these."

"Adele, please be careful," Alex said, trying to sound calm. "That gun has a very sensitive trigger."

Adele ignored him. "I've gotten tired of having to pick up after you, Gordon. You keep making these foolish mistakes with women, putting yourself in positions where they can harm you. I don't know why Daddy ever thought you'd be a good judge. I'm not sure why I didn't think of this sooner. You've made enough money for me to live on comfortably for the rest of my life, especially when I cash out your interest in Kemble, Laughton, Mercer, and Duff. I'll be quite the well-to-do widow, won't I?" She slowly raised the gun until it was pointed squarely at Barclay's face.

"Adele, *no!*" Barclay yelled out.

"Annie, get down!" Alex screamed as he rushed forward at Barclay's wife. Annie hit the floor a split second before she heard the single shot, then the sound of the gun hitting the floor. When she looked up, Alex was restraining Adele, the gun at their feet. They were staring at Gordon Barclay. He had fallen back against the tweed sofa, his eyes open, staring at the ceiling. Where his throat used to be there was only a pulpy mass of crimson blood.

Chapter 24

"And in closing, Fred, I think I'm speaking for every single employee of Kemble, Laughton, Mercer, and Duff when I say that it just won't be the same here without you." Sitting at a table in the ballroom of the Cascade Club, Annie listened with half an ear as, one by one, all of the senior partners in the firm stood up to give their tributes to Fred Duff on his retirement. Vivian, in a powder-blue knit sweater set, dabbed at her eyes with a hanky as she held Fred's hand and listened to the speeches.

Only the week before they'd heard about the deal the prosecutor's office had cut with Adele Barclay. She'd agreed to plead guilty to the murders of Nancy Gulliver and Deborah Silver in exchange for a thirty-year sentence at one of the more luxurious minimum-security prisons for women. She'd no doubt spend the rest of her life teaching cooking and craft classes to her fellow inmates.

No charges were filed for the death of Lucy Watney, as there was no evidence that a murder had even been committed, but both Alex and Annie took comfort in the fact that they finally knew the truth about what had happened.

Alex's role in the shooting of Barclay had confused prosecutors at first when they learned how little experience Adele had with handguns. But remarkably hers were the only prints on the weapon, and all charges against Alex were dismissed on the grounds of self-defense. Not having seen the fatal shot, Annie tried not to think about the fact that it might not have been Adele who aimed the weapon at Barclay's throat.

It was finally Fred's turn to speak. He walked to the podium without the use of his cane and clicked off the microphone muttering something about hating the dang contraptions. It hardly mattered. His voice was strong enough to reach to the back of the room without any difficulty.

His farewell speech was a bit on the long side, but as Annie glanced around the room she could see that no one minded. Vivian's weren't the only moist eyes in the house. Fred concluded by saying, "This is the start of a new era for Kemble, Laughton, Mercer, and Duff. The upcoming merger with the Los Angeles–based firm of Fenortner, Sussman, and Klein will make this outfit the largest on the West Coast and the third largest in the nation. It makes for a damned bright future, and one that we never could have dreamed of back in forty-six when four young G.I.s home from the war decided it might be fun to start our own law firm.

"But I also know that it's time for this old dinosaur to be put out to pasture. I can't say it well enough, but you've all been like a family to me. Thank you so much."

Fred tried to brush away the standing ovation of his colleagues, walking back to his seat where he gave Vivian a kiss and a hug. Seeing them, Annie wondered once again if she'd ever find the kind of love they shared. She'd gotten a letter from David Courtney that morning and, after reading it about a dozen times, still didn't know whether to be happy or depressed by it. He'd decided to take a one-year teaching job in Hawaii, agreeing that it was better if he wasn't around while she reevaluated what she wanted. He ended the letter by saying, "Even though it might not work out for us, kid, I hope you've learned you can't run away from love. It will always track you down."

All those years Annie had always thought her father had run

away from love. Now she knew that wasn't true. She hoped
the next time the opportunity arose, she'd be able to follow
David's advice.

She turned when she felt a tap on her shoulder. "Jed, I didn't
know you'd come."

Joel had gotten up to look for a pitcher of ice water and Jed
flopped down in his empty chair. "Hey, I couldn't miss the
sendoff for old Fred. Even though seeing all these geezers does
sort of give me the creeps. I can't say I miss the pompous
asses."

"So how's it going on the job front? Any nibbles?"

Jed looked around furtively. "Actually, that was the other
reason I came tonight. I wanted to talk to you and Joel. Hey,
there y'are, big guy. What d'ya say the three of us step out into
the hallway a second?" Joel, looking a little befuddled, followed, carrying his water pitcher and a glass. Jed's eyes were
alight with excitement.

"Okay, here's the story. I know that your merger is up in
the air right now, because the new folks from L.A. would have
to approve it all over again. But hell, you guys don't want to
work for a thousand-person firm anyway, right?"

Annie and Joel exchanged glances. They'd discussed the situation but hadn't come up with any great alternatives. Cash
flow was still a significant problem.

As if reading their minds, Jed said, "I want to start a firm.
Now, before you say anything, I know it sounds kind of
crazy, but here's how it would work. You guys have done it
before, so you know how to run a small firm. I've talked to
some of the insurance clients I used to work for, and now that
Gordon's out of the picture they'd be willing to send me their
business. But wait, here's the clincher. Dad says he'll loan me
as much money as I need, interest free, as long as I associate
with someone who's really good at keeping track of details."

Annie and Jed both turned to look at Joel. "Detail" was, after
all, practically his middle name. Annie raised her eyebrows.
"Think we could convince Val to come out of retirement?"

"It's possible," said Joel, pondering the possibilities.

"There's lots of downtown office space available. Here, I've already worked out some of the start-up costs." Jed handed Joel a computer printout. "We could call it anything you like," he said, eager as a puppy. "MacPherson, Feinstein, and Dela-court. How's that sound?"

Joel had pulled a calculator out of his pocket and was furiously computing. He nodded slowly. "You know, it might just work."

Annie smiled. "It just might at that."

About the Author

Although born and raised in southern California, Janet L. Smith has applied for naturalization as a northwest native. She has lived in Seattle for the past twelve years. After graduating from law school at the University of Washington, she practiced law for five years with a large regional law firm, spent several years as an administrative law judge for the state of Washington, and is now a trial attorney with a small firm.